There's Wild, Then There's You

M. LEIGHTON

BERKLEY BOOKS, NEW YORK

THE BERKLEY PUBLISHING GROUP
Published by the Penguin Group
Penguin Group (USA)
375 Hudson Street, New York, New York 10014

USA • Canada • UK • Ireland • Australia • New Zealand • India • South Africa • China

penguin.com

A Penguin Random House Company

This book is an original publication of The Berkley Publishing Group.

Library of Congress Cataloging-in-Publication Data

Leighton, M.
There's wild, then there's you / M. Leighton.
Pages cm—(A Wild Ones)
ISBN 978-0-425-26782-0 (Berkley trade paperback)
1. Rock musicians—Fiction. 2. Horses—Breeding—Fiction. 3. Ranch Life—Fiction. I. Title.
PS3612.E3588T44 2014
813'.6—dc23 2014004661

PUBLISHING HISTORY
Berkley trade paperback edition / June 2014

PRINTED IN THE UNITED STATES OF AMERICA

10 9 8 7 6 5 4 3 2 1

Cover art by ImageBrief.com/Greg Daniels
Cover design by Lesley Worrell

M. LEIGHTON IS

"INSANELY INTENSE."
—The Bookish Babe

"FREAKIN' HOT!"
—Nette's Bookshelf

AND "SERIOUSLY SCANDALICIOUS."
—Scandalicious Book Reviews

PRAISE FOR *SOME LIKE IT WILD*

"*Some Like It Wild* left me feeling breathlessly happy . . . the exact same feeling I had when I read *The Wild Ones*. M. Leighton has done it again—she's written the perfect, sexy love story!"

—*New York Times* bestselling author Courtney Cole

"Sizzles with passion and romance . . . Leighton's intensely sensuous novel alternates between Laney and Jake's first-person perspectives, creating a heart-wrenching emotional story. Fans and newcomers will eagerly await the next book in the series." —*Publishers Weekly*

"This is my first read by M. Leighton, it won't be my last. Laney and Jake's journey to their HEA was sexy, fun, and emotional."

—*Guilty Pleasures Reviews*

"*Some Like It Wild* charms and delights much like its hero Jake Theopolis does." —*Fresh Fiction*

PRAISE FOR *THE WILD ONES*

"This book is worth every second I spent reading it. Ms. Leighton is a phenomenal writer and I cannot give her enough praise."

—*Bookish Temptations*

continued . . .

"Hands down one of the hottest books I've read all summer . . . Complete with love, secrets, dreams and hidden pasts! *The Wild Ones* is romantic, sexy and absolutely perfect! Drop everything and read this RIGHT NOW!"

—*The Bookish Brunette*

"I can honestly tell you that this is one of my top books of the year and easily one of my new all-time favorites. I couldn't put the book down."

—*The Autumn Review*

"You will laugh, swoon, and even shed a few tears. M. Leighton knows how to write an amazing story. Get your copy of *The Wild Ones* today. You will not regret it."

—*Between the Page Reviews*

"This book was one of the best books I've read this year. It may sound like just a love triangle on the surface but inside there's so much more going on."

—*The Book Vixen*

"One of the best books I've read this year so far." —*Sim Sational Books*

PRAISE FOR M. LEIGHTON'S BAD BOYS NOVELS *DOWN TO YOU*, *UP TO ME*, AND *EVERYTHING FOR US*

"Scorching hot . . . insanely intense . . . and it is shocking. *Shocking!*"

—*The Bookish Babe*

"I definitely did NOT see the twists coming." —*The Book List Reviews*

"Brilliant." —*The Book Goddess*

"Leighton never gives the reader a chance to catch their breath . . . Yes, there is sex, OMG tongue hanging out of mouth, scorching sex."

—*Literati Literature Lovers*

"Well, I drank this one down in one huge gulp . . . and it was delicious . . . seriously *scandalicious.*" —*Scandalicious Book Reviews*

"Delicious . . . I stopped reading in order to grab a cold beer and cool off . . . the twists and turns on the plot line are brilliant." —*Review Enthusiast*

"OMG! It was freakin' hot!" —*Nette's Bookshelf*

"Steamy, sexy, and super hot! M. Leighton completely and absolutely knocked [it] out of the park." —*The Bookish Brunette*

"Scorching hot . . . an emotional roller coaster." —*Reading Angel*

"I devoured it, and I'm pretty sure you will too." —*For Love and Books*

"Prepare yourself to be blown away." —*My Keeper Shelf*

"I loved it . . . bring on the Davenport boys." —*Smexy Books*

To my wonderful husband
for putting up with me and my neurotic ways.
I love you, babe!

To the awesome God that provides, no matter the need.
Thank you. Always.

ONE: *Violet*

One by one, I watch the people in the rows in front of me stand up and introduce themselves.

Oh, sweet Jesus! How do I get myself into these messes?

I don't know why I even ask. I already know. I help people. It's not only what I do; it's who I am.

By day, I'm a social worker, finally able to do what I went to school for four years to do—help people. But by night, I'm a chauffeur, a counselor, a nurse, a guardian, a suicide hotline, and, tonight, an addict.

As the first person in my row stands, my stomach turns a flip and I look around once more for my best friend, Tia. The only reason I'm here is for moral support. *Her* moral support. And she hasn't even shown up yet.

That's what I get for trying to help her when she obviously doesn't want it.

Tia's fiancé, Dennis, insisted that before they get married, Tia attend at least ten sessions at an addicts meeting. That might sound ridiculous to some people, but it's probably not that much to ask, considering that Tia has cheated on him not one, not two, not three, not even four times. But six. Six times in three years, Tia has gotten drunk and slept with someone else. She regrets it immediately. Cries over it, apologizes for it, always confesses it, but it never seems to stop her when she feels a wild hair come on and a hot guy happens to be near. It doesn't help that she's gorgeous. With long, blond hair and pale blue eyes, Tia looks just like a Barbie doll. She has insanely big boobs, an enviably tiny waist, and ridiculously long legs. It's a package that draws the eye of practically every male within a ten-mile radius. And that only worsens Tia's . . . weakness. She loves first kisses. And butterflies. And excitement. And vodka. That combination lands her in more trouble than I care to comment on. It also lands me in more trouble than I care to comment on.

Like finding myself *next* in a long line of people standing up to explain who they are and why they're here. My mind is whirling as I listen to the lady beside me explain that her name is Rhianne and that she's been an addict for eleven years. People clap (why, I'm not sure), and she smiles before taking her seat again. Then the room falls quiet and every eye turns to me. My stomach drops into my shoes.

My turn.

Slowly, I stand. I give the guy at the head of the room a shaky smile, and he nods me on in encouragement. I clear my throat and wipe my damp palms on my jeans. I glance quickly around at all the attentive faces, wishing silently that this moment was already over.

Just a few more seconds and it will be . . .

It's when my eyes collide with breathtakingly pale blue ones that I nearly forget where I am and what I'm supposed to be saying. Lucky for me, my speech is short. And exactly 50 percent *un*true.

"Hi. My name is Violet, and I'm a sex addict."

TWO: *Jet*

The monotony and the hopelessness of the night take an immediate turn for the better when she stands up. I watch the tiny brunette fiddle with her fingers as she looks around. She seems shy, which isn't a trait I'd associate with people like the ones in this room. But she's here for a reason, which intrigues the hell out of me.

I sit up a little straighter as I watch her. She's actually really hot—dark auburn hair pulled back into a twist, creamy skin flushed around her cheeks, straight nose tucked nervously toward her chest, and pearly white teeth biting into her lush lower lip.

Her figure is small but proportionate—round tits, flat stomach, firm ass, long, long legs. Looking at her makes me *glad* to have found her *here*. I know for sure she likes one thing. And she likes it *a lot*. I can sympathize with that.

I watch her wipe her palms nervously on her jeans. She looks around and I wait for her eyes to make their way to me. I feel like I *need* to see them, like I *need* to see the rest of the package. What will they look like? What will they *say*?

When her quick scan reaches me, it pauses. For maybe a hundredth of a second. And I realize that her eyes are exactly what I was hoping they'd be, even though I didn't know I was really hoping they'd be *anything*.

They're a pale, silvery gray. Smoky. Sexy. It's in them that I can see why she's here. There's something wild about those eyes, something that says she's hiding a little devil inside that hot-yet-innocent librarian exterior, and it's just dying to make its way out.

"Hi. My name is Violet, and I'm a sex addict."

I feel like groaning. God, that voice! It's low and husky, the kind that's meant to say dirty things in the dark. It goes perfectly with her eyes. I have no doubt there will be a lot of wet dreams featuring that voice tonight.

I'm even more intrigued now. This woman is an unusual and very attractive blend of chaste and fiery, a combination I've never before encountered—and that's saying a lot. I've tasted pretty much every type of woman this world has to offer. Or at least I thought I had.

Wouldn't you know I'd finally find someone who really *interests me* here, *of all places.*

My eyes don't leave her until she disappears back into the crowd that sits between us. Even as other people rise to speak, and even though it's undoubtedly inadvisable, I know I'll see Violet, Sex Addict again. Up close and personal. And soon.

THREE: *Violet*

I can't get to the door fast enough. I'm irritated, I'm humiliated, and I'm a terrible liar. Trying to keep my head down and my feet moving quickly, I steadily make my way through the crowd.

Someone pushes open the exit, letting in the cool, crisp night air. It ruffles my hair and draws me toward it like a moth to the flame. That's freedom just up ahead and I'm scrambling for it.

But I'm not scrambling fast enough.

A few feet before I reach my goal, someone steps into my path. I see denim-clad legs right in my way. And they aren't moving.

I glance up to find the meeting coordinator, Lyle, standing in front of me, smiling. "Don't run off. At least give me a chance to welcome you to the meeting and explain a little about what we do." He gestures to a table. It's surrounded by chatting addicts and laden with cookies, cups, and a big urn of coffee. "Can I buy you a drink?"

I refrain from commenting on his poor choice of phrasing. Ironically, it sounds like a cheesy pick-up line. From the coordinator of a sex addicts meeting. *At* the meeting.

If that ain't funny . . .

But rather than commenting on his gall, I smile and dig deep for some courage and a really good story. "Oh, there's no need. I've been to dozens of these," I say with a casual wave of my hand. "I've been . . . uh . . . in control now for three years, so there's no need for you to waste your time on me when there are so many others here that might need you."

I give him a friendly nod and start to move around him. "That's great news! Congratulations! Our group could use someone just like you. We have folks in varying stages of the twelve steps, but few in your position that still attend meetings."

I feel a surge of panic coming on. I thought a story like that would make me *less* of a target or spectacle, not opt me into something worse.

In my head, I curse my best friend and her loose-and-free tendencies. I should've known she'd never show up tonight. Yet here I am, lying to a room full of sex addicts, making up stories about mastering a sex problem that I don't have and never expect to.

I *am* glad, however, that my lie sounded convincing. Probably because it wasn't *really* a lie. At least not all of it. Since my ex, Connelly, and I broke up three years ago, I haven't been with anyone, so basically what I said was true. It's just the "addict" part that's a bit of a stretch.

Or a lot of a stretch.

I loved Connelly, but never in a million years could he have turned me into a sex fiend. Our sex life was more of an obligation. Or a gift. A concession—*my* concession to *him*. I did it because I knew he liked it, not because I really got much out of it. I'm sure the other people in this room would laugh their butts off if they knew the *real* me—lukewarm in the sack, with no intentions of heating up.

But they won't. Mainly because once I leave here—if I can manage to get out—I'm never coming back. Tia can suck it up and come by herself. I did!

"I'd love to," I say, trying not to stumble over the blatant lie (I would much rather have a root canal), "but I have some place I need to be."

Lyle frowns at me, but doesn't question me further. "Oh, okay. Well, I hope we'll see you again. This crowd could benefit from someone like you. It's good to see victors. Those who have overcome." His smile makes me feel even worse about my deception, but I don't let it sway me.

"Thank you. I, uh, I . . . sorry, I need to go."

I move around him, refocusing on the door. When I'm within a few inches of it, the tension already beginning to drain from my limbs, someone else steps right between me and freedom.

Again, I stop. But this time I stop not because I can't move past the obstacle, but because, for just a moment, I don't want to.

Those eyes . . . I recognize them instantly. I might dream about them later. I might remember them forever. They belong to the guy who was watching me when I stood up. They were disconcerting then, but now . . . seeing them with the rest of him . . . they're a thousand times worse.

Or maybe a thousand times better.

Tall and striking, he oozes the very sex appeal that makes him fit right in with this type of group. I doubt for a second that he's even real, that he's even human. That he's anything more than a figment of my imagination. Everything about him is an invitation—his eyes, his smile, his posture. From his spiky black hair and dazzling blue eyes to his perfect lips and politely casual smile, he appeals to me like no one has ever appealed to me before. But he reeks of danger and hedonism, two things I avoid like the plague. Two things I've never wanted *not* to avoid.

Until now.

As we stare at each other, I wonder if he's going to speak to me. And, if so, what he might say. I mean, we *are* at an SAA meeting. I'm sure picking up the other attendees is at the very least frowned upon. Before I can get too carried away pondering it, though, he smiles courteously and steps aside, stretching out his arm to push open the door for me.

I'm admittedly a little disappointed, which is stupid. I ought to be *glad* he's aiding in my escape, not hindering it. And yet, as I return his smile and step forward, I'm not. Not at all. So caught up in my thoughts and my fascination am I, it's no wonder that I get tangled in my own feet when I pass him, tripping and nearly falling right into him.

Fast as lightning, his hands reach out to catch me, righting me before I can make an even bigger fool of myself.

"Ohmigod, I'm so sorry," I say, feeling my cheeks burst into blood-red flame. I keep my eyes cast down as I lean back, once again stable on my feet.

"Please don't apologize," his deep voice rumbles.

I lick my lips before I raise my eyes to his. Part of me knows I should turn and run, foregoing common courtesies and niceties. Something in me, some deep and rarely used instinct that lives within, knows that once I meet those eyes, I'll be forever lost. It makes no sense, but I know it like I know my name and my eye color and the way my hair flips out on the ends when it's rainy outside.

Despite my better judgment, I do it. I look up and up and up until I reach a blue so fathomless I feel like I could dive into it and never reach the bottom. Like I could drown and never even know it.

But I can't do that. I can't dive in. Not with a guy like this. I've seen what someone like this can do to a person—turn that which was once whole and capable into nothing more than scattered pieces of wreckage and ruin.

"I'm Jet," he offers softly, his eyes never leaving mine.

Jet. Even his name is sexy, which makes me more uncomfortable.

Ridiculous! my rational, level-headed, slightly bitter side scoffs. It pipes up with its less bedazzled perspective, reminding me that guys like this are nothing more than predators. The love 'em and leave 'em type. And he's obviously worse than most, as evidenced by his attendance here. Apparently, he's got a *real* problem.

I give him a tight smile as I straighten away from him. "Violet. Nice to meet you," I say, hurrying to continue. "Excuse me please."

I slip on my familiar, no-nonsense persona like a protective shield, like the armor that has kept me from harm all these years. It has never failed me before; I don't expect it to now.

My head is high, my spine is rigid, and my imperviousness is firmly in place as I move past the dark and damaged stranger. With every step I take, I determine to put him out of my mind and never think of him again.

Until he speaks once more. His words make dents in my breastplate like armor-piercing rounds.

"It's short," he calls from a few steps behind me.

Confused, I turn.

Knowing I shouldn't, *still* I turn.

"Pardon?"

"My name. It's short."

"Short for what?"

I watch as he moves toward me, narrowing the space I only just created. He stops within inches and bends slightly forward, one side of his mouth pulling up into a self-deprecating grin. "Jethro."

And, just like that, he's human. And vulnerable. And slightly imperfect. And even more dangerous to me than he was before.

FOUR: *Jet*

I thought at first she was going to just walk away. Ignore me. And that's never happened before. Never. I tell myself that's why I told her my name. My *real* name. Normally, I guard that like I guard my heart—with a grip like a bear trap, ready to take off the limbs of any who might seek to uncover it. Yet I just handed it over to this girl. Because she wasn't responding to me.

What kind of messed-up egotistical shit is that?

But my instinct was obviously spot-on. My unusual and notably impulsive revelation worked. I see the change on her face, in her eyes the instant my words penetrate the wall she was erecting.

Her grin is small, but open and sympathetic. "Really?"

I give her an exaggerated sigh. "Really. See why I go by 'Jet'?"

Her smile widens, bringing out a dimple at one corner of her mouth. My first thought is that I'd like to lick it. My second is to wonder what she'd do if I did. Slap me? Cuss me out? Kiss me? Take me outside and beg me to get between those long legs? With a walking, talking contradiction like this woman, it's hard to say, but I'm very anxious to find out.

FIVE: *Violet*

For a few seconds, my heart feels light. I'm not thinking of serious things or concentrating on being responsible. For a few seconds, I'm not feeling defensive or calculating ways I can avoid being sucked into some destructive habit. No, for just a few seconds, I feel happy and worry-free. Playful. Impulsive. More like the friends and family I've been surrounded by all my life, the ones who never consider consequences or stress about tomorrow.

But that's not me. It never has been. I'm not *that girl*—one that would hang around a Sex Addicts Anonymous meeting for *any* length of time to talk to *anybody*. I've never found someone that interesting. Or found myself this interest*ed*. And yet, here I am, thinking I'd like nothing more than to stand here and talk to this handsome stranger who suddenly seems to be more than meets the eye.

With the DANGER! DANGER! DANGER! alerts going off

like crazy in my head, I remind myself that this is the kind of thing that could get a girl into trouble. I've seen it far too many times.

It takes great effort to tear my eyes away from his, but I do it. I expect to feel instantly clearheaded and more like myself, but I don't. I can still see the piercing blue as if I were still staring into it.

Not willing to risk looking up again, I keep my head down, making a big production out of digging through my purse for my keys.

"Well, it was nice to meet you, Jet." I glance up only long enough to move past him. "Enjoy your night."

The nip of the night air cools my heated cheeks when I plunge myself out into the dark. As much as I want to leave that meeting, and the deception and the humiliation of it behind, it's hard for me not to look back. I know Jet is standing in the doorway watching me. Not only can I hear the sounds from inside and smell the aroma of the coffee, I can feel his eyes on me, warm against the cool air.

I'm smart enough to know that's not a good sign.

"Where *were* you?" I ask Tia when she finally answers her phone.

"What?"

"Where were you tonight?"

Her reply is quick and unconcerned. "With Dennis, like I was supposed to be. Like I still am. Where were you?"

"Ti-a! Seriously?"

"Seriously, what? What's your damage?"

"My damage is that I just had to get up in front of a group of people and claim to be a sex addict because I went as moral support for *somebody* who didn't even bother to show up!"

"Oh shit! Was that tonight?"

"Yes, Tia. It was tonight. I told you this morning that it was tonight. I told you yesterday at lunch that it was tonight. Did I need to scribble it on a Post-it note and stick it to your forehead?"

"Vi, I'm so sorry! I swear I didn't space on purpose. You know my memory sucks."

"I know. That's why I reminded you. Twice."

"You know I'm not very organized either." I can hear the pout in her voice.

I sigh. She's right. I know all these things about her, and I should've expected this. It's typical of Tia, and I'm sure it's one of the reasons I'm so drawn to her. She's kind of a mess, which is my specialty, something I learned early in life. Besides that, she's been my best friend since we were kids. I can't *not* love her. "I know you didn't do it on purpose. I'm just . . . frustrated."

The line goes silent for several seconds before Tia speaks. Her voice is small, like a little girl's. "Was it awful?"

I have to be careful how I answer her. It would take very little to discourage her from *ever* going. Even though I know she loves Dennis and I believe he's good for her, Tia isn't exactly the type that will make herself miserable to please someone else. But she needs this. Dennis or not, she needs this.

So I fib. Just a little. "No, it wasn't that bad. I just hated having to be there alone."

I can almost hear her pushing her lower lip out farther in a bigger pout. "I'm the worst best friend ever."

"No, you're not. You're just . . . free-spirited."

"I'm a total moron."

"Don't say things like that," I chastise lovingly. Tia has enough self-esteem issues courtesy of her villain of a father. I'm convinced it's part of the reason that she acts the way she does. She has a wonderful heart. She just has some problems with self-control and with finding comfort and validation in the arms of random men whenever she's feeling down. "You are smart and beautiful, and you can do this. You can do it for Dennis, and you can do it for yourself. And I'll be right there beside you the whole way."

"You will?" I can tell by her tone that she still needs some convincing, still needs some motivation.

"I will. And you just might enjoy the scenery."

I cringe even as I say the words. I hate to use hot guys as bait to get her to the meetings, and I wouldn't if I didn't believe that she needed to be there. But I *do* believe she needs help. Help that neither Dennis nor I can give her. If these meetings don't open her eyes, I don't know what will.

"Ohmigod, I *know* you didn't just lure me to a sex addicts meeting using hot guys as bait."

I grin. "Maybe. Is it working?"

There's a very short pause. "Hell yeah, it's working!"

We both laugh.

"So does that mean you're going next week?" I'm willing to continue the ruse I started if it means helping my friend.

"If you'll go back with me, I will."

"I told you I would."

"Then yes, I'll go. Far be it for me to miss some interesting eye candy."

"Yeah, I know. That would be a travesty," I add sarcastically.

"I try to explain this to Dennis, but he just doesn't get it."

I snort and shake my head. "I can't imagine why."

I hear the muted bleep of another call coming in and hold out my phone to check the number. Even though it's not in my list of contacts, I recognize it. I've seen it pop up far too many times *not to* recognize it.

"I've got to go. I've got another call coming in."

"At almost ten o'clock on a Thursday night? Who could that be?" I don't answer. I know once she thinks about it, she'll know. "Oh," she finally says. "Damn. Here I thought maybe you'd picked up a hottie from that meeting."

"Not hardly," I say derisively. Based on my normal total and complete lack of a social life, Tia and I both know that's preposterous. What Tia *doesn't* know is that tonight I actually considered it. Even though it was just for a heartbeat, I actually ran into someone who made me forget all my million and one reasons to keep to myself.

"You take such good care of him, Vi. He's lucky to have you. We all are."

"Thanks, chickie," I say on a sigh, already dreading the night ahead. "I'll call you tomorrow."

"Let me know if you need help with him."

"I will. Thanks."

"Love you," Tia says sincerely.

"Love you, too."

I hit the swap button and answer the unwelcome second call. "Hello?"

"Hey, Vi. It's Stan. He hit his stride a little early tonight. Passed out on the bar about fifteen minutes ago. Think you can come get him?"

I swallow every comment, every emotion, even the simple sigh that is begging for release, and I answer calmly. "Sure, Stan. Give me ten minutes. I'm on the other side of town."

"Sounds good. See you then."

He hangs up, and I finally start my car. I'm still in the parking lot outside the SAA meeting. I refuse to admit that I might—just *might*—have been watching the door to see if I could catch another glimpse of Jet. I refuse to admit it because that would be pathetic. And immature. And much more emotional than I ever get. I'm too levelheaded to let a guy like Jet get under my skin. Or *any* guy for that matter. Getting too involved, too dependent on a man for happiness leads to trouble. Trouble I've seen and trouble I don't need. So I avoid them. Unless it's to help them—professionally. Otherwise, it's just not worth it.

I keep telling myself that as I drive across the small town of Greenfield, South Carolina, to the Teak Tavern, my father's watering hole of choice. His other favorite bar-type place in town is called Lucky's, but Dad was banned from there a long time ago.

I see his truck outside. It's parked straight inside the lines of the space, which tells me he was okay when he left the house. At least he wasn't out drinking and driving *before* he hit the tavern. He's done that before, and it both infuriates *and* distresses me. It would be a tragedy in every way if he hit someone and hurt them. Not only for the victim and their family, but for Dad as well. He's still pretty fragile emotionally and that would do him in for sure.

I pull up along the curb, close to the front door and cut the engine. I've learned all the best tricks for getting him out the door and home quickly and safely. Having the car close is step number one.

I see Dad as soon as I walk into the tavern. He's sitting on a stool, slumped over onto the bar, mouth hanging open, snoring like a freight train. At least this one won't be a violent, argumentative episode. I hope not, anyway. When he's already passed out, that's usually a good sign. It's when he's awake and running his mouth that poses a problem most of the time.

I walk in, greeting Stan as I pass. "Thanks for calling me, Stan."

He smiles as he dries a glass with his white bar towel. He reminds me of Sam from one of my Dad's favorite old shows, *Cheers*, anyway, but he looks even more like him when he dries glassware. "Not a problem, Vi," he replies pleasantly. "Always a pleasure to see you."

Even though Stan is a good ten years older than my twenty-two, I get the feeling that he's attracted to me. He always watches me with an extremely . . . appreciative look in his eye. Not that it matters, because I'm *so* not interested. So. Not. Interested.

I walk to the end of the bar where my father is passed out and lay my hand gently on his arm, doing my best not to startle him. The most I can hope for is that he'll wake up just enough to get to the car and then pass out again until I can get him home. "Dad, wake up. It's time to go home."

He grunts, but makes no move to sit up or even adjust his position. I give him a little shake. "Dad. My car's parked outside. Time to go home."

I hear his tearful moan and he slurs, "I don't wanna go home."

I fight the guilt that swells in my gut like a sponge in water. "Why not?" I ask. I know the answer already, but my point is not to ask him questions I need answers to. My point is just to get him talking. If I can keep him somewhat involved in the conscious world around him, I'll have a better chance of getting him up and to the car.

"All alone. Everyone left me," he mutters, rolling his head to the side to glare at me with one unfocused green eye.

"I didn't leave you, Dad. I just moved out. There's a difference."

"No, there's not."

"Yes, there is. I'm only a couple of miles away and I still see you almost every day."

"But you left."

"I didn't leave. I grew up, Dad. I would never leave you."

He lifts his head and stares up at me, tears filling his remorseful eyes. "I know you wouldn't, Vi. I'm just lonely."

My heart aches for him. He drives me crazy sometimes, but I love him and I wish there was something I could do to help fill the space that my mother left when she bailed for good four years ago.

"I know you are. That's why I come over so often. I see you more now than when I lived there."

And that's true. There were many days when I'd leave before he got up and he'd be gone by the time I got home, but now I go by almost every day to take him lunch wherever he's cutting grass or pulling weeds for his landscaping business. I make the effort because I worry about him. And, evidently, it's a valid worry.

"It's just not the same. The house is so big. And empty."

"I'll come by more at night, Dad. I promise. But right now, let's get you to bed. You need your rest. It won't do for you to be tired tomorrow."

When he gets like this, a soft, motherly approach works wonders.

"No, I don't want to be tired," he says brokenly.

"I know. What do you say we get out of here?"

My father nods his rusty orange head and slides off the barstool, grabbing onto the brass bar rail for balance until he gets his equilibrium. I wait patiently, just like I always do. Dad moves at his own pace, just like he always does. It only makes him mad if I try to rush him. I learned that the hard way.

After six excruciating minutes of watching him take a step, sway, catch himself, and then occasionally stop to slap someone on the back and ask them what they're drinking, we finally make it out the door to my waiting car. Once he's safely inside, I run around to the driver's side and slide in behind the wheel. He's snoring before I even start the engine.

SIX: *Jet*

The other guys in the band tease me about being such a lucky bastard. I've never really thought of myself as lucky, but this . . . this makes me wonder if maybe they're right. Tonight, I can see why they'd say that.

I've never been in this little market before, so I'm forced to walk the main aisle and look down each row in search of the beer cooler. It's not in the very front *or* the very back, which is unusual, I think. I probably would've ended up leaving, frustrated, had I not seen the beautiful Violet, Sex Addict standing in the coffee aisle. Needless to say, at this point, I'd like to shake the hand of the dumbass who arranged the goods this way. If he (or she) hadn't, I'd never have seen her.

After about a heartbeat and a half of thought, I hang a right and saunter down the aisle, stopping beside her like I'm looking for coffee, too. She ignores me at first, but finally, nearly a full minute later, she gives in and glances over.

From the corner of my eye, I see her do a double take and then turn to stare straight ahead. A few seconds later, she casually takes a step away, down the aisle. Suppressing a grin, I take an equally casual step to follow her. I see her raise her hand to tap a finger against her chin, like she's debating, and then she takes another step away. Warming to the little cat and mouse thing we've got going on, I take another step toward her.

I see her glance quickly in my direction again, so I turn to her and say, "Ma'am, could you please stop crowding me?"

Her muted gray eyes go round for one indignant second before I see a playful light turn them to soft puffs of pale smoke. Seeing the change makes me feel strangely gratified. I get the feeling she doesn't play or tease often.

"Of course! Pardon me. I *do* apologize for being such an aisle hog," she teases, a grin flirting with her lips as she slides farther away.

I shuffle down the aisle after her.

"Don't you just hate it when people get in your space when you're trying to pick out coffee?" I complain jokingly. "God, it's so distracting. Especially when they smell really nice."

Soft color blooms in her cheeks, making my groin ache. I can all but picture her face flushed like that, right in the middle of an orgasm. Her lush lips parted, her brow slightly puckered, her smooth skin shiny with sweat.

Aw hell!

I shift from one foot to the other, trying to alleviate some of the strain behind my zipper. I can't remember the last time a woman even *came close* to giving me an unexpected hard-on in public. I'm up for some risky public foolin' around as much as the next guy, but this kind of thing could get embarrassing. And that doesn't happen to me often. Part of that might be because I don't embarrass easily.

I struggle to get my libido under control. That's another thing that doesn't happen to me often. I mean, women excite me—most *all* women, every size and shape—but I'm a little desensitized because I usually get what I want. Females don't deny me. They never have. But this girl, I know she would. She would shoot me down if I even *attempted* to engage her. And, like any stubborn or forbidden fruit, that makes her even more irresistible. And that *really* excites me!

I give her an easy smile, but I see that she's taking on that apprehensiveness again, probably getting ready to make her excuses to get away. Naturally, my ego steps in and I preempt her, continuing before she has a chance to cut me off. "Well, enjoy your shopping."

I turn to walk away, but stop when I hear her confused voice. "Aren't you going to get some coffee?"

"Nah. I just saw you standing there and thought I'd come by and be friendly." I pause, holding her gaze for several seconds. "I mean, if you can't be friendly with the people who know your deepest, darkest secrets then who *can* you be friendly with?"

She nods slowly. "I guess I never thought of it that way."

I give her a lopsided grin. "Well then I've done my good deed for the day. Next time, it'll be your turn. Give and take. Part of the process."

"The process?" she says, her brows drawing together.

"You know, the process of overcoming. Helping each other along the way, making it through. Being a shoulder or a friendly face, whatever is needed."

"Oh, right right. I'm sorry. It's just . . . it's been a long night."

"Well, hang in there. And if you need to talk, I'm a great listener."

"Thanks, but I really need to be getting home." Violet reaches for a container of coffee and starts to back away. "I appreciate the offer, though. It's . . . it's very kind of you."

I shrug. "Not necessary. Just doin' my part."

She nods and smiles, finally turning to walk away. I try not to watch her ass as she goes.

I fail miserably.

SEVEN: *Violet*

I roll over, turning away from the sun that's streaming through the window. Every muscle aches as I shift and turn, this way and that, trying to resituate. Dad's voice startles me and I jump, flipping over and causing a painful twinge to reverberate along my spine.

"You stayed," he observes simply.

"Yeah, I . . . uh . . . I was tired and didn't want to drive home."

"On a good day, I could *walk* to your house. It's not that far."

"And your point would be . . . ?"

"That you weren't too tired to drive the very short distance home. I know why you stayed. You stayed because of me. And slept on this awful couch," he says, his eyes full of guilt and regret. "I'm so sorry, Vi. I did it again, didn't I?"

I sigh and ease slowly into a sitting position. I can't really deny it.

I *did* stay because of him. And I *did* sleep on this awful couch because of him.

"It's not a big deal, Dad."

"It's a big deal to me. How many times have you slept on that couch just to keep an eye on me? To take care of me when I get sick or stop me from going right back out the door and getting in my truck and hurting someone? You practically grew up on that thing, guarding the front door."

"It's not a big deal," I repeat, wondering if my aching back will ever agree. The couch is old and the cushions lost their gusto about a hundred years ago. Now they sag toward the middle, dragging whoever is unfortunate enough to lie atop it into an uncomfortable U shape. Not a good thing for a side sleeper like me.

"I . . . I wish I could do better, honey," he says tearfully.

I know his distress is genuine. I honestly believe he *wants* to do better. It's simply beyond him to do so. He's been this way for far too long. But more importantly, I think he's lost the will to fight it. When it became obvious that my mother had finally left *for good*, he stopped having long periods of living a healthy life. Now, he just gets by in between bouts.

The problem is that I'm not the most influential woman in his life. Never have been, never will be. My mother holds that position. I've always just sort of held him together until she comes back. Until she didn't. He's been in a downward spiral ever since.

"I know, Dad. It's okay. But you're still making progress. Just don't give up."

"Cutting back to only torturing your daughter a couple of times a month is hardly what I'd call progress."

"Dad," I say in a stern yet loving voice, "when it's down from twice a *week*, it is most definitely progress."

He smiles weakly. "If I could just forget about her, maybe I'd be able to kick it completely."

"I have faith in you. I don't think you'll ever forget, but I don't think you *need* to. One day, you'll master these new coping skills, and you won't feel the need to drown your sorrow over losing her. You'll be able to deal with it in a healthy way."

"I wish I was half the man you think I am, Vi."

"I love you for who you already are, Dad. But that doesn't mean I don't see the potential for you to be happy and well-adjusted one day."

"I hope you're right. And I know if there's a chance that I could be, it would be because of you. I don't know what I'd do without you."

I stand, folding the beige throw I used as a cover all night and then draping it over the back of the couch. I walk to my dad, reaching around his big shoulders to hug him. "Lucky for you, you never have to worry about that. I'm not going anywhere."

"I hope, for your sake, that's not true. I want you to have a happy life one day, honey."

"I *do* have a happy life, Dad. I have a job I love, family I adore, and friends to keep me busy. What more could I ask for?"

"You're a social worker. All you do is listen to helpless people talk about their hopeless problems all day."

"But I'm good at it, Dad. I'm a problem fixer. I love to help people."

"It's because you've been doing it your whole life. You *had to be* good at it."

"*However* I got where I am, I'm happy with the result. There's nothing wrong with liking to help people."

"What about a boyfriend?"

"That'll happen one day, but I'm not going to rush it." I don't add the part about how a man in my life is trouble I don't need. I've seen what love can do to a person. It makes them weak and frail and can utterly ruin their life. It can be as destructive as any addiction. Look at my dad, for Pete's sake! Thanks, but no thanks.

"That's because you're smart. You'll do it the right way and it'll last forever."

I say nothing, just smile up into his haggard face. "How about some coffee? I saw that you were out and I went to the store last night. I got your favorite."

His smile is lighter when he says, "I know. I've already got it in the machine. The water is heating as we speak."

I raise my eyebrows in surprised appreciation. "Well, didn't you wake up feisty?"

"Sometimes people can surprise you in a good way, Vi. Don't ever forget that."

Again, I say nothing, but I'm silently hoping for the day that begins to happen.

EIGHT: *Jet*

I'm a little surprised when I find myself parked in front of the building that, after business hours, becomes the weekly meeting place for SAA. I wasn't sure I'd come back tonight, that it would be worth it. But after spending the better part of a week thinking of dove gray eyes and a shy smile, I don't think there was any real way I'd miss this. I just hope she's here.

I walk in and take a seat, nodding to the people who look my way. All the men look antsy, like they've got a monkey on their back and they just entered the gorilla cage. And I'm sure that's how they feel, like they're tiptoeing around, waiting to get torn apart by their needs. It doesn't help that there's a shitload of ass walking around.

To be a support group for people who are addicted to sex, there are an awful lot of women here. Some of them look as though they aren't very committed to being celibate, even for a day, which I find curious. I can't decide if they're the ones who have been coming here the longest, who have suffered through the hardest part of their dry spell, or if they're new to the program and the edge just hasn't worn off yet. Either way, it's an interesting mix in here. The one thing we all have in common—male, female, new, or old—is excess. We *all* know about excess. What fewer people know, especially people in a room like this, is moderation. I can relate to that most of all. I know very little about denying myself. And, if I'm being honest, I'm not really keen on the idea of learning.

I keep a casual eye on the door, waiting for Violet, Sex Addict to appear. I glance at the wall clock again. Three minutes until the meeting starts. Maybe she isn't going to show. Being in her position, having conquered her desires, she might not need regular support. But, as cruel as it sounds, I hope she does. At least enough to bring her back in here tonight.

NINE: *Violet*

"I don't know how I get myself into these messes," I mumble as I lead Tia through the door and into the stuffy SAA meeting room.

"You're not in a mess, Vi. You're at a meeting with your best friend as a show of support. We're both doing this for the people we love. End of story. Neither of us needs to be here, but that doesn't mean we can't fit in. Just relax. The hard part's over for *you*."

I ignore Tia's comment about not needing to be here. Little does she know, but she *very much* needs to be here. "Tia, these people think I'm a long-standing sex addict who has somehow managed to kick my addiction. Trust me, the hard part is *far* from over. What if they ask me questions?" I hiss.

"Lie."

"I'm a terrible liar! You know that!"

Tia pulls on my arm to stop me before we are surrounded by too many ears. "Look, you've worked with all sorts of twisted people. Just channel some of that emotional shit you get to hear every day and you'll be fine. It's me you should be worried about anyway."

I say nothing. I *am* actually worried about Tia. I'm afraid that nothing will make her see what's really going on. I'm afraid that her denial will prevent her from seeing how much she has in common with these people, and that she'll live the rest of her life missing out on the important things if she doesn't learn to control herself. If she can't ever *see* her weaknesses, she won't ever be able to overcome them.

Whoever said admitting you have a problem is the first step was a friggin' genius!

Before I can formulate an appropriate response, Lyle, the meeting coordinator, takes the podium.

"Welcome, everyone. Can you please take your seats?"

As Tia and I are making our way to two empty chairs on the back row, I look up and my eyes collide with warm blue ones. My gait falters as we stare at each other. He nods once and then looks away.

I purposely keep my eyes trained straight ahead until we are seated. Tia leans over and whispers in my ear, "Holy Mary mother of God, you weren't kidding about hot guys, were you?"

I shush her and tip my head toward the front of the room, hoping she'll drop it and pay attention like she needs to.

No such luck.

"Do you know him, Vi? Did you meet him last week? Who is he?"

"No, I don't know him. I met him briefly last week. His name is Jet. Now zip it and pay attention," I say with mock severity. Even if

I did want to talk to her about Jet, which I don't, I don't want to talk about it *now*. Not only is that rude, but the last thing I need to do is draw attention to myself.

As he did last week, Lyle asks if there is anyone that's new to this particular meeting. Two people raise their hands. Evidently there's a never-ending supply of sex addicts. Lyle welcomes them and then moves through a brief explanation of the SAA philosophy, which is based on the Alcoholics Anonymous 12-Step program.

I try to listen, but I can't seem to focus on what he's saying for long. I find myself watching Jet from the corner of my eye. I can just make him out between two people if they both shift the right way. I see his head move several times as though he might be turning to look at me, but I can't be sure. And I *won't* be sure either. I can't risk looking directly at him and getting caught. Instead, I stare straight ahead like I'm deeply interested in what's going on at the front of the room.

Eventually, we make it through to the part where everyone stands up and says their little piece. Some have a longer, more in depth story to tell, which terrifies me. I don't want anyone to ask me for *my* story. Because, you know, I *don't have one*.

My anxiety rises the closer it gets to being my turn. Tia is to my left, which means that she goes first, though. Leave it to her to make it worse and give me something else to freak out about.

She stands after the person to *her* left sits back down. I can tell by her posturing that she's treating this like her time in the spotlight rather than the humiliating experience that it is. She smooths her tight jeans and gives everyone a beaming smile. Internally, I shake my head. The *least* she could do is *pretend* she's here for help. As it is, flipping her hair and pulling her shirt down tight, she looks like the only thing she's trying to do is make a good showing for the masculine population in the room.

Taking a deep breath, Tia puffs out her already-ample chest and begins in her charming way. "Hi, my name is Tia, and I'm a sex addict. Ummm, I never really saw that I had a problem until I met this wonderful woman." She pauses to cast an amazingly convincing smile of gratitude down upon me. "She has helped me so much. If it weren't for Violet, I'd still be living in my old ways. It's through her strength and with her support that I'm here tonight. "

Well, at least that part's true, I think to myself as I struggle to keep the cringe off my face. Meanwhile, Tia is eating up having a roomful of eyes trained on her. She really should've been an actress. She's already got the self-control issues and the narcissism down pat.

She bends down and kisses my cheek then turns to give the audience a tearful smile. All that's missing is for her to take a bow. They clap for her as she takes her seat, and then all eyes turn toward me.

I stand, a blush stinging my cheeks as I do. I glance around the room, determined to casually skim over Jet. But when my eyes meet his, they stop, refusing to go any further. He's watching me, his gaze intense. I feel a warm flush pour through me, despite the cool temperature of the room, and I squirm uncomfortably.

I waste valuable time chastising myself, arguing that I should *not* be getting any kind of warm fuzzies over a guy in a place like this, one who has a problem like the one he's got. He's trouble that I don't need. He's a kind of broken that I can't fix.

"Violet, why don't you tell us a little bit about your journey," Lyle suggests when my silence drags on too long.

My mind spins in a panic and I feel my heartbeat as though it's hammering right behind my eyes. "I'd love to, Lyle, but I'd like tonight to be about my friend Tia, if you don't mind. She's heard my story a thousand times, and I'd rather this be the beginning of her own journey."

Lyle smiles in his softly accepting way and nods at me. "What an amazing sponsor you must be, Violet."

"Oh, I'm not her sponsor," I correct before I have time to think better of it. Then, when I do, I could kick myself.

"Well, her loss is our gain. You'd be a great sponsor."

I give him an uneasy smile and take my seat, silently cursing Tia for making this nightmare that much worse.

On edge, I'm ready to deflect and defend for the rest of the night, but, thankfully, the need doesn't arise. I must've said just the right thing. No one else asks me anything for the remainder of the session.

Until Tia and I are headed for the door.

"Violet," I hear a deep and oddly familiar voice say just as we are on our way out the door.

I look back to see Jet making his way toward me, two coffee cups in hand. He gives me a lopsided grin when he reaches me, handing me one of them. "I thought I'd buy you a drink," he says casually. "Because I *know* you drink coffee."

I return his smile, taking the cup yet knowing I won't drink a drop of the steaming contents. It would keep me up all night. "Yes, I do. Thank you."

"Vi," I hear from the other side of the partially open door. "You coming?" It's Tia. I glance behind me in time to see her poke her head back inside. Her eyes meet mine for a fraction of a second before they rise and widen. I know exactly who they're trained on behind me. I feel a surge of possessive jealousy well up inside me, which is very unusual. I chalk it up to wanting to keep Jet to myself so that neither he *nor* Tia does something stupid.

At least that's what I tell myself.

Tia walks slowly back into the room, her hips already adopting that swivel they get when she's interested in someone. I turn toward her when she stops in front of me. I see her flash her most dazzling smile over my shoulder.

"Tia, right?" Jet says from behind me. I see his muscular forearm shoot out past me at my side as he leans forward to offer his hand, his chest pressing into my back.

"Yes. You remembered," Tia says, happily sliding her palm over his.

"I'm Jet. It's nice to meet you."

"Likewise," she drawls, all but salivating. It isn't hard to picture her with the toothy grin of a great white shark, sharp teeth flashing in the light as it opens its mouth to gulp down its prey.

Jet's next words surprise me. "Tia, would you mind if I borrowed Violet? I promise to bring her right back."

His words surprise Tia, too, as evidenced by the way they round in confusion. She's not accustomed to anyone else getting the least bit of attention when she's around. She's beautiful, vivacious, and extremely flirtatious. When she sets her sights on something, she unerringly gets it.

And I can't help but wonder if now they'll be set on Jet.

Still, Tia recovers quickly and graciously agrees. "Of course not. I don't mind sharing."

There's no mistaking what she *really* means by that comment. I glance back at Jet. It's obvious by the wink he gives Tia that *he* didn't miss it either. Rather than respond, however, he just looks down at me as though she never spoke. He tips his head toward the wall behind us. "Do you mind?"

I'm so caught off guard, I don't think to do anything but agree. "Of course not."

All I can think of are Tia's eyes on me as Jet lays his hand on the small of my back and guides me away from her. He leads me to a corner that's fairly private—well, as private as two people can be when surrounded by a roomful of ears and eyes.

When he stops, leaning casually against the concrete block and smiling down at me, I forget all about Tia. And everyone else in the room, for that matter. The only person I'm aware of is Jet—Jet with his piercing eyes, Jet with his heart-stopping smile. Jet with his bag full of problems that somehow make him real and more attractive than any other man I've known.

"Look, I, uh . . . I was wondering . . ."

He trails off. I wait for him to continue.

I don't mind waiting. If he never said another word, I'm not sure I'd care. I could stare at him, stare into those amazing, fathomless eyes for days on end and never utter a single complaint. When he finally speaks, I struggle to focus on his words.

Jet takes a deep breath and blurts, "Would you be my sponsor? I know it's not the normal practice since we are the opposite sex, but you're pretty much the only one in our group who *could* do it."

My mind is filled with the sound of screeching brakes. His words are like a concrete barrier in front of the speeding car of my silent fawning.

"Jet, I—"

"I know it's probably a headache for you to even consider it, but let me tell you first how much I would appreciate it. I promise not to bother you every day like some people might. I'm very familiar with my . . . triggers, and it's during those times that I could really use a little help. Sometimes just an ear, sometimes maybe a visit to keep me focused on what I need to be focused on. I swear I won't be a full-time job."

When he finishes, Jet gives me a wry yet charming smile. It reminds me that, while he's amazingly handsome and charismatic as all hell, he's *just a guy*. Human. Like the rest of us. He's just a little weaker in some areas than the majority of the population, but at least he's smart enough to realize it and try to get some help. And whether he knows it or not, he's speaking my language. I'm nothing if not helpful.

I sigh, worrying my lip as I nervously contemplate all the hundred and one ways this could go awry. I *want* to help him. I do. And a big part of me is already saying yes. I mean, how hard could it be to make sure the guy goes home alone?

But the more reserved part of me is reminding me that I'd be doing this under false pretenses. It's all a lie on my end. This could blow up in my face in the worst possible way. And end up hurting *him*.

With Jet watching me as I deliberate, I try to formulate an appropriately easy letdown. Unfortunately, that gives Tia just enough time to jump in and make my life a little harder than it was fifteen seconds ago.

"Of course she will," Tia says, stepping up to us from where she was standing closer to the door.

Jet and I start to respond at the same time.

"Tia, I—" I begin.

"I don't want to impose if you think—" Jet says.

But Tia interrupts us both.

"I don't want to hear excuses. This isn't the place for excuses, right? This is a place where we can be real with each other, where we come for help. Jet, Vi is an amazing person and such a great fixer. And you need fixing. This is right up her alley," she says, turning to smile meaningfully into my eyes. "She's helped me so much, and I know she can help you, too. She's just shy. Once you get past that, I think you two will really be able to . . . connect."

Ohmigod! Tia!

Jet turns his penetrating gaze back to me. The hopeful yet hesitant look in them is the very reason that I *want* to agree. "I really could use the help."

I look back and forth between Jet and Tia. I tell myself that I really *can't* say no now. If I protest too much, it might seem suspicious. Plus, this might be a great way to keep Tia coming to the meetings.

Yeah, that's what I tell myself. The problem is that I'm a little too pleased to agree. And that is *not* a good sign.

"I'll do it," I say, turning to Tia. "And since Tia will be coming back each week, she can help encourage you. These meetings are very important after all."

Tia's laugh is the nonverbal equivalent of a *Touché!* I give her my sweetest, most innocuous smile. "See, Violet, you're always thinking."

A short, uncomfortable silence falls between the three of us. Jet is the first to break it. "There's more," he says, clearing his throat. "One of the reasons I wanted to ask you tonight is that tomorrow night is one of those times that's particularly hard for me. I wondered if maybe you would . . . if you could . . ."

"Of course she will," Tia chimes in again, overenthusiastic. Now she's doing it just to needle me. I see the challenge light her eyes. She's enjoying this.

"We *both* will," I add, sending a subtle glare at Tia. "Weekends are hard for Tia, too. This will be good for her."

Tia punches me playfully on the shoulder. "Youuu," she starts through gritted teeth, her smile notably forced, "you're such a little . . . *helper.*"

I almost laugh. I have no doubt that sentence ended much differently in her head. But this is what she gets for putting her manipulative nose in my business. "That's me."

"Great, then let me give you the address," Jet says. "Do you have your phone with you?"

"My phone?" I ask, not really understanding why he'd need that to give me an address.

"Yes, your phone," he repeats with a grin. "I thought we could exchange numbers and then I'd text you the address so you'd have it tomorrow. Isn't that pretty standard with this kind of thing? That we exchange phone numbers so that I can call you if I get into trouble?"

I shake my head and wave him off casually, like I'm just being absentminded. "Right, right. Of course. I'm just a little . . . it's been a long day."

In my head, I smack my forehead. That's almost exactly what I said at the store last week. If I'm to continue this charade, I'll have to come up with something better than "a long day" to excuse my lack of knowledge.

I dig out my phone and hand it to Jet. I try not to focus too much on how big and perfectly formed his hands are, or how nimbly his fingers move over the screen of my smartphone. It's not like me to feel this kind of instant attraction—or really, very much attraction *at all*—to a guy. To say I'm flustered would be a grave understatement.

When Jet finishes, he hands me back my phone and then punches something into his own. A few seconds later, my phone bleeps with an incoming text. I glance down to see his name and number pop up.

"Around ten?" he asks.

I open the text, not recognizing the address. But at least I won't be going by myself.

I glance up at Jet. "I'll be there."

The smile he gives me could stop a car. Or my heart. Or maybe both. "Great. I look forward to it."

I'm a little concerned by the fact that, now, I do, too.

TEN: *Jet*

I've never really felt like a piece of shit before. Not until tonight.

I mean, I'm always up front with women about who I am and what I want. They know what to expect. They know me. Or at least the me that they see onstage.

But not Violet. Not only is she nothing like the women I'm used to, but she has no idea who I am or what I'm like. And what kinds of despicable things I'm capable of. Not really.

Tonight was an all-time low for me, though. I really didn't think I'd feel this bad about it, so I'm a little surprised. I think the worst part, the part that makes me feel the shittiest, is that I'm not going to call it off. I could tell her not to come, but I won't. Why? Because there's something I want *more* than I want to feel good about myself.

This isn't about success or proving a point or winning. This is about me wanting a woman. One woman in particular.

Violet. I want Violet, and I'll do whatever it takes to have her. Period. End of story. And *that* is who I am. *That* is the *real* me.

ELEVEN: *Violet*

"What *is* this place?" I ask Tia when we pull up outside a huge, elaborately decorated red barn.

"It's the old Pfizer barn. Have you never been out here before?"

"No, should I have?"

Tia rolls her eyes. "Good God, you really *do* need to get out more. They've been renting this place out for parties for, what, five or six years now?"

"Some of us have better things to do than party in old barns," I snap, unable to keep the bitterness out of my voice.

Tia starts backpedaling immediately, sympathy dripping from her tone. "I'm sorry, Vi. I know you've never really had time for fun."

I send a frown over to Tia as I cut the engine. "I don't want your pity, Tia. That's not what I was getting at. I *chose* to do what I did. I was simply reminding you of that, reminding you of why I'm so clueless about Greenfield pop culture."

"I know. And I know it was your choice. Well, sorta." Tia turns in her seat to face me. "Don't forget, Vi, I've known you since we were kids, since that first summer your dad had to bring you over to my house while he was mowing the grass. You were sick and he was afraid to leave you, afraid your mom wouldn't come back. You've spent most of your life taking care of everybody else. As you got older, maybe it was a choice, but when you were younger it wasn't. I remember all the things we invited you to do that you *couldn't* do because either you were afraid to leave your dad or you were worried that your cousin might do something stupid. That's no way to grow up, Violet."

"I *like* helping people, Tia. You know that. It's who I am."

"I know that, but at times, it's been to the exclusion of everything else, every*one* else. It's not healthy for you not to have a life of your own. You need time to do the things that make *you* happy."

"I *do* have time for things that make me happy."

"Name one."

"I baked a caramel apple spice cake last weekend using a recipe I found online, one I'd been dying to try. You know how much I love to bake."

"Yes, I know that. But why were you doing it? Why were you baking rather than us going shopping like you had planned for three weeks? Who was the cake for?"

I pause. I know that telling her the truth will only make her point for her. "It was for me. And Dad."

"Viii," Tia warns, looking at me from narrowed eyes.

"Fine. It was for a new landscaping client Dad is trying to sign."

"See? Everyone and their crisis comes *before* you. Everyone."

I don't bother to mention that I do a lot for Tia, too. She definitely benefits from my desire to help people and fix their problems.

"There's nothing wrong with that, Tia. It doesn't make me a monster."

"No, it just keeps you from finding your *own* happiness in life."

"Helping people *does* make me happy."

"But I know you want more. You *have* to want more."

"What if I don't? What if this is all I'd like to do for the rest of my life? Is that so terrible?"

Sadness fills Tia's eyes. "No, it's not so terrible, Vi. I just hate to see you end up alone. That's all."

"There are worse things than ending up alone, Tia."

"Don't you ever want to fall in love?"

I look closely at my best friend and, for once, I'm brutally honest. "I don't think I do." She gasps in outrage. I knew she would never understand. "Maybe I don't want to pin all my hopes and dreams and happiness on one person. Maybe I don't want to give them the power to destroy me. Maybe I don't want to need someone like that. Maybe I want to be strong enough to stand on my own."

Tia's brow wrinkles. "You think love makes you weak?"

"Doesn't it?"

"Of course not. Look at me and Dennis. Look how happy we are."

"Are you, Tia? Are you really? Is Dennis? Do you know what it does to him every time you cheat on him? Do you know how much it hurts him? Can't you see how crushed he is when it happens?"

Tia tilts her head and looks at me like I'm being a difficult child. "That's not the way it is, Violet, and you know it. Dennis knows that I'm not really interested in another man the way I am in him. Those were just . . . they were just . . . flings."

"To *you* maybe, but Tia, they're killing Dennis. Why do you think the SAA meetings were even suggested? Did you think he was just trying to be mean? To get back at you?"

"No, I . . ."

I can see by the look on her face that she's never really considered Dennis's true feelings. Not really. And it's not that Tia is an awful person, or that she's heartless. She's just weak. She's addicted to attention and approval, both things she never got from her dad. And getting them from Dennis just isn't enough, not when she's feeling low. Like most addicts, there's a physical component to the addiction, but most of it is psychological. Emotional.

The mood in the car is somber and serious, even more so than what is usual for me. I feel the need to lift it. And lift Tia. This is *not* why I brought her along. Yes, I want her to open her eyes and *really see* herself and her . . . proclivities, but I would never hurt her to do it.

So I change the subject.

"Well, Miss Social Butterfly, now's your chance to show me how the fun half live. Let's go get me into some more trouble."

I say the last with as much playfulness as I can muster, but it's too soon. Tia is still stinging.

"That's my fault, too, isn't it, Vi?"

Her chin trembles like she's on the verge of tears. As is my nature, I want to make her feel better. I reach over and grab her hand, wiggling it back and forth. "Nah. I was getting bored with my deception-free, sex-addict-free evenings. I needed a little som'n som'n."

Tia's smile is tremulous, but I know by her teasing that she'll soon be over this little setback. "Well, you're in luck. I just so happen to know a guy who can give you a little som'n som'n."

"Geez, Tia, the guy's a sex addict. Isn't that kind of like shooting fish in a barrel? Singling out the weak one in the herd and all that?"

"Hey, I'm only looking out for you. I'm not worried about the weak one *or* the herd. I'm your friend. The least I can do is get you an orgasm before that thing freezes up on you."

"Tia!"

"Don't 'Tia' me! I remember how things were with you and Connelly. He fired you up about as much as an Eskimo in midwinter. But not all men are like that. And if I was a betting girl, which I'm not because I don't need to add gambling to my list of problems, I'd bet you anything that Jet could make your panties spontaneously combust with a snap of his fingers. From *across the room*." She's nodding her head to emphasize her point.

I just shake my head. "You're one twisted girl. And I like my panties just the way they are, thank you very much."

She sighs and rolls her eyes like I'm a lost cause. "That tells me all I need to know."

"And what, exactly, is that?"

"That this is an emergency. Tonight is more than just an outing with my bestie. Tonight begins the 'Save the Vagina' campaign."

With a nod, Tia unfolds her long legs from my passenger seat, gets out, and closes the door behind her. I see her dig her underwear out of her crack before she turns and bends down to smile at me through the window.

I hear her muffled words as she mouths at me, "My ass loves these things like a fat kid loves chocolate."

Again, I shake my head. I do that a lot around Tia.

TWELVE: *Jet*

I see her the instant she walks in. Obviously, I've been watching for her, but I would've spotted her anyway. There's something about Violet, Sex Addict that just draws me. I don't know what the hell it is, but I've got a pretty good idea that it has at least a *little* something to do with her favorite pastime.

I weave my way through the crowd toward her. She and her friend haven't moved beyond the door. They're just standing in the entrance, looking around with wide eyes. Tia looks like she's about to laugh. Violet looks like she's about to bolt.

"Welcome, ladies," I say when I stop in front of them. I make eye contact with Violet's turbulent gray ones. "Thank you so much for coming."

"Is this," she begins in a hushed voice, her eyes shifting left and right before returning to me. "What *is* this?"

"It's a bachelor party," I say with a cringe. "One of my best friends from high school is getting married, and this isn't something I could really say 'no' to, you know?"

She nods slowly, looking around the wildly decorated barn interior. Among the various sizes, shapes, and positions of blow-up dolls that are dotted throughout the room, there are balloons made from condoms, an ice sculpture of a busty naked woman, and a service staff of girls that look like Playboy bunnies. It's any man's waking fantasy.

I can see by the shock on her face that this is hardly what Violet, Sex Addict was expecting.

"I'm sorry I didn't warn you. I was afraid you wouldn't come. And I really, *really* needed you to be here."

Her eyes finally make their way back to mine, and she smiles tentatively. "No, it's fine. I can see why this kind of thing would be hard for you. So I'm fine. Really."

"Are you sure?"

She takes a deep breath and nods. "Yeah, I'm sure."

I glance over her shoulder at the wide, exhilarated eyes of her friend. "Is she gonna be okay?"

Violet glances back as well, then shrugs at me. "I sure hope so."

Just as I'm about to escort them to the bar, one of Jake's friends whose name I can't remember makes a lunge for Tia.

"Hey," he slurs, righting himself and petting her arm like his favorite fur jacket, "are you one of the strippers? Holy shit, I hope so. There's nothing that would make this night more perfect than seeing your luscious tits and those long—"

"Stop right there, man," I say to him, tugging him back from Tia, "these are my guests. They're not the entertainment. Take your drunken pawing somewhere else, all right?"

He turns bleary eyes on me. "Hey, who asked you? I was talking to the *lllady*."

"No, you were about to get the piss slapped out of you. Do you really think she looks interested in talking to you?"

The guy slowly turns his head from me to Tia, back to me, and then back to Tia again.

"Damn, I'm sorry," he says, stumbling forward as if to hug her.

"That's enough, dude. Time for you to go find someone else to talk to," I tell him, grabbing his upper arm.

He stumbles, knocking Violet, Sex Addict into my arms. The shock I feel at the contact ricochets through me, taking me by surprise. Inadvertently, I pause, giving the other guy just the edge he needs.

"Mind your own business, asshole," he mumbles, wheeling around and swinging his right arm in the wide arc of a backhand aimed at my head. I duck it easily, but I don't move quickly enough to catch the left-handed follow-through. The one that catches Violet right in the side of the head.

A surge of violence rips through me when I feel her slam into me. I see red, and am all but ready to tear this guy's throat out when Violet, Sex Addict straightens away from me and addresses the asshole.

"What's your name?" she asks loudly, moving out of the line of fire, yet close enough to be face-to-face with the drunken shit-for-brains.

At first, he doesn't answer. I'm sure adrenaline is pumping through his veins, and this wasn't what he was expecting after throwing the first punch. He watches Violet for several seconds with a confused expression before he finally answers, "Gary."

"Gary," Violet begins with a calm, reasonable voice. "While I'm sure Tia is flattered by your . . . compliments, she's got a fiancé whom she loves very much. We came here to visit our friend, Jet, and that's what we'd like to do now. I'd be forever grateful if you could point me in the direction of the bar so I could get some ice for this," she says, smiling as she points to the side of her head.

Gary responds immediately. "Did I hit you? I swear to God I didn't meant to hit you. I was aiming for this—"

Before he can get all belligerent again, Violet interrupts in her soothing way. "I know you didn't, Gary. I'm fine. I'd just like to get a little ice. Now," she says, gently taking his arm and turning him away from us to face into the room, "could you point it out to me, please?"

Wobbling unsteadily on his feet, Gary points in the direction of the bar that sits a few feet from the back wall. It's impossible to miss as soon as you walk in, and I'm sure Violet *didn't* miss it. It's just serving her purpose very well right now to let Gary help her.

Violet smiles up at him, patting his arm like he's a wayward child. "Thank you, Gary. Now, it looks like someone over there is trying to get your attention." She nods toward a group of guys pointing at Gary and laughing.

"Heyyy, Todd!" Gary exclaims loudly, throwing his arm into the air in greeting. He lumbers off and, just like that, the crisis is averted.

When Violet turns back to me, she looks cool as a cucumber.

"Damn, that was impressive," I observe.

She shrugs, but even in the low light, I can see the pink stain enter her cheeks. "It was no big deal."

Before I can give it a second thought, I reach up to stroke one satiny side of her face. "Maybe not to you . . ."

She stares up into my eyes and, for a second, we're just two people who are incredibly attracted to one another. We're not addicts or posers, or liars or cheaters. We're not people with issues or those who keep secrets. We're just a guy and a girl who feel an undeniable chemistry.

But then, as I watch, her carefully constructed cool, unaffected exterior drops down like a protective blanket, reminding me of how *I'm* supposed to be behaving—like someone who's *not* trying to get her into my bed.

"Sorry," I whisper, not *totally* insincerely. I take a step back from Violet, giving her the space she needs before she asks for it, and I take her hand. "Come on. Let's get you some ice."

"Really, it's not—" she begins, only to be interrupted by her lively friend.

"Holy shit, Vi! You took that punch like a champ!"

"Thanks, Tia. That's something I've always wanted to hear."

Someone calls out to Tia and she stops, looking around for the face that goes with the voice. It's evident the moment she spots the owner that he is familiar to her. Her face lights up and she squeals, "Annndy!" and then takes off across the room toward yet another guy that I don't know.

I glance down at Violet. With a somewhat resigned expression, she's watching her go. I squeeze her fingers. "Don't worry. I won't leave you."

Her smile is small, but she nods, and we continue on toward the bar.

THIRTEEN: *Violet*

When we stop at the bar, I glance back over my shoulder to make sure I can still see Tia. Coming here *at all* was probably a bad idea. Coming here *with her* was probably flat-out stupid. This night might well end in disaster.

If Jet thinks this is the kind of place that might spell trouble for him, then the same goes for Tia. Maybe even more so. She's in a room full of horny, drunk men and she's one of only a handful of females. And, from what I can see, quite a few of the guys are young and attractive. That plus alcohol is not a good combo for Tia's self-control.

"She'll be fine. We won't let her get into trouble," Jet says from my side, drawing my eyes back to him. Even in this low light, I'm awestruck by how handsome he is and how incredibly dumb it was for me to engage in *any* kind of relationship with him. He practically oozes heartbreaker.

"*We* won't?" I ask, grinning over the "we" part.

Jet shrugs and throws me a sheepish grin. "Okay, maybe I should've said you've got your hands full tonight." I smile and nod, agreeing wholeheartedly. "But I promise to be on my best behavior, if that helps." He pauses, clearing his throat. "Seriously, though, it makes a difference that you're here. Just you *being* here is . . . is . . ." The way he's watching me makes me feel breathless and giddy, like I'm in some kind of strangely thrilling dream, one where there are no consequences. Only this isn't a dream. And getting involved with Jet in any romantic way would come with very real and very painful consequences, I'm sure. "Well, it helps. I'll just say that."

"Isn't that why you asked me to come?"

He watches me for several long seconds before shaking his head. For some reason, I don't believe him when he says, "Yes, it was." It's almost as though he silently finishes the thought with, *wasn't it?*

We stand at the bar, staring at each other, lost in our own moment, when the bartender speaks. "What can I get you?"

Jet answers him without taking his eyes off mine, which is, somehow, very disconcerting. "We'll start with some ice first."

The way he says it—his voice low and velvety, his eyes boring hot holes into mine—makes it sound like he has very naughty plans for that ice. Or is that just the way *I* heard it?

It takes all my strength to argue. "No, no. Please. That's not necessary."

"It's the least I can do."

"No, really. It doesn't hurt and I'd rather not draw any attention to it." The more I think about having to ice my head at a party, the more humiliating the prospect becomes.

Jet's eyes narrow on me. "To *it* or to *you*?"

I resist the urge to look away. "Either," I say with a casual smile.

He says nothing for the longest time, just watches me. When he does speak, his voice is thoughtful. "Then what will you have to drink, lovely Violet?"

I feel a little thrill vibrate along my nerve ends and land in the very pit of my stomach. Maybe I didn't imagine his intonation about the ice. "I'll have a Coke."

Jet raises one brow. "Just a Coke? Nothing in it?"

"Nope. Just ice."

Jet turns to the bartender and orders a Coke for me and a beer for himself. I feel both bereft and focused without his eyes on me. But when he returns his attention to me, and I'm as mesmerized as ever, I'm strangely relieved to be caught in his web again.

"Don't you drink?"

"Yes, of course. I just ordered a Coke."

Jet grins, and my heart trips over itself. "I love a smart-ass."

"Glad to hear it," I offer, with a grin of my own. I know I shouldn't be indulging in playful banter with Jet. I know I shouldn't. And yet . . .

"But I'm not that easily put off. Why don't you drink?"

"Are you asking if I have a problem with alcohol?"

"Do you?"

"No."

"Then why don't you drink?"

"I don't like feeling like I'm not in control."

"Having one drink doesn't mean that you're not in control."

"But it could lead to more."

"Sometimes more isn't a bad thing. It's the 'too much' that seems to be problematic."

"To me, that's like playing with fire. Pushing the limits to see how far you can go before you've gone too far and can't find your way back."

Jet's eyes are the most intense thing I've ever seen. "And you don't like to play with fire?"

"No."

"Not even a little?"

"No."

"So your philosophy in life is to abstain from everything on the off chance that you could become addicted?"

As difficult as it is to think straight around him, I do my best to digest his words, his real meaning and respond. "Essentially, yes."

"Well, I know there's at least one thing you can't resist," he says with a wink.

I cock my head to the side, feeling careless for maybe the first time in my entire life. "You don't think I can resist you?"

"What makes you think I was talking about me?"

There's a dare in his eyes.

It takes a few seconds for me to remember I'm supposed to be a sex addict. He thinks I have a hard time resisting sex.

I let out a slow, even breath. "I try not to let *anything* get under my skin anymore."

Jet nods, his gaze still holding mine, refusing to let go. "Maybe you can teach me that trick," he says softly.

"You have to want it."

"Oh, I want it." Something tells me he's not referring to restraint.

"That makes the rest easier."

"The rest?"

"Saying no."

Staring at me over the bottle as he tips it up, Jet takes a drink of his beer. "Yeah, that's where I have a little trouble. I don't like that word."

"Well, you'd better get used to it."

"Are you gonna teach me that, too?"

My heart is pounding. For the space of a breath, I think that I don't want him to say no. Not to me. I don't want him to resist me. Just like *I* don't want to resist *him*.

It's just that I *need* to. It's the smart, prudent choice for me, the only one that will ensure self-preservation. And that's always been my main goal—to defend against any weakness that might destroy me.

The problem is, this is the first time I've ever wanted to give in. That should scare me. And it does.

Another problem is it also excites me.

When Jet led me, drinks in hand, to the semicircle of sofas placed around the center of the room, I never expected him to sit beside me the whole night. Yet that's what he's done. For two hours now, he's lounged beside me, his arm draped casually over the back of the couch, fingertips barely grazing my shoulder. I'm sure that I should protest, that I should *mind*. But I don't. I don't protest, and I very much don't mind.

Within minutes of us sitting down, others started to follow suit, sprawling on the other sofas, gathering around Jet like cheerleaders around the quarterback. I would think it bizarre if I didn't completely understand it. Jet has a charisma about him, a magnetism that draws people in. I can see it in their eyes as they watch him, listen to him, interact with him.

Jet doesn't seem the least bit affected by it, but I'm sure he notices. I have no doubt he knows exactly how people respond to him.

Especially women.

I can feel the eyes of every female in the place on me, stabbing me with knives of envy. Even the ones that are ostensibly here with *other men* seem to be waiting for the moment when Jet will leave my side so they can swoop in and make their move.

I'm relieved that Tia has stayed within eyesight. I haven't been able to tell how much she's drinking, but she seems in control, like she's just having fun socializing. I hope that's all it is.

A loud siren sounds and a red strobe light starts to flash on the makeshift stage set in front of the couches. Along the back wall, a curtain that I hadn't even noticed before parts to reveal a huge plaster cake on wheels. Two guys wheel it to the center of the stage and jump down to scoot onto the rapidly filling couches.

The music gets louder and the lights dim even more as people start to clap and cheer. Someone brings a folding chair and sets it directly in front of the cake. Seconds later, three guys escort the man I presume is the groom-to-be to the chair and push him down into it.

"Jake! Jake! Jake!" the crowd chants. Jake, a ridiculously handsome guy wearing a fireman's hat and a big smile, shakes his head.

"Oh, no! The only girl I'm interested in is meeting me at the church tomorrow."

A mixture of boos and claps ring out. A red-haired guy steps up and whispers something in his ear and then slaps him on the back good-naturedly.

"He'll tough it out. No need to worry," the smiling auburn-haired man yells as he turns toward the rest of the room. I can see that he's quite good-looking, too. It makes me wonder if all of Jet's friends are hot.

He hands Jake a shot of amber liquid, clinking the glass with the one he's holding, and they both down the liquor in one smooth drink.

They both holler and laugh, the one guy backing away and announcing, "Jake Theopolis, ladies and gentlemen." He makes his way back to a gorgeous, exotic-looking brunette, one of the few "other" women here. It's obvious by the way he looks at her and then bends to kiss her that he's very much taken.

The crowd cheers again, but not nearly as much as they do when the top of the cake pops off.

I'm not surprised when a beautiful blonde arises, wearing nothing from the waist up but pasties. Gracefully, she climbs out of the cake and slinks her way down to Jake where he's seated in the chair. That's obviously the hot seat.

Behind them, another girl jumps up in the cake, this one a brunette who is also wearing only pasties. After she climbs out, another arises, making me wonder how much room there is inside that cake. But I don't wonder for long. While the blonde is busy with the guest of honor, the only male in the room who looks like he's really not interested, the other two girls get about their business—mingling. I see the brunette's eyes scan the crowd and come to a screeching halt when they reach Jet. She visibly veers toward him.

With her loose-hipped walk, she struts straight to Jet. I feel his hand clamp down on my shoulder and I glance over at him. His face gives away nothing, but I can only imagine how hard this is for *any* man, much less one who has a weakness when it comes to sex.

The brunette bends to slide her hands up Jet's thighs, reaching for his free hand and tugging. When he doesn't move, she leans in to whisper something in his ear. She straightens, still holding his hand, still tugging. Jet gives her a polite smile and shakes his head. While she is perceptibly disappointed, the girl doesn't continue to try to change his mind. Her eyes flicker to me once and then she concedes, moving to the guy sitting closest to Jet on the other side, putting her wiles to work on him right away. When she leans forward to flash her ample cleavage in *his* face, I notice that her eyes are still on Jet.

I focus on Jet to gauge his reaction, but he's still staring straight ahead. When I glance toward the stage area again, it's to see the redhead is now approaching. She, too, attempts to lure Jet into doing . . . something. Whatever it is that guys do with these types of girls at bachelor parties. But again, he resists.

He says nothing and neither do I. I question whether it's going to be like this all night, but then the music changes. I'm relieved when it seems to signal that this portion of the night's . . . entertainment has come to an end. But it doesn't really. It only triggers another surprise.

All the service girls, the ones who look like pinup bunnies, file into a single line in front of the stage. With a crescendo in the new song, each reaches for the center of her little satiny outfit and pull. It breaks away, leaving each woman in only her fishnets, some tiny black panties, and black sparkly pasties.

As they stand before the crowd, posing in their feminine beauty, I scan their faces. It's with growing dread that I see that a few of them are already eyeing Jet. It doesn't take a genius to figure out why he is prone to excess. If this is the way women react to him on a regular basis, which I suspect it is to some degree, it's no wonder he has trouble saying no.

I see a particularly interested waitress with short brown hair glancing repeatedly at Jet. So when the girls disperse, I'm not the least bit surprised to see her make a beeline for him.

I glance at Jet again. His face is set in stone, still showing no reaction whatsoever. If it weren't for the tic at his jawline, I would think he's made of steel. But that tiny tell is all it takes to show me what's really going on inside him.

I lean up slightly, scooting to the edge of the cushion, uncertain whether I can sit through another girl throwing herself at Jet. Unwittingly, I draw his eyes. In them, I see the battle that's waging.

And that's why I act.

At least that's the reason I give myself.

I tell myself that I want to help, but that I just don't know how. And that *that* is why, without second-guessing it, I turn my body and stretch across him, pressing my chest to his, and I kiss him.

At first Jet doesn't move. I think he's as surprised as I am. But it only takes a fraction of a second for him to recover. And I know the moment that he does. I know because that's the very instant that I'm as lost to his allure as everyone else in this place.

His lips soften first. I feel the change and it startles me, shaking me from my insanity. I start to pull away, but Jet's big hands come to either side of my neck, his fingers sliding into the hair at my nape to hold me still.

He tilts his head, drawing me further into the kiss. I feel his lips part and, as though they move independently of thought, mine part as well. When his tongue slips between them, I sigh into his mouth, reveling in the taste of him—the tang of beer, a dash of mint, and a dark sweetness that's as dangerous as the man himself.

His tongue licks at mine, tasting me in long, leisurely strokes then moving to explore the inside of my mouth. I melt into him, enjoying the way he moans against my lips. I swallow it, taking in some part of him that makes me feel dangerous and exhilarated.

I don't know when he turns and pulls me into his lap; I just become aware of the hardness against my hip and the warm hand that's roaming my back and side.

Jet sucks my lower lip into his mouth, taking it gently between his teeth. When he releases it, I open my eyes to look at him, feeling dazed and heavy of limb. He's watching me, his eyes a deeper, warmer blue.

Everything around me is muted. I don't hear the music or the voices. I don't pay attention to the people. There is only me and Jet, and the heat that's raging between us.

Quietly, he watches me. Quietly, I watch him right back.

Without his mouth pressed to mine, my lips feel dry. I wet them with my tongue, drawing Jet's gaze.

"Don't do that," he whispers.

"Don't do what?"

"Don't show me your tongue. It's all I can do not to stand up with you in my arms and carry you to a dark corner and taste everything that you're hiding from me."

At his words, an uncharacteristic heat pours through me, flooding my core. "I'm sorry. I wasn't trying to make it harder on you."

Suddenly, I feel silly. What was I thinking? Why would I imagine this could be helpful to him, to someone who struggles with an addiction to sex?

"I know you're not. You're trying to help me. And I'm grateful. Truly. You're different than these girls," he says earnestly.

"Yes, I'm different. I'm not dangerous to you. They are," I reply.

Jet's voice drops into a low rumble. "What if I told you that you might be *more* dangerous?"

"I'd tell you that you were wrong."

"I'm not so sure," he muses, his eyes roving my face. I don't know how to respond to that, so I say nothing. He continues. "I'd be a liar if I told you that I'm not attracted to you. If I told you that I didn't want you."

I shouldn't want to hear those words. They shouldn't give me any pleasure at all. But they do. Oh, how they do!

"But you know we can't do this," I state, quashing the excitement that his words brings.

His smile is small and wry. "Exactly. But that doesn't mean I didn't enjoy this, or that I don't still enjoy your company." He pauses, his thumb rubbing back and forth over the skin of my arm as his eyes search mine. "I'm glad you came."

I don't want to admit that I am, too, so I deflect. "I'm glad I could help."

Before Jet can respond, a meaty arm wraps around his neck from behind. A few seconds later, a broad, ruddy face topped with a clump of thick strawberry hair appears beside Jet's head.

"Caught you another one, did ya?" comes the gruff voice that perfectly matches the bear likeness of its owner.

"Shut it, Harley. This is Violet."

Harley looks duly unimpressed. "And who is Violet?" he asks, directing his question to me.

Jet turns his head and glares at Harley. "We met at a . . . meeting." The way he says "meeting" so meaningfully makes me think Harley might know about Jet's problem.

As if to confirm my suspicion, Harley slowly starts to nod, returning Jet's look. "Ohhh, I see. Well, it's nice to meet you, Violet. I'm Harley, Jet's manager."

I reach forward to grab the calloused hand the big man extends toward me. "It's nice to meet you, Harley."

"Oooh, that voice," he says, closing his eyes like he's in ecstasy.

"Don't even think about it, old man."

Harley tries to look offended, and I smile at his theatrics. "Old man? I'm hardly old, *pup*," he says, giving Jet a tighter squeeze. When Jet makes a strangling sound, Harley returns his attention to me. "Don't believe a word he says, Violet," Harley warns. "This boy could charm the panties off a nun."

Jet reaches back to playfully wrap Harley's head in the curve of his bent arm, locking it down with a tug of his hand. "She didn't ask for your bullshit take, dimwit."

I feel the need to explain. "You should know, Harley, that contrary to how this must look, he's not trying to get anywhere near my panties, so I don't think I have anything to worry about," I tease.

Harley's expression sobers the tiniest bit, giving me a chill. "Oh, you should worry, sweetheart."

Before I can respond, Jet easily pushes Harley back and stands with me in his arms, slowly letting my legs slide down his until my feet are firmly on the ground. I'm torn between wondering at his reaction to Harley's last comment and swooning at the contact with his tall, hard frame.

"Don't pay him any attention, Violet. He lost his mind years ago," Jet says.

I glance behind him to see Harley studying Jet's back. He meets my eyes over Jet's shoulder, and I see some genuine concern.

Yes, it seems he does *know about Jet's problem.*

I smile reassuringly at Harley. "Don't worry about me, Harley. I'm pretty hard to charm."

"I think that ship has sailed," he mutters. And then, without another word, Harley turns and walks away.

FOURTEEN: *Jet*

If I weren't so enjoying Violet's tiny, voluptuous body pressed against mine, I might be inclined to walk right over and punch Harley in his big mouth. But as it is, I see something unsettled rolling over her face like fog over water and I know I've got some damage control to do.

Damn it!

"You'll have to excuse Harley. He's old and crazy as hell, and his sense of humor is . . . unusual."

She looks at me with all the seriousness I've seen in her before. "Maybe he wasn't joking."

"*We* don't think it was funny, but *he* probably thinks it was," I respond nonchalantly.

Violet slides her eyes away from mine and I know the setback is official.

Shit!

"I should check on Tia," she says quietly, glancing everywhere *except* at me.

"Violet, Harley—"

"There she is," she says, pointing to her friend who is obviously having fun with some guys over at the bar.

With that, she just turns and walks away. I do the only thing I can and follow her. When we get closer to the bar, Violet's friend looks up and sees her. She throws her arm up and starts waving. "Vi! Vi! Over here."

Her spastic motions throw off her balance and she tips over on her stool. I hear her squeal as she goes down. Violet runs through the crowd to get to her, but I'm not worried. I can hear the girl laughing.

"Are you okay?" Violet asks, reaching down to help her friend to her feet.

"Never been better, Vi," she replies, her tongue noticeably thick. "Lemme introduce you to some of my father's cronies' sons. Alvin, Simon, and Theodore," she slurs, ticking them off and then collapsing into peals of high-pitched laughter. She cups her hand around her mouth and whispers loudly to Violet, "They're not really chipmunks, Vi."

"I figured as much," Violet says patiently, dusting debris off Tia's leg from where she fell. "I think it's time to go, don't you?"

Her friend's face crumbles into a devastated expression. "Oh, no! Not yet," she whines to Violet.

"Yes, I think we'd better. You won't be able to walk if we stay much longer."

"Yes, I will. I'm fine. Give me a sobriety test," she says, tripping as she moves away from the bar. "That doesn't count. Alvin tripped me." Over her shoulder, she sends a wink at "Alvin."

"Tia, seriously, it's time to go. Can you make it to the car?"

She scowls. "Of course I can make it to the car. I'm not a child."

Tia strikes out across the wood planks of the barn floor, weaving unstably and bumping into one of the half-naked waitresses currently entertaining two drooling idiots.

"Hey, watch it!" the girl exclaims, glaring at the drunken Tia.

Violet rushes in, steadying her friend and giving the waitress an apologetic smile. "I'm so sorry. She's had a little too much to drink." For her trouble, she gets a glare from both Tia and the waitress. "Here," she tells Tia, scooting up under her much taller friend's arm to help her walk, "lean on me."

And just like that, I see who Violet really is. To the bone, she's a sponsor. An anchor. A fixer. Just like Tia said. She sees a broken, disadvantaged, or otherwise distressed person and she feels the need to swoop in and help them, however she can. And that's what she's doing with me. She's trying to fix me.

And I'm taking advantage of that.

Impulsively, I stride over and take Violet's arm, moving her out of the way. "Let me," I say, bending to throw Tia over my shoulder and carry her to the door.

Tia giggles nonstop all the way across the room. I hear Violet, obviously shuffling to keep up, whispering to Tia, "Stop laughing or you'll make yourself throw up."

She's obviously been through this with her friend countless times. And her friend is obviously the most selfish bitch in the world to never consider what Violet goes through for her.

When I reach the door, Violet swings around in front of me, pulling it open and stepping outside ahead of me.

"Where are you parked?" I ask.

"Over there," she says, pointing to the back of the parking lot, to the darkest part.

I strike out across the gravel, getting more and more irritated with the girl I'm carrying. I hear the crunch of Violet's footsteps as she hurries along behind me.

"You really didn't have to do this," she says from behind me.

"I know."

She falls silent for a few steps. "You can put her down. We can make it to the car just fine."

"No. I've got her," I reply. "Which car is yours?"

"The silver coupe."

I scan the cars until I find it and head that way. When we reach it, I set Tia on her feet and lean her up against the driver's side door. I turn to Violet and hold out my hand. "Keys."

Wordlessly, she hands me the keys. I hit the remote button until I see the lock in the back door pop up. I open it and then turn to heft Tia up again and lay her in the backseat.

"Watch her head," Violet says.

I resist the urge to bang her head on the inside of the door on purpose. It might make *me* feel better, but it would definitely *not* endear me to Violet. And I don't need any more setbacks tonight.

"I will."

I get Tia situated and shut the door. Gently. Then I turn to Violet. "Where are you headed?"

"Home."

"Do you two live together?"

"Oh, no. I mean, I'll drop her off and then head home."

"I'll follow you. In case you need some help."

"You don't have to do that."

"I don't mind. I think you could use an extra hand."

"It's really not necessary. I can handle her."

"I'm sure you're very practiced at it. Nevertheless, I'll follow you."

"Jet, seriously, you—"

I hold Violet's keys up in the air, far over her head where she has no hope of reaching them. "It's that or I'm driving, which means I'll have to hitchhike to get back here."

Violet tilts her head to one side, obviously exasperated. "Jet . . ."

"Violet . . ."

Finally, after watching me for several long seconds, she shakes her head in resignation. "Fine," she says, holding out her hand for her keys.

I smile in satisfaction and give them to her.

"I'm very persistent."

"I can see that," she responds. Her tone is dry, but I can see the twitch at the corners of her mouth. She's trying not to grin. I can't stop myself from reaching out to brush the little dimple that appears at the edge of her lips.

"You'd do well to remember that."

My action changes the mood instantly. I'd like to run with it, press things with her just a little farther. But I'm savvy enough to know now's not the time. The risk outweighs the benefit. No, tonight I need to be on my best behavior so that I don't scare her off.

I step back and give her a very casual, "Lead the way," before I turn and make my way to my own vehicle.

When I hear Violet's motor start, I think to myself that I can't remember the last time I was this enthused about something.

I should feel like shit about that. But I don't—at least not right this minute.

I'm just that much of a selfish asshole.

FIFTEEN: *Violet*

All the way to Tia's house, my eyes keep flickering to the headlights in my rearview mirror. As terrible as it sounds, I think I'd pretty much forgotten Tia was in the backseat until she moans, "I feel sick."

That is a very harsh reminder.

"Just a couple more minutes and you'll be home. Try to sleep."

I've been through this numerous times with Tia. And with my dad. They're both the same in that if they keep their eyes closed and try to sleep, they won't puke. But just as soon as they sit up and try to wake up for the ride home . . .

I hear her mumble something unintelligible, but then she falls silent. In my head, I'm crossing my fingers that she doesn't get sick. I breathe a sigh of relief when I hear her soft snoring.

I'm thankful when I finally pull to a stop along the curb in front of her apartment building. I hurry to shut off the engine and make my way to Tia in the backseat before Jet can. I feel bad enough as it is.

I've got her hands and am pulling her into a sitting position when Jet pushes me gently aside.

"Here, let me."

I don't argue. Evidently, it won't do me any good. Instead, I get Tia's purse from my trunk, where we locked our things, and I dig out her keys. I lead Jet to her first-story unit and let us in, flipping on a light so that he doesn't trip as he carries her to bed.

In her room, I pull back the covers and stand aside for Jet to deposit her on the bed. I pull off her shoes before I straighten out her legs and throw the covers over her.

We're backing out her bedroom door when I hear her pitiful voice. "Violet, I'm gonna be sick."

With a sigh, I go back in, helping her to her feet and to the bathroom. I barely have enough time to raise the lid before she falls down onto her knees in front of the toilet and pukes her guts out.

I grab a washcloth and wet it before I kneel beside her, pulling back her hair and wiping her mouth when she turns her head to the side. Her eyes are closed and her breath smells like vomit when she says, "I love you, Vi."

"I love you, too, Tia."

To make sure she's not going to get sick again, I wait for several minutes before I suggest going back to bed. By that point, she's ready.

"Okay," she agrees, turning to crawl back into her bedroom. When she reaches the bed, she pulls herself up into it and rolls onto her side, starting to snore almost immediately.

I take the wet washcloth back into the bathroom and wash it out before flushing the toilet, spraying air freshener and closing the door behind me. I head for the living room, stopping when I see Jet leaning against the doorjamb, arms and ankles crossed.

I put my finger over my lips. "Shhh," I whisper, stepping out of the bedroom and closing the door behind me. "She'll be fine now, but just to be safe, I think I'll stay here tonight."

Jet says nothing. He just watches me, a strange expression on his shadowed face. Finally, an uncomfortable amount of time later, he says, "She doesn't deserve you."

"Yes, she does. She's a good person. A good friend. She just has some . . . problems."

"Are you always around to bail her out? To keep her out of trouble?"

"Oh, no. She gets in plenty that I don't know about until *after* the fact."

"I bet you patch her up even then, don't you?"

I frown up at Jet. "Of course I do. She's my best friend and I love her. Why wouldn't I?"

"Because some people are beyond help."

"I don't believe that."

"Yet, some part of you has to realize that what I'm saying is true. How long has this been going on between you two?"

Too long, I feel like saying. But I don't.

"It doesn't matter. I won't give up on her."

One corner of Jet's mouth turns up in a wry smile. "Until the bitter end, is that it?"

I get the feeling he doesn't approve. I raise my chin defiantly. Jet's opinion of me doesn't matter. I can't let it.

"Always."

He makes a noise in the back of his throat as he shakes his head, stepping closer to me. I stand my ground and hold his gaze.

When he stops in front of me, he stares down into my face for the longest time before he raises his hand and brushes the backs of his fingers down my cheek.

"Violet, the soft, delicate flower that is stronger than steel. Strong enough to support everyone around her. But are you strong enough to fix the whole world, beautiful?"

Something in his voice sounds . . . pensive. And doubtful. It gives me chills.

"I don't need to fix the world," I reply quietly, not knowing what else to say.

"Then can you fix me?" he asks, his eyes burning into mine.

I see him glance down at my mouth. My lips tingle in response and I hold my breath. I know he's going to kiss me. And that I'm going to let him.

Jet lowers his head, tilting his face just enough to graze my cheek with his lips.

"Goodnight, Violet. Sleep well."

And then he turns around and walks out the door, closing it tightly behind him.

The ring of my phone wakes me. My first thought, which is both bothersome *and* ridiculous, is that it might be Jet. I try to get to it before it stops ringing. I scramble to untangle myself from the blanket that somehow twisted itself around my body and one of Tia's couch cushions, binding us together. By the time I get to my phone to answer it, I'm out of breath and very much awake. I let out a sigh of disappointment when I look down and see my father's number on the lighted screen.

With a complete and utter lack of enthusiasm, I slide my finger across the green square to unlock the phone, hearing a cheerful, "Good morning, sunshine" as my father greets me. I feel like growling, not answering in kind.

"Hey, Dad," is my tepid reply.

"Could I swap you a hot cup of coffee for a quick ride to Summerton?"

I'm grouchy, and this was not how I'd hoped my day might start. My mouth falls open. Summerton is not a quick ride. Twenty minutes is *not* a quick ride. I bite back my knee-jerk complaint in favor of, "Has something happened to your truck?"

"Nothing extensive, I don't think. I'm pretty sure it's only the spark plugs. I just don't have time to fix them this morning before I have to be at my new account."

This brightens my mood. "You got it?"

I can hear the pride and pleasure in his voice. "Yep. Sure did. Aren't you proud of your old man this morning?"

"I was proud of you yesterday morning, Dad, but I'm really, really happy for you."

"I knew you would be. And I'm sorry to call and be such a bother on your day off, but I'm kind of in a pinch."

I smother my sigh and add as much chipper to my voice as I can muster. "I'm at Tia's. Can you give me fifteen minutes?"

There's a hissing sound as he draws air through his teeth. "Wellll . . ."

"Okay, I'll be there in ten then."

"See you in ten."

Luckily Tia lives closer to Dad than I do, so although I'm a little more rushed at ten minutes, I still have time to dig out my toothbrush from the cosmetics bag I keep under her bathroom sink. A clean mouth and brushed hair is as much as I can manage, however, before I have to leave. Last night's makeup held up pretty well, and that's fortunate because it'll have to do. This is as good as it's gonna get.

Tia's still snoring, face buried in her pillow, when I slip quietly out her front door and hurry to my car.

Twenty-five minutes later, I've got a backseat full of lawn tools, a Weed eater in my trunk and I'm following Dad's directions to get to the home for which he's been contracted to do the landscaping. At my father's suggestion, rather than driving all the way around the smooth, cement circle that sweeps in front of the beautiful three-story Mediterranean-style house, I simply pull up at the curb along the street to let him out.

"Wow, this place is gonna take you forever to maintain," I tell Dad as I survey the expanse of lawn and all the elaborately planted beds.

"Thank God someone had already mowed it just before I got the contract, so I just have to do the trim work and some weeding in the beds this week."

"Just. You say that like this is a cottage, not a mansion."

My father turns a happy smile on me. "Lucky for me, I love what I do."

I feel his pleasure reflect on my face. "I know you do, Dad. And I'm glad. Otherwise, this would be one seriously crappy Saturday."

He shrugs. "Well, it would've been just the one. Normally, I'll come on Tuesdays, but since he'd already had *some* work done, this is more of an in-between visit." My father lowers his voice and speaks in a conspiratorial tone. "Honestly, I think he's testing me."

"Why would he do that?"

Dad frowns. "I don't know. This one's pretty shrewd, I'd say. Cold even."

"Money does that to some people."

"Nah. What is it they say? Having money just allows some people to be the assholes that they were always meant to be."

"Da-ad!" He gives me a chuckle and a cute grin when I slap his arm playfully. "Come on. I'll help you unload."

I put the car in park and get out to unload some of the tools and Dad's gloves while he gets the Weed eater and the gas can out of the back. I can only imagine how long it will take me to get that oil-and-gas smell out of my car. "So, how long do you want me to wait before I come back to get you?" I ask, dusting the pieces of grass off my hands, afraid to even think about trying to clean out my backseat.

He glances around the grounds and bobbles his head back and forth. "Ehhh, how about two hours?"

"Is that all? This is an awful lot of yard, Dad."

"It's in good shape, though. I think I can get everything done by then."

"Do you want me to stay and help? I mean, that's not very long. It would probably be easier for me to help than to go all the way back to Greenfield."

"Dressed like that?"

I glance down at my clothes from last night. My black jeans and boots, and my white, off-the-shoulder shirt. "Okay, so it's not ideal, but I don't mind if you don't mind."

Dad shakes his head. "No, sweetheart, you go on home. I don't want you out here working in the dirt and ruining your clothes. I'll have this done in no time. I appreciate you chauffeuring me around."

"I'm not chauffeuring you, Dad. I'm always happy to help. You know that."

His smile is sweet and loving. "I know that, Vi. You're a jewel."

"Or a flower," I tease, backing toward my car.

"Violet?" a different voice calls.

My heart stops. I don't have to turn around to know who's behind me, who just spoke my name. It's likely I'll never forget the sound of that voice.

I turn to find Jet sitting at the end of the driveway, in what looks like the little black car he followed me to Tia's in last night. My brain is firing off in a hundred different directions—the way I look, the fact that I'm wearing last night's clothes, the fact that my father is standing right behind me, why Jet is here, the way I look, the way I look, the way I look.

"Jet. What are you doing here?"

One side of his mouth pulls up into an unhappy smirk. "My, uh, my father lives here."

My mouth drops open. I snap it shut as quickly as I can, but I'm certain Jet saw it.

"Your father? Lives *here*?"

"Yep, 'fraid so."

"Who's your friend?" my dad asks, moving in behind me.

My heart starts to race as I think of all the ways this simple interaction could go so terribly wrong. For one thing, Dad can never know where I met Jet. Explaining that to my father would be the most humiliating nightmare known to man. Secondly, there's the fact that the most important thing Jet knows about me is nothing but a lie.

Yeah, there's that . . .

My heart races for a whole different reason when Jet puts his car in park and gets out and comes around to where my father and I are standing. His dark, shaggy hair is still damp from his shower, and his black tank top under a leather jacket makes him look more dangerous than ever. All he needs is a motorcycle to round out the picture of the quintessential bad boy.

"Jet Blevins," he says when he reaches us, nodding to my father and extending his hand.

My father returns the gesture. "Royce Wilson, Violet's father."

"Nice to meet you, sir."

After a few seconds of unnerving silence, my father speaks again, letting me off the hook. "Well, I'd better get to work, hon. Two hours?"

I smile, my body flooded with relief. "Two hours."

Dad kisses me on the cheek, grabs his pruners, and walks away, leaving me and Jet standing side by side, watching him go.

"So, what's two hours?"

"He had some car trouble this morning. I'm gonna give him a ride back home in two hours."

"What will you be doing in the meantime?"

I shrug. "Heading back to Greenfield, I guess."

"Big plans for the day?"

I shrug a second time. "Not really."

"Why don't you save yourself some gas, then, and let me buy you a cup of coffee?"

I want to say yes. I can't think of anything I'd like better than to spend the morning with Jet. But my biggest concern is that I shouldn't want to, but even that's not as compelling a reason as the one that brings a burst of heat to my cheeks.

"Um, I'd love to, but . . . ummm, I uh . . ."

"Yesss . . ." Jet prompts.

"Well, it's just that I . . . I mean, I didn't have time to . . ." I feel my face get hotter.

How embarrassing.

Jet smiles. "Wow, this must be *really* good." He crosses his arms like he's settling in for a great story.

"What do you mean?"

"It must be a really good excuse in the making."

"Oh, it's nothing like that. I assure you. It'll be very . . . obvious that it's true."

"*If* you tell me, that is."

I give him a sassy grin. "You want it? Fine. I haven't showered yet this morning. Dad called and woke me up at Tia's and I had to leave straightaway and get him. This is last night's hair *and* makeup, and I'm sure you've already recognized the clothes."

Jet's smile widens. "Is that what you're worried about?" He waves me off, reaching for my hand. "Come on. You look better in day-old makeup than most women do after a day at the salon."

I resist, tugging on his hand. "Seriously, I'm a mess. I can't go out in public like this!"

Jet doesn't even pause; he just keeps dragging me toward the curb, toward my car. "We'll hide in a corner then."

I hate to admit, even to myself, how appealing that sounds. How appealing and how . . . intimate.

"Jet, I really don't—"

He reaches in to cut off the engine and pull my keys from the ignition. He grabs my purse from the back floorboard, locks the door, and slams it shut.

He finally stops to look at me and give me his full attention as he hands me my purse. "I can tell by looking at you that the *only* thing you need right now is coffee."

"And a shower," I add.

Jet's voice is low and his eyes are warm. "I'm trying not to think too much about you in the shower. Mind taking it easy on a guy?"

I feel hot and breathless at his insinuation, and it's all I can do not to let it show on my face. "Sorry," I mutter.

"God," he whispers, taking my hand and turning away. "We gotta get out of here."

I don't argue anymore. There's no point, and I don't really want to anyway.

Jet opens the passenger side door for me, closing it snugly behind me once I'm inside. As I buckle up, I watch Jet through the windshield. I try not to pay attention to the smooth way he walks as he rounds the hood, or to the way his low-riding jeans sit on his lean hips, but it's impossible not to notice.

When he slides in behind the steering wheel, he gives me a mischievous grin. "There's no escaping me now," he says, shifting into gear and easing out into the road. "For the next two hours, you're all mine."

As we speed off down the street, I can't help thinking that I don't mind the sound of that. Not one bit.

SIXTEEN: *Jet*

I know I made the right decision the instant I sit down across from Violet in the back corner booth of the little locally owned coffee shop I picked. It's not nearly as busy as the bigger-name ones, and it's twice as intimate. The coffee's not bad either.

I watch Violet as she takes a hesitant sip of her frothy drink. She smacks her lips a few times, tasting the blend, and then looks up at me with wide, pleased eyes. "This is really good."

I smile, feeling it all the way into my balls when she drags her tongue along her upper lip to lap up the sweet foam residue there.

"I'm glad you like it," I finally say.

She taps the end of the tiny straw sticking up from the other side of her cup. "Wanna taste?

I lean forward, narrowing my eyes on her. "Do you do that on purpose?"

She frowns. "Do what?"

"Ask me things like that? Knowing that I'd love nothing more than to have a taste?"

Nervously, Violet tucks her hair behind one ear and takes another sip of her coffee. "Sorry. That sounded bad."

"I wouldn't say that. At least not bad in a *bad* way. It sounded bad in a good way. A *very* good way." Her cheeks turn pink, something I'm quickly becoming incredibly fond of. "There it is."

"There what is?"

"That blush. I love it when you blush."

"Why? I hate it."

"It reminds me of other things I like about you. Things that are different from other women."

"Like what? A crippling social ineptitude?"

"That might *seem* like the case, but I happen to know differently."

"You do? And how is that?"

"You forget, I know your secret. I know what you're hiding behind that blush."

"Maybe I'm not hiding anything."

"I doubt it. Everyone's hiding something."

"That's an awfully jaded viewpoint, don't you think?"

I shrug. "Maybe. But it's true, jaded or not."

"And just what are *you* hiding?"

I don't respond. I just watch her. Obviously, I can't tell her my biggest secret. She'd be out the door in two seconds flat. "Ask me anything," I respond.

"I just did."

I grin, nodding at her quick mind. "Ask me anything *specific*."

She narrows her eyes on me like she's debating how ruthless to be. I'm not sure what to think of where she starts. I don't know what that says about her, but I like the fact that she seems to want to get to know me. Even though I shouldn't, I like it a lot.

"What's it like living in that big, beautiful house?"

"I wouldn't know. My father lives there. I don't."

"You didn't grow up there?"

"Hell no! My father and his new wife moved in there a few years ago."

"Ohhh. You don't sound too happy about that."

"I'm not. He cheated on my mom at least a dozen times. But this last one had money, so he decided he'd keep her around. Instead of his *real* family, of course."

Violet's eyes are full of sympathy when she reaches across the table to wind her fingers around mine. "I'm sorry I brought it up. We can talk about something else."

"No, it's fine. I'm more mad about it than anything."

"I don't suppose I need to ask why."

"Probably not. I'd say half the country can relate to the whole thing. He married the perfect woman, one who worshipped the ground he walked on, gave him three healthy kids, took care of his house, cooked his meals, and treated him like a king. But it was just never enough. He couldn't seem to stop his wandering eye. Just couldn't say no."

"Do you blame him for *your* problem?" she asks.

At first, I'm confused. I want to ask her, *What problem?* But then I remember.

I can't keep the sneer out of my voice. "I'm nothing like him."

Violet is perceptive enough to know when to stop, so she does. "Oh, okay."

I wait several seconds before continuing. I don't *owe* her any explanations, but I feel the need to give her one anyway. It bothers me that she'd even suggest such a thing—that I might resemble my father in any way.

"My father hurt people with his ways."

"But you don't." It's not a question, but it feels like one.

"No, I don't."

She's tentative when she asks, like she knows I'm sensitive and she's trying to be as gentle as possible, "What about your mother? Does it hurt her?"

Violet is tweaking the only real raw nerve that I have—my conscience. And, even though I'm *trying* not to let it bother me, it's still pissing me off.

"What I do is none of her business," I reply firmly.

"Then I'm sure she's fine with it," Violet replies.

She glances down at her coffee and leaves me to think. Her words say one thing, but her tone says something else.

"Why should she not be?"

Why can't I let this go?

Violet shrugs. "Well, if she sees you following in his footsteps, I could see how it would bother her. Or hurt her."

"For one thing, I'm not following in his footsteps, but even if I was, I'm not doing it to *her*."

"But you're her child. I'm sure she would want more for you. It might hurt her to think of you ending up like him. Or for your children to end up feeling like you do. It's a vicious cycle, and I'm sure she knows that."

My smile is tight when I say, "Damn. I didn't realize I'd get coffee *and* therapy."

She has the good grace to look sheepish. "Sorry. Occupational hazard."

"And what occupation is that?" I ask, more eager at the moment to get the focus off me than anything.

"Social worker. Not that we do therapy. I just hear a lot and see a lot. A *lot*," she finishes.

"I bet you do. So tell me about the background of a social worker. What was *your* perfect childhood like?"

To end up with a sexual addiction, it must have been a bitch.

Suddenly, Violet seems inordinately interested in her napkin. "I've been surrounded by addiction in one form or another my whole life. My mother is a rock band groupie. She has all the habits to go along with the lifestyle. She couldn't even stop using drugs and drinking long enough to carry my younger sister to term. Marlene was born with a heart defect. She died at sixteen months. Mom just couldn't make the transition to settled life. She'd disappear for months at a time then show back up like nothing happened. Until four years ago. She left and never came back."

Now I feel like a dick. "Violet, I shouldn't have—"

She holds up her hand. "No, it's fine. It's no secret. I'm used to it. My father has a drinking problem. Both my aunts have substance abuse problems. My cousin is addicted to painkillers and men. Even my best friend has a pretty significant impulse control problem. I guess I learned at an early age to look beyond the surface, to look for the reasons and the causes, to try and figure out why so I could help fix it. But I shouldn't have done that to you. Your reasons and causes are none of my business. I'm very sorry."

"Violet, please. Don't be. I was an asshole, and you didn't deserve that."

"I shouldn't have pried."

"It's fine. And the reason I reacted the way I did is because you were right. It *does* hurt my mother. And I feel like shit about it." I take a deep breath and lean back against the cool wood of the booth. "I don't know what the hell is wrong with me. I guess I just like to get lost in things that feel good. That take me away from everything that sucks. Maybe *that's* the real weakness my father left me—that I can't face the hard stuff in life. That I'll find something to drown it in—a bottle, a woman, a song."

Every word that's coming out of my mouth feels like it's being dragged out from under a mountain of repressed emotional baggage. And it disturbs the piss out of me to know that every word of it is true.

"Nobody likes the hard stuff. We all cope in different ways, some good and some bad. The trick is to do something about the bad ones once you recognize them."

I nod slowly, taking in the new dimension I'm seeing to this increasingly interesting female. Not only is she gorgeous and sexy and a little bit shy, but she's smart and has it together in a way that I don't see in women very often.

Before I even realize what I'm doing, I give her something truly honest. "You're a pretty amazing woman, Violet. Wilson, is it?"

She smiles, a radiant, relieved smile that mirrors the . . . lighter feeling that's taken over my gut. Evidently confession really *is* good for the soul.

"Thank you, Jet. Blevins, is it?"

"Yes," I laugh. "It's very nice to meet you."

"And it's very nice to meet you," she returns in her shy way.

As I stare at her from across the table, I wonder for the first time if maybe the guys were right. Maybe even *I'm* not *that* cold.

Or maybe I am. Because I still *want* her. I want her *more* than I want to tell her the truth.

SEVENTEEN: *Violet*

It's been ages since I've spilled my guts like I did with Jet over coffee last weekend. On the one hand, I feel good. Still. All these days later. I feel lighter, cleansed. But on the other hand, I know it's a huge mistake to get too close to him, to let him in when the basis of our entire association is a lie. That could be devastating for someone like him, someone who's just looking for some help. For that reason, I've decided to be extra careful and not let him get too close.

As I drive to a client's house, I let my mind wander to the SAA meeting tonight. I tell myself that there's nothing wrong with looking forward to it. Not only am I helping my best friend and supporting her by going, but I'm helping Jet, too. I *should* be excited about going. I should feel exhilarated. Because I'm doing something good for others. Helping them. Fixing them. Enjoying the company of them in the meantime is only a bonus. Nothing to be concerned about.

At least that's what I tell myself. I ignore the fact that my stomach is jittery just thinking of seeing him again tonight. I ignore the fact that I can't seem to forget the way his lips felt on mine or the way his body fit against me. I push all that aside and remind myself that I'm just helping.

Just helping. Just helping, I chant, hoping that the ache I feel behind my eyes won't erupt into a full-blown headache.

My phone rings, jarring me out of my thoughts. I glance down at it as I roll slowly toward a stop sign.

I sigh. A deep sigh.

I can't help it. I feel forty pounds heavier than I did ten seconds ago and I haven't even answered the phone yet. For one millisecond, I consider *not* answering. But that's just not who I am.

I hit the talk button. "Hello?"

"Violet?" comes a tiny voice.

"Hi, DeeDee. How are you?" The question is a nicety, a courtesy. I'm pretty sure I don't really *want* to know the answer. DeeDee is my much-older cousin. She is addicted to painkillers, she's an undiagnosed hypochondriac, and the only goal of her existence is to have a man in her life at all times. Even if it's a crappy man.

Normally, her calls involve some kind of drama that ends with me going to her apartment to rescue her from someone or something. Just another family member I'm trying to help. Or fix. Or, in some cases, just survive.

"I'm just awful," she whines, her voice trembling.

"What's the matter?"

I listen to her draw a deep, steadying breath as I pull into the driveway at my client's house. Rather than getting out of the car, I simply cut the engine and lean my head back against the seat, bracing myself for the onslaught to come.

"Well, I ran out of toilet paper last week and I didn't have enough money for gas to get to the store, so I used paper towels instead."

"DeeDee, please tell me you're kidding."

"Why would I joke about something like that?" she asks, truly perplexed. "Well, evidently all those paper towels stopped up the pipes and the sewer started backing up. Violet, the smell was terrible!"

"I imagine that it was," I commiserate, glad she can't see me shaking my head and pinching the bridge of my nose to fend off the migraine that is now more an inevitability than a possibility.

"I called the landlord and he sent Maintenance up to fix it. They couldn't get it unclogged even after they pulled up the toilet, so they had to leave it like that until a plumber could come. Those rascals opened up the floodgates for those fumes and, after a few days, I started feeling sick and getting headaches. I felt so weak I could barely get off the couch." DeeDee says this like it's an abnormal thing, but considering her long list of pseudo-medical problems, she spends more days on the couch than not.

"Did you go to the doctor? Maybe you're getting sick."

"I *did* go to the emergency room, and you'll never believe what they told me." I think to myself, *Probably not.* But I refrain from voicing that thought. Instead, I wait for her to tell me, which she always does. "They told me I have methane gas poisoning. Those maintenance men could've killed me, Violet!" she cries shrilly. Everything with DeeDee is a matter of life and death. Like everything else about her personality, there is no middle ground. It's high or low, wonderful or horrible, black or white.

"What did they suggest you do?"

"They said I need to get out of there until they fix that mess and let the place air out."

I can feel my day taking a turn for the worse. "When was this?"

Shamefully, I'm praying that she'll say this was days ago and that the danger has passed, and that she's back in her apartment again. But I realize this is likely a stretch.

"Last night."

I sigh. Again. I can't help it. I know what's coming. I'm going to offer her a place to stay, because that's who I am. And she's going to accept it, because that's who she is. And she's going to turn my neat, orderly home and life into a pigsty in two point two seconds, because that's the way it goes. She doesn't know the meaning of the word *clean* and I'd say she hasn't even seen a broom in a year or more.

But then, miracle of miracles, she continues, saving my Thursday from the apocalypse of houseguests. "But John, the guy who lives in 3C that I was telling you about, offered to let me stay with him so I could be close to all my stuff."

"John? The one who told you he has a problem with his temper? That John?"

"Yes. He's never gotten hateful or mean with me, though."

"But that doesn't mean he won't. You barely know him, DeeDee. Do you think this is smart? Why don't you just come and stay with me?"

DeeDee has the best track record in the history of track records for picking the absolute *worst* man in a fifty-mile radius and attaching herself to him. She's been married more times than I can count and is convinced that she cannot have a happy life if it doesn't have a man in it.

"I'll be fine. I think there really might be something between us, Vi."

"But DeeDee, you said he—"

"He might be the one," she interrupts, triggering a cringe-hiss-sigh combo in me. I've heard this *too many* times before. They're all "the one," and yet not one of them sticks around.

"But what if he's not? What if he really *does* have some anger issues? What then?"

"I can leave anytime I want. He's not *making* me stay there."

"I know, DeeDee, but—"

"It'll be fine, worrywart," she assures in her completely oblivious fashion. When she's like this, she can't be reasoned with. Even less so than on a normal day.

"Will you call if you need me? If he gets rough or mad or starts to spout off, will you call me? I can come straight over and get you."

"I'll call if he gets rough, Vi, but he won't. I guarantee it."

"You've known the guy for a couple of months and gone out on two dates that didn't go well. How can you guarantee it?"

"A woman just knows these things," she declares mystically.

Oh Lord!

"How about I come by and check on you later?"

"I won't be there. John is taking me out to dinner tonight."

"Then tomorrow?"

"He's taking me to get groceries. I told him I'd buy since I'll be there eating his food. I'm gonna show him what a great cook I am."

I hold my tongue. There's no point in arguing with her when she gets her sights set on something. Or some*one.* I just sit quietly in the silent interior of my car, waiting for her to get to the reason she called. She *has to* need something.

"But there is one thing . . ."

And there it is . . .

"What's that, DeeDee?"

"I just bought all my medications a few days ago, so I really don't have any money to *buy* the groceries. Do you have a few dollars you could spare? Just until I get my check?"

DeeDee receives aid from everyone that will help her—the state, the federal government, the local churches, and, of course, family. "Family" in this case translates to me. Everyone else is pretty much tired of her never-ending state of distress, but I just can't turn my back on her. She's family. And that's not what family does. Family sticks around when everyone else leaves. At least they're supposed to. Most of mine just haven't figured that out yet.

"I'll bring something by after work."

"Just put it in my mail slot. I'll be back and forth most of the day."

"Okay. Just . . . just be careful, okay?"

"I'm always careful, hon."

I swallow the derisive snort before it can make its way out. "Call if you need me," I say, totally unnecessarily. DeeDee *always* calls if she needs *anything.*

"Oh, I will." And I have no doubt she will. I just hope it's not from the hospital or from a battered women's shelter.

After I hang up, I sit in the quiet, reminding myself that I love this, that I love helping people. It takes several minutes of convincing before I feel patient enough to go in to my client's house. As I walk toward the front door, I hear a screaming child and I know this is going to be one long and nasty Thursday.

I'm feeling a little off-kilter by the time Tia and I reach the meeting. I don't know why, but I suddenly feel stupid for rushing home to take a shower and taking special care with my hair and makeup tonight. I wouldn't normally do that, and I know it has everything to do with the prospect of seeing Jet.

I feel even worse about my silly decision when, fifteen minutes into the meeting, Jet still hasn't shown.

Part of me is a little worried that something has happened. I mean, he seemed pretty serious about the process thus far. Another part of me is disappointed that maybe he's pulled the wool over my eyes, that I believed him because I *wanted* to believe him, wanted to believe that there's hope for him. I now realize I was a little too personally invested in that hope.

The biggest part of me, however, is upset that I don't get to see him, and that he didn't want to see me enough to come to this meeting. And *that* is unlike me, which shows me that I *really was* getting too close. For that reason alone, this is probably a good thing. Tonight, I'm officially pulling the plug on being his sponsor. If he's not any more committed to healing than this, I'm not going to waste my time.

Even though I'm not a real sponsor and I've lied to him from the very beginning, I think.

I refuse to let the guilt I feel over that take hold, though. This is all for the best. I just need to see Tia through these meetings and then put it all behind me. The end.

If only it were that easy. Because it's not.

By the time the meeting is closing, I'm feeling antsy and angry and in the midst of a desperate need to blow off steam, something I've never really felt before. Normally, I cope well with whatever comes my way. But tonight, that's not the case. I don't know how to explain the particulars of it, I just know that I want to go out and prove something to somebody, whether it's me or someone else, or the world at large.

When Tia and I are settled in my car, I turn to her. "Do you wanna go somewhere?"

She frowns. "Like where?"

I shrug. "I don't know. Just somewhere. I wanna do . . . something."

"Huh?" She's looking at me like I've grown a second head. Even Tia realizes this isn't like me.

"I don't know. I feel . . . antsy. I just wanna go somewhere and do something."

"Like where? You mean like a bar or a club or something?" She looks doubtful because I've *never* wanted to do those things.

Until tonight.

"Yeah, maybe something like that."

"Why?"

"Tia, I don't know. Why are you asking so many questions? You're the party girl. Can't you just run with this, like you usually do?"

"I've always done this part solo. Or with other friends—friends who go out. Never with you. You're throwing off my game."

"Well maybe that's a good thing. Maybe, for once, you don't need game. Maybe *I* need game."

"What the hell has gotten into you?"

"I don't know. And I don't want to spend the rest of the night thinking about it. Now are we going somewhere or not?"

Her eyes get wide and she holds up her hands. "Okay, okay, okay. Untwist the panties. We'll go out. Damn."

"Good," I tell her with a relieved smile. I start the engine and back out of the parking lot. "Where to?"

"For what you're wanting, the only place to go is Summerton. So head for the interstate."

I do. And I feel better already.

Nearly half an hour later, I'm pulling into the large and packed parking lot of a bar called Whiskey River. It only occurs to me when we're getting out of the car and I straighten my skinny jeans and deep V-neck shirt that I might not be dressed appropriately for an outing such as this.

"Am I dressed okay for this place? I mean, it's not like I—"

Tia smiles at me over the top of the car. "Oh no. Trust me. You're dressed just fine."

It's as we're making our way to the front doors that Tia stops, gasping and reaching out to grab my arm.

"What is it?" I ask, my eyes following hers to the enormous lighted sign near the door that announces the band Saltwater Creek is playing tonight.

"Holy hot damn and mother of all things sexy, I *knew* I'd seen that guy somewhere!"

"Who? What are you talking about?"

Tia doesn't answer. She just looks over at me and smiles the biggest, most satisfied grin I think I've ever seen her wear.

"You'll see. Come on."

With that, she takes my hand and practically drags me through the front door and past the ID checkpoint.

Once we're inside, I see that the big room is divided into two halves, separated by a humongous bar area. I can hear loud music and screaming arising from my left. It's my guess that's where this Saltwater Creek band is playing.

I try to get a peek at the stage, but Tia is pulling me around to the opposite side of the bar, where my view is obstructed. She gets the attention of the bartender, quite easily I might add, and orders two melon balls.

"Two?"

She ignores me until the bartender sets the twin bright green drinks in front of her and Tia pays. She picks them up and holds one out to me.

I shake my head. "You know I don't drink."

"Tonight you do. *You* are the one who insisted that we do this. If you wanna cut loose, this is where you're starting—with a drink. This one is like training wheels. There's only enough alcohol in here to give a buzz to you or a toddler."

"Then why are you drinking one?"

"Because if your tolerance is *worse* than a toddler's, then someone's gonna have to drive you home. But I have faith in you. If this one does what I think it will, you'll just be . . . relaxed, and I'll order a vodka tonic next go-round."

"There's no need for that."

"Are you kidding me? It's your first night out on the town. Ever. It would be a travesty for me *not* to celebrate."

"How is it that *you* get to celebrate *my* liberation?"

"Solidarity, that's how."

I roll my eyes and take a tentative sip of the drink. Despite its off-putting color, it actually tastes really good. I can't detect the alcohol at all.

Tia's watching me like a hawk, of course. "Okay, now I've tried it. Can we go check out this band of yours?"

"It's not *my* band. And don't tell Dennis. He hated that I used to follow them so much, so I quit for the most part. In fact, this is only the second time I've seen them since Collin, the old lead singer, was replaced."

"Then let's go listen. It sounds like they do a great job of covering old rock songs." They were finishing up a Great White song when we came in. Now they started a Def Leppard song called "Animal" that I love.

"Not until you finish."

"Ti-a!"

"Don't argue. Drink."

I take a bigger sip of my drink, then another one bigger still, until I'm sucking liquid out from around the ice cubes. "Happy?" I ask, holding up the empty glass for her inspection.

"Yep," she replies. "Okay, wild thing, here we go."

Again, she takes my hand and pulls me through the crowd. We go around the back of the bar, which still blocks my view, until we are at the rear of a crowd of people, all standing.

"Excuse me," Tia says as she nudges and wiggles her way through the crush of bodies, tugging me along behind her. I turn this way and that, trying to be mindful of people and their drinks. It's when we stop, flirting with the edge of a group of thrashing females of various ages near the stage, each vying for the attention of the band, that I begin to focus on what they're saying. It's then that I realize whose *specific* attention they're vying for. I hear one name over and over again.

Jet.

That's when I look up. And I see him.

Jet. *My* Jet.

I hardly recognize him. But, then again, I couldn't mistake him. The way he moves, the way his voice sounds, the way I feel when I look at him—it's all *too* familiar.

But this isn't the guy I've come to know. This guy is wild and likely drunk. He's got a guitar strap over one shoulder and he's wearing a torn tank top that shows an intricate tattoo on his right arm and shoulder. I've never seen it before because he's always dressed like a normal person when I see him. But not tonight. Because tonight he's not a normal person. He's a rocker. Living the life of a rocker, right down to the screaming groupies.

As I watch, dumbstruck, one of the girls in the crowd somehow makes her way up onstage. She runs to Jet and shamelessly plasters her barely clothed body to his side, writhing against him. He smiles at her, wrapping one arm around her waist as she kisses his neck and puts her hands in the tear of his shirt near his chest.

I see the flash of metal at one exposed nipple. And then I see the ripple of his abdominal muscles as the girl glides her hands all over his belly. It's when she brazenly reaches between his legs to cup him that I feel my stomach turn, and the true weight of what I'm seeing settles down on my shoulders. On my heart.

So this is the *real* Jet. This is who he is when he's not at SAA meetings and visiting his rich father. And lying to me.

I feel an ache in my chest when Jet launches into the chorus of "Animal." The words are perfect for the scene before me, for the way he's acting. It's like this person—fueled only by what he wants and what he needs, by his inner animal—is a total stranger to me, like I've never met him. The Jet I thought I knew, the one I was excited about helping and spending time with and getting to know, is dead. Or maybe he never existed at all.

In my mind's eye, I see this realization like the flames of a raging fire, consuming my misconceptions and leaving me with only smoke and ash. It brings a sick feeling to my gut and tears to my eyes. I don't know why I feel so wounded and betrayed, but I do. There's no question.

I'm backing away from the stage, away from Jet, drowning in my disillusion, when he looks up to scan the crowd. I know the instant his eyes find me. Even if they didn't stop on me, I would know. I can *feel* them. They light up my insides like napalm, fiery and destructive.

My chest is tight as I turn away. A fist of unusual and unwelcome emotion is lodged in my throat, and I can't get away fast enough.

Weaving through the bodies as quickly as I can, I make my way to the door. It's only when I'm outside in the crisp air, surrounded by nothing but night and humiliation, that I remember I didn't come here alone. Before I can think to go back in after her, I feel a hand on my shoulder and turn to see Tia behind me. Sorrow is on her face. Sorrow for me. And it only adds to my embarrassment.

"I'm sorry, Vi. If I had known sooner, I would've warned you."

My belly churns as I put all my focus into being nonchalant. "It's fine, Tia. He's obviously not the kind of person I need to waste my time helping. Better to find out now than later."

I give Tia my easy, confident smile, but I feel it waver. Although the words spill smoothly from my lips because they are 100 percent true, they leave a taste in my mouth that's like battery acid.

I try my smile again, turning toward the car. "Let's go home. I think I'm ready for bed now."

I have to make myself *not* run to the car.

EIGHTEEN: *Jet*

I'm comfortable in my fog. I've numbed the guilt I felt over skipping the SAA meeting, and now I'm in the one place where nothing else matters. I'm on a stage, surrounded by people who want me. My head is buzzing with alcohol, my blood is singing with music, and my pulse is thumping with the energy of the crowd. There is no better feeling than being right here, right now. Dazed. Comfortable. Free.

The faces in front of the stage are a blur, and that's just how I like it. I don't need faces to go with these women. All I need are their hands and their mouths and their bodies. Their adoration. Their anonymity.

Our security guys know to let one hottie up onstage every now and then. It keeps the others wild, and I sure as hell don't mind it. These girls are ready and willing. Very ready. And very, very willing.

When the nice-looking blonde crawls up onstage and heads for me, I brace myself, ready for her to slam up against me in a crush of big tits, long legs, and lips that never stop.

I sing the words by heart, barely focusing on them as the chick at my side drags her fingers over my nipple ring and teases my cock through my zipper. She's straddling my leg, practically humping it. I can feel the damp heat from between her thighs all the way through my jeans.

She lets her hands wander as I let my eyes wander, not trying too hard to see through the haze.

Until I spot familiar smoky eyes set in a hauntingly beautiful face, watching me with all the disgust and disappointment that I so often see in the mirror.

Even from the stage, I see the tears fill her eyes. Every drop of moisture rocks me to my core. Of all the shamed looks I've seen in my mother's eyes, none of them have ever felt like they were tearing out my heart. None of them.

I push the horny chick off my leg and glance to my left, giving Trent in Security a nod. He rushes out to remove the girl and take her backstage. Automatically, my eyes go back to where Violet was, but she's already gone. When I find her again, she's pushing her way through the crowd. It's obvious that she's trying to get away. That she *wants* to get away. She wants to get away from me.

NINETEEN: *Violet*

Not only have I refused to cry, to shed one single tear over something that wasn't even *anything*, but I've also decided not to sleep evidently. I've been lying here for over two hours, trying to relax and clear my mind enough to drift off, but it's becoming obvious that it's just not going to happen. Sitting up, I reach over to snap on my bedside light and drag a paperback from my nightstand drawer.

Despite my feelings on love and relationships, I can't resist a good romantic read. Whether it's because the characters always find their happy ending or because I like getting lost in a fictional world with fictional problems, I don't know. Either way, they're my drug of choice whenever I need to escape.

Ten minutes later, I'm just beginning to fall into the arms of a gorgeous man when I hear my doorbell. I glance over at the pale blue LED numbers on my bedside clock. Two things register. Number one, it's after one in the morning. Number two, the color isn't that far off from Jet's eyes.

The pang in my chest is short-lived by the immediate onset of worry. It's far too late for me to be getting a visitor. Something's wrong. What if someone is hurt? What if something has happened to my dad or Tia? What if DeeDee finally made her worst choice yet?

My pulse is racing as I leap out of bed and race to the front door, pausing only for a heartbeat to glance out the peephole. It barely registers that it's Jet and that I probably shouldn't open the door or even give him the time of day. I only act.

I fling open the door. "What's wrong? Is someone hurt?"

"I guess that depends on what you say next," Jet answers slowly, his tone quiet and reserved.

I take a deep breath, giving my flustered mind time to settle down and process before I speak. I reach for coldness, but I can't seem to find it. Only hurt, and a little aggravation.

"You mean whether I tell you to leave or I just cut to the chase and call the cops?"

A bit of an exaggerated response, but Jet didn't do himself any favors by getting my feathers further ruffled in the middle of the night when I have to work tomorrow. I'm hardly feeling charitable.

"Not quite the choices I was hoping for."

"Rest assured, your hopes are no concern of mine."

"I deserve that, Violet. I know I do, but would you please just give me a chance to explain?"

"I don't think an explanation is necessary. Everything was pretty clear from where I was standing."

I hate that there's hurt in my voice. I don't want it there. I don't want to *feel* it, much less show it.

"Can I at least come in? For just a few minutes?" When I don't move to respond or to let him in, he adds, "Please."

With a heavy sigh, I step aside so that he can enter. I've loved my little house from the first moment I set foot inside the cozy living room. I've never thought of it as small until tonight. But Jet's presence is so big, so much larger than life, it overwhelms the space and makes it feel tiny in comparison.

"How did you find me, by the way?" I ask as I walk over to curl up on one end of my comfy chocolate-colored couch. I am hyperaware of my bare legs and arms, and the thin material of my sleep shorts and T-shirt.

"Tia. She wasn't thrilled with a late-night visit, and neither was her boyfriend."

"Dennis was there?" I ask, smothering a cringe. "Oh, boy."

"I'm not worried about Dennis. Or Tia. I'm worried about you."

"You might not be, but I am. Tia hasn't exactly always been faithful to Dennis, and you showing up at her door in the middle of the night won't do either of them any favors."

Jet sighs. "Something else I need to apologize for then." He sits on the edge of the sofa, his body angled toward mine, his elbows on his knees. "Look, this isn't going the way I had planned."

"You had a plan?"

"Well, no. I just left as soon as our set was over and headed straight here. I didn't really think about what I would say. I just knew I needed to see you. To talk to you. To explain."

His eyes are as sincere as his words. Once again, he's the Jet I met at SAA, not the one I saw onstage tonight. But I resist the urge to soften toward him, reminding myself that this *is* the same guy. One I can't trust.

"There's no need. Really. It's not like we were dating or I have some kind of claim on you." And that's true. There's really no *logical* reason for me to be upset.

"Regardless, seeing that look on your face tonight bothered me."

"What look?"

"That hurt look. And that disappointed, disgusted look."

"I wasn't—"

"You were, Violet. You can deny it all you want, but I still saw it. I'm all too familiar with that look. It's just never . . . never . . ."

"Never what?" I prompt.

I watch Jet's eyes melt into puddles of pain and regret. "It's never hurt *me* before. Made me feel shitty, yes. Guilty as hell, yes. But it's never made me feel like it did tonight."

"Well, it shouldn't. You don't owe me anything."

"Maybe not, but I'd appreciate it if you'd humor me anyway."

"Fine. Say what you need to." I try to keep my frigid exterior in place, even though I can feel my inner ice melting with every word that comes out of his mouth.

"I was being completely honest with you last weekend when I told you that I drown out my problems, that I'm like my father in that way. But my ocean is the stage." Jet stands and walks slowly to my unlit fireplace to stare into the cold, dark heart of it. "I'm not an alcoholic, but I have a drinking problem. I'm not a narcissist, but I have an ego problem. I'm not a drug abuser, but I have a drug problem. The drugs

I use just aren't ones that are smoked or shot up. They're the ones that come in the form of women who want nothing more than to please me and fans who want nothing more than to hear me. Music that I can lose myself in. A place where I can be someone else who has no problems and doesn't give a shit about consequences. *That* is my addiction. *That* is my weakness."

I forget for a moment how hurt and betrayed I've felt all night. "Does that really work? Does it really make you feel better?"

"Maybe for a little while. And that used to be enough. But . . ."

"But?"

Jet turns to look at me, his eyes deep and glistening and sincere. "But tonight it wasn't. Tonight it felt like *exactly* what it was. Fake. Shallow. Temporary."

I know my heart shouldn't speed up this way. I shouldn't react to the look in his eyes or the gentle huskiness in his voice.

And yet I do. I just can't seem to help myself.

"Maybe one day you'll stop. Maybe you'll find some better way to cope, something that's more important to you than escaping."

"I've never wanted that before. Never looked for it. But being with you, just the little time we've spent together, makes me think I could be different. That I could be the person that I used to want to be."

"And who's that?"

One side of his mouth quirks up into a slightly bitter grin. "I used to want to be a songwriter. Being in the spotlight was never my intention. It just sort of . . . happened. The crazier shit got at home, the more I felt like I needed to get away." He sits down on the couch again, leaning his head back and stretching his legs out in front of himself as he stares at the ceiling. "Shortly after Dad left, Mom told me she didn't want me around my two younger brothers. They're twelve and fourteen now. She told me that until I got my shit together, she didn't want them exposed to my 'ways,' that one negative male role model was enough. For a while, I quit everything. I went back to school, got a few more of my architecture classes under my belt. That was my second choice, if I couldn't write music. But then Collin, the lead singer of Saltwater Creek, left, and they asked me to come on full time. The gigs got better, the fans got better, which meant more money. But that also meant I could dive right into all the things that made me the person she hated. Just like my dad." Jet laughs, the sound bitter. "I just didn't really realize it until I told you. I guess I've been drowning that out, too."

"Are you beginning to realize that drowning your problems in *what*ever and *who*ever isn't going to fix them?"

Jet rolls his head on the cushion to look over at me. His eyes are dark and pensive in the low light coming from my open bedroom door. "I don't think I ever expected it to. It was more a convenient way to be happy in the meantime."

"In the meantime of what?"

"Finding a way to be a better person."

That statement tweaks my unwilling heart a little. "Jet, having addictions or issues or overwhelming problems in your life doesn't make you a bad person. We're all works in progress. But now that you're aware of what's going on, maybe you can take steps to fix *yourself*."

"Why do you think I picked you?" he asks softly.

"Having a sponsor isn't the answer to all your problems, Jet, but maybe it's a start to getting back on the right path."

"Maybe I wasn't talking about you as my sponsor," he whispers.

"Jet, I . . . I can't . . . I mean, we can't . . ."

"Don't start freakin' out," he warns with a crooked smile. "I'm not expecting anything. I know you're doing this for . . . whatever reason you're doing it. And I won't take advantage of your kindness. But I feel like I should at least be honest with you about how I feel." Jet raises his head and leans toward me on the couch. He's not close enough to kiss me, but he's close enough to touch. And that's what he does. He reaches for my hand where it's resting on my leg. He takes it in his and starts stroking my fingers, one by one, as he speaks. His eyes are downcast, watching our hands, but being free of his hypnotic gaze doesn't mean I'm free of the spell he's weaving. My heart speeds up. "From the moment you stood up in that meeting, I was attracted to you. I won't lie. But then when I spoke to you, I was intrigued, too. I felt more drawn to you with every second we spent together. And tonight," he says, pausing as if it hurts him to speak of it, "tonight it killed me to look up and see your face. To know that I put that hurt and disappointment there. The last thing I want to do is hurt you."

"Jet, I—" I begin, but he cuts me off.

"It's what I do, Violet," he confesses, his eyes finally rising to meet mine. "I hurt people. I don't do it on purpose. It's always just been a result of the way I am and the things I do. The worst part is, I've never really cared before. Not until you. I don't *want* to hurt you. But I'm afraid that no matter how much I need you, no matter how much I *want you* in my life, it won't matter. I'm afraid I'll end up hurting you anyway. And I'd rather get my ass kicked every day for the rest of my life than to see that look on your face again."

I appreciate what Jet is saying, but this reminds me why I can't get emotionally involved with him. I don't need that kind of trouble in my life. But I can't walk away either. I've lied to the guy, and now he's depending on me to support him. There's absolutely no way that I could live with myself if I didn't at least try to help him.

"Jet, I appreciate your honesty. I really do. And I appreciate your concern, but you aren't going to hurt me because I'm not going to let you. I avoid getting too attached and too involved with people for this very reason. I've seen what caring too much, what getting too invested and falling in love can do to people. I don't want any part of that. But that's something I consider a strength in myself, especially in a case like this—my emotional distance. I can help you without getting too involved. This just reminds me of where I stand and the way things have to be. So thank you for that."

And that's mostly true. This has served as a great reiteration of why I can't enjoy him and his company *too much*.

The smile that curves his lips doesn't reach his eyes, which makes me curious what I've said that bothers him. But I won't ask. I don't need to know. This is the way things have to be. Period.

"So as long as I don't fall in love with you, we're good to go," he says. I ignore the way my pulse jumps at his words.

I return his smile. "Exactly. Although I don't think that's going to be a problem for you."

"And why do you think that?"

"A guy like you probably has several types of women, and I'd be willing to bet I don't fit the description of *any* of them." My laugh is casual, even though the truth behind the words stings.

"I don't think I really knew what my type was until I met you."

My breath catches in my throat. I don't know what to say to that.

And I hate that I want Jet to kiss me right now. And I hate *even more* how *much* I want him to kiss me right now.

After several seconds, I recover. Somewhat. "Jet, if I'm to help you, you probably shouldn't say things like that."

"Are you saying you won't help me if I'm honest with you about how I feel?"

When put like that, I sound like a douche if I say yes.

"No, but . . ."

"Does it make you uncomfortable?"

"No, it just . . ."

"Does it make you feel something you don't want to feel?"

He's being so honest with me, my answer is swift and true. It has to be. "Probably."

Jet's smile is dazzling. "I can't say I'm disappointed to hear that. But my guess is that I'd better leave well enough alone tonight. Don't want to push my luck."

He makes no move to get up, however, so, reluctantly, I push myself to my feet. "That's probably a good idea," I tease, with a smile, hoping he can't see how shaky I am.

Jet gets up and makes his way to the door, turning as he pulls it open. My lungs completely shut down with the desire for him to kiss me and the fear that he might do exactly that.

"I know it's awfully soon and probably ballsy as hell to ask, but I've got back-to-back gigs this weekend. I don't suppose you could find time in your schedule to come help a guy out, could you?" Just the thought of what I saw tonight and how I felt about it make me want to decline, but this is what I *need* to be doing—helping him. "It would really be a big thing for me. Seems like a lot of bad in my life is wrapped up in that stage."

"Then why keep it up?"

Jet sighs. "Well, I need to work, obviously. And I love music. I'm still hoping to get some notice for my songs, and this is great exposure for 'em, so . . . And I don't want to spend my life running from weakness. That's not the answer any more than embracing it is."

"No, you're right. And I get that. I agree. If you have to be there, and this is what's toughest, then of course I'll come."

"Thank you," he says quietly, his eyes dropping to my mouth. Once again, my lungs just seize right up. "You know, I've never thought violet was a color that had much light in it. But now, I'll probably never look at it the same way again." He reaches up to trace a single fingertip from the corner of my eye all the way to the tip of my chin. "Could be that I'll never look at a lot of things the same way again."

I can't tell if he sways toward me or if *I* sway toward *him*. Either way, his lips get close enough for me to feel the warmth of them. Just for a second. And then he pulls away and whispers, "Good night, Violet."

As much as I want to stand in the doorway and watch him go, I don't. I'm chilly and I need to close the door. The strange thing is, I don't feel any warmer once I close it. And if I'm being honest, I know exactly why. Jet left and took his warmth with him.

And I don't want to be honest about it.

TWENTY: *Jet*

In a way I hope Violet doesn't show up.

What the hell are you doing, man?

The more I learn about her, the more I know she deserves better than me. Than what I can give her. Than what I'm already giving her. As I listen to the guys warming up on stage, I think to myself that they'll be happy to know that they were right about me. I *do* have my limits. There *are* some things I feel like shit about doing.

Violet Wilson is one of them.

I resist the urge to throw my guitar at the wall. Why now? Why her? Why couldn't I have met her under different circumstances?

I close my eyes and take a deep breath, calming myself before I go out.

Maybe I wouldn't have batted an eye.

Nah, I definitely would've noticed her. But maybe I wouldn't have persisted beyond her cool demeanor. Or maybe that would've intrigued me, just like it did. Who knows?

I hear the familiar notes of our first cover song begin and I put all the futile questions out of my mind. The facts are that it is what it is, and I am where I am. And I'm not going back now. Violet is in the unfortunate position of being something that I want. Something I want *bad*. And I'm a selfish dickhole. What's new?

I take the stage. Within seconds of stepping out, I feel all other thought drift away. All I see, hear, and feel is adoration. Like I'm having an out-of-body experience. Like I'm someone else, for just a little while. It's the best drug known to man.

I walk to the mic and stop. All the house lights shut off. The crowd gets quiet. My fingers hover eagerly over the strings of my guitar. The *tap tap tap* of the drum is the only sound that penetrates the silent scream of anticipation in the room. I close my eyes and soak it all in, not even trying to deny the pleasure of *this*. *All this.*

Eight beats later, with my pulse humming and the energy rising, the lights come back on with the bang of the music. Without even giving it thought, my fingers float over the strings of my instrument as I let the tide of screams wash over me.

But then I see her. And everything changes.

In the rush of the moment, I'd forgotten Violet would be here. In the blink of an eye, I was someone else, someone who doesn't know her. But here in the next blink, I see her, and I don't want to be him anymore.

When I begin to sing, *There she stood* . . . I've never *felt* the words more. It feels like I'm singing to Violet. Whether she knows it or not.

TWENTY-ONE: *Violet*

Watching Jet this time is totally different than stumbling upon him last night. Not only is this a much bigger venue, but this time I'm prepared for what I'm about to see. This time, I get to enjoy it. I get to enjoy *him*.

His voice is incredible. It's deep and smooth, and it brings chills out more times than I can count. And the way he plays his guitar is so natural, like he doesn't even have to think about it.

But more than all that, I can see that Jet is a true performer. This may not be what he *wants* to do with his life, but he's good at it. And I can see why he likes it.

The women just go wild over him. And he works them like a magician works a wand. He makes eye contact with them as he sings. He smiles and gestures. He drives them wild.

How do I know this? Because every time he does it to me, I feel like melting. A couple of times he has met my eyes and winked at me during certain lyrics. I'm trying not to read too much into it, but it's hard not to. And he looks at me often, more often than he does anyone else. Of course, he *should*. I'm like his focal point in Lamaze.

But still, I feel it. I feel his charisma, his magnetism and I'm drawn. As much as I don't want to be, I'm definitely drawn.

A couple of times women have gotten onstage, much like the one I saw last night. But tonight, Jet kindly hands them off to Security, a fact that pleases me more than I'd like to admit.

It's when the lights dim and Jet exchanges his bass for an acoustic guitar and sits on the edge of the stage that I realize I'm not as strong as I thought I was.

After he gets situated, a spotlight clicks on and focuses its radiance on Jet. With his head bent as he adjusts the strings on his guitar, his hair looks like an ink spill in the light. Everyone around me is quiet as we wait, mesmerized by nothing more than his presence.

He closes his eyes with the first strum of his guitar. The simple sound vibrates through me, pulling me into its rhythm, into the song. Into Jet.

He tips his head back, turning his face into the light as he picks out notes. When he opens his eyes, staring out into the brightness, they glisten like pale blue diamonds. He turns them onto the crowd for a few seconds, until he begins to sing.

That's when they find me. And I forget that we're in a room full of people and that I shouldn't be feeling this way about him. I'm simply lost. Lost to the moment, lost to the feeling. Lost to Jet.

Smoothly, he begins to sing the words to "Through Glass." The lyrics float around me. His voice slides through me. But it's Jet . . . It's whatever makes Jet *Jet* that weaves a spell around me, a spell like silk ribbon that holds me right here. Right now. Right where he wants me, and right where I want to be.

His eyes never leave mine as he sings. Not once. He doesn't glance down or around, doesn't look at anyone else. Not for a single second. And no one steps between us. It's like the ocean of people parted in reverence of what's happening, and that no one would dare to interrupt it.

When he strums the last chord, no one moves. Not Jet, not me, not the people in the crowd. We all stay perfectly still, watching him watch me.

Jet doesn't smile or wink or make this moment cute or contrived. He just stares at me like he's seeing me for the first time. Or maybe that he's *feeling* me for the first time. Like I'm feeling him.

It's the tap of the drums that bring an end to my thrall. The spotlight shuts off and the dim house lights come back on. Another song is beginning around us, but none will ever compare to the beauty of this one. Of this one song. And how Jet sang it to me.

I didn't talk to Jet before the show, and I didn't think to ask what I was supposed to do after. But since someone was waiting for me when I arrived to bring me close to the stage, I should've known someone would be waiting for me afterward as well, to take me away from it.

It turns out it's the same guy, too. Trent, I think he said his name was. Evidently he works security for the band. And he must also handle Jet's women, because he's the one Jet would hand them off to when they'd crawl onstage.

"Violet," he says when he touches my arm, "come on. Let's get you backstage."

I nod and move to follow him, feeling more like a wallflower than ever. I want to shrink away from all the glares and odd looks I get from the women I pass. There's no doubt every one of them would like to be going where I'm going, and it's suddenly easy for me to see how a man could get lost in this, lost in this kind of adulation. Especially when so many of the girls are young, beautiful, and scantily clad.

Trent leads me through a series of doors to one that says AUTHORIZED PERSONNEL ONLY. There's a uniformed guard standing to the left. Trent flashes his pass at the stone-faced man, gets a curt nod, and then we walk right in.

Beyond the door is yet another world I'm totally unfamiliar with. There are girls everywhere, but back here, it doesn't seem like *they* are the problem. It's the guys.

I see the various band members scattered throughout the room. One of the other guitar players has a girl bent over his arm, kissing her and feeling her up like they're in private. I glance quickly away, feeling the blush sting my cheeks.

I scan the rest of the room, taking it in with equal embarrassment. The guy who plays guitar and the keyboard is having his picture taken by a delirious girl who can't be a day over twenty. He has a female under each arm. One is licking his nipple, the other is kissing his neck and has her hand on his crotch. Just beyond them is a couch where a beautiful blonde is sitting, head thrown back, chest puffed out, letting the drummer pour champagne all over her breasts.

It's plain to see that she's wearing nothing but hard nipples under her tight, white T-shirt.

My heart is pounding as I keep searching for Jet, fearing that I won't find him, yet terrified I will. But when I do, it's to see him coming out of what looks to be a bathroom, rubbing a towel over his bare chest. His hair is wet, like he just stuck his head in the sink, which he might have.

He steps out and glances around the room, his eyes not stopping on any particular vignette. He doesn't seem to be surprised by what's going on, which is very telling.

Finally, his eyes find me. They light up, which makes my stomach roll over, and then a smile spreads across his face and he makes his way across the room toward me.

I can't help but admire him as he walks. Aside from his stunning face, Jet is absolute physical perfection. His shoulders are impossibly wide and muscular, making his narrow waist look even trimmer. His chest is smooth and broad, and both nipples are pierced. His stomach is flat and rippling with muscles that draw my eye even farther down.

At the bottom of his abdomen is a tattoo that I didn't see through the holes in his tank top last night. It runs across his belly, disappearing below the low-hanging band of his black pants. It's only when my eyes drift farther down that I notice Jet has stopped walking.

In shock and horrified dismay, I jerk my eyes up to his. They aren't laughing or playful, teasing or light. They're serious. And intense. And as hot as the flames that are inked up his ribs.

My mouth gets dry and I remind myself over and over again why I'm here and why I absolutely *cannot* get involved. Some part of me is crying out that it's too late, it's too late, but I ignore that voice. I ignore that cry. I'm still in control. I don't have to walk away.

Finally Jet starts to move again. Air gets trapped inside my lungs when he stops in front of me, looking down into my face yet not saying a word. I wet my dry lips with the tip of my tongue, and I see Jet's brilliant blue eyes drop to watch me, making my whole mouth tingle in awareness.

"You were phenomenal," I offer when the silence is just too much, too *intense* to bear.

His gaze rises back to mine and I see his expression soften. "Thank you. The only thing that could've made tonight better is if I'd been singing my own songs."

"I thought you got to perform some of your original music?"

"Most of the time I do, but this venue wanted all cover songs."

"I'm sorry."

With a wry smile, Jet reaches out to brush my bangs out of my eyes. "Don't be. Tonight was the best night I've had in a long time."

My heart thunders inside my chest. "And why is that?"

He steps closer still, his thighs just barely brushing mine. I know I should retreat. I know I should keep this more . . . *clinical* and less emotional, but for the life of me, I can't seem to find the will to make my legs move. I don't think I even really want to.

"Seeing you out there made it—"

"Who's this?" the band's drummer asks loudly, coming up behind Jet to lean in over his shoulder, beer bottle in one hand, cigarette in the other.

I feel as much as hear Jet's sigh. His warm breath dances over my lips and brings chills to my arms.

So close . . .

"This is Violet. Violet, this is Grady, the drummer."

Grady sticks his cigarette back in his mouth long enough to offer me his sticky right hand. "Pleasure, Violet. You don't look like the . . . usual kinds of girls we see back here. Are you from the Red Cross or something? Because I would happily donate any of my . . . fluids to your cause," he leers.

My mouth drops open a fraction of an inch. Jet shakes Grady off him and pushes him back with an elbow to his gut. "Man, go the hell away! What's the matter with you?"

"What?" Grady asks, an innocuous expression settling on his face. "I was just kidding. I thought she was . . . she was . . ."

Although Grady is very obviously well on his way to being drunk, I can see that he genuinely thought his proposition would be accepted.

"It's all right, Grady. I can only imagine what goes on in these rooms. No harm, no foul. I know Jet from . . . we met at a . . . group activity."

Grady's brows shoot up, and I blush. I should've kept my mouth shut. I was going to say "meeting," but realized that might sound suspicious if Jet didn't want anyone to know.

"A 'group activity'? Holy shit, I'm the best team player you've ever met!"

I can't help but laugh at his enthusiasm. "Not *that* kind of group activity."

"Oh. Damn," he mutters, deflated. "Well, whatever kind of group thing it is, if everyone else looks like you, count me in." He pauses as if to reconsider. "Unless it has anything to do with ogling danglers. I don't swing that way."

"Neither do I, dumbass, and that's not what she means anyway. We met at a . . . meeting."

Jet looks meaningfully at Grady, and, after a few seconds, Grady finally seems to get it.

"Ahhh, I see," he says in realization. Then, as if something else occurred to him, he says a brighter, "Oh! Really? This is—"

"I think you've made this awkward enough, Grady. Why don't you tell Violet good night? I'm sure she's more than ready to go home."

"Aren't you going to introduce her around?"

Jet sighs and runs his fingers through his damp hair. He glances back at me and asks, "Do you mind?"

"Of course not," I say politely, even though I'm very much ready to leave.

Jet takes my hand and we walk to the center of the room. He looks around at his bandmates, as do I. Strangely, they all look the same—dark hair, rocker clothes, tattoos, and piercings. And all draped in women. Even Grady has already made his way back to the girl with the champagne-soaked shirt.

Seeing that they're all otherwise occupied with their . . . entertainment, Jet glances down at me and grins, saying, "Maybe I should do formal introductions another time."

I smile up at him. "Maybe that's best."

"How 'bout I just point 'em out?"

"That works."

I watch him survey his friends. He starts to his left, pointing to the band member who *did* have a girl under each arm. Now, however, he's juggling three, as the one who was taking pictures has joined in the fun. "That's Leo. He does a little of everything."

"I can see that."

Jet grins as he continues. "He plays, keyboard, jumps in on vocals. He's a really funny guy," Jet says, his smile turning wry, "you just can't tell it right now."

"Oh, I can tell. He looks like he put the *fun* in *funny*," I say dryly.

Jet laughs. "He's not usually quite *this* much fun. He's got a lot going on. Probably blowing off some steam." He turns his attention to the next person sprawled out on the furniture, one I've already met. "You met Grady. He's the drummer."

"Yes, how could I forget?"

"That guy," he says, pointing to the one who had his tongue stuck down some poor girl's throat five minutes ago and is now firing up a bong with a totally different one, "is Sam. He plays bass and pretty much anything else with strings." He moves quickly on from Sam, pointing over to two guys talking in the corner. They look embroiled in something serious. Probably business. "And you met Harley at the bachelor party. He's our manager. That's Trent he's talking to. You met him already, too." Trent is the enormous security guard.

"Yes, I remember them both."

He finally turns back to me. "So that's it. That's everybody. For now anyway. Seems like there's always somebody coming or going. Might be a whole different place back here in a week."

"They're just as I imagined rock stars to be," I say uncomfortably.

Jet frowns down at me. "Are you okay?"

I shrug. "I'm fine. I'm just ready to go whenever you are."

"How about now?"

I sigh in relief. "Now sounds good."

With my hand still in his, he grabs his shirt and leads me out the back entrance and around the building to the parking lot. He pauses only long enough to slip on his shirt, then takes my hand again and we continue our silent walk to my car, where he stops and gestures for my keys. I give them to him. He unlocks the door and holds it open for me.

"Why don't you follow me back to Greenfield? There's a place I want to show you."

I nod, keeping my smile to a polite curve rather than the beam it feels like. I'm glad the night isn't over. I don't want it to be.

"Okay. I'll be right behind you."

"I'll pull around and flash my lights, okay? Give me five minutes."

I nod and slide behind the wheel. Jet closes my door and winks at me through the driver's side window as he backs away. The gesture sets the butterflies in my stomach aflutter. My pulse is humming along nicely by the time he turns to jog back the way we came.

Three minutes later, I see Jet's car as he weaves through the rows to get to me. As promised, he flashes his lights as he passes. I can see his smile as he drives by. My butterflies react accordingly.

I follow him all the way back to Greenfield. My mind has wandered the entire way, guessing where he might be taking me, reveling in the anticipation of it. When he pulls into the dark parking lot of a park near the middle school, I'm a bit more confused than excited.

Jet parks and then gets out and comes to open my door when my engine is shut off. He doesn't say a word, doesn't offer an explanation, just takes my hand and leads me through the darkness and the trees to a set of swings that face the playground and the front of the school beyond.

He holds a swing for me and I sit in it, wrapping my fingers around the cool metal chain and pushing off. Gently, I move back and forth as Jet takes the one next to me. His feet don't leave the ground as he sways, and his eyes don't leave the shadowy, moonlit view ahead.

"Is something wrong?" I finally ask.

He's silent for a long time. So long, in fact, I wonder if he heard me at all. But then, minutes later, I hear his quiet response.

"I'm sorry I brought you backstage tonight."

"Why?"

"You told me about your mom and her . . . problems. It was incredibly insensitive for me to expose you to that shit tonight. Rockers, drugs, the stuff with the women. God, Violet, how could I be so stupid?"

"You're not—"

"I want you to know that it was just inconsiderate on my part, and it won't happen again."

"Hey," I say, stopping my swing and reaching for his arm. "Don't beat yourself up over it. I'm a big girl. My mom's problems are *hers*, not mine. I'm fine. Really."

Jet sighs and stares up at the star-studded sky. "I'm trying to do better, but times like tonight make me think I'll never be anything more than a selfish asshole."

"You're not a selfish asshole, Jet," I declare vehemently.

He falls silent again, and I hold my tongue, not knowing what to say now.

"I come here to see my brothers," he begins. Finally.

"Your brothers?"

"Yeah. I told you that my mother won't let me see them until I get my shit together. So I've been coming here to see them. Chad, the oldest, brings Todd out here after school so he can play for a while before they go home. Mom kinda went apeshit after Dad left and she's pretty tough on 'em. She doesn't know I see them, of course. I made them promise not to tell her."

"But you love them. That's not selfish."

Jet turns his eyes on me. He stares deep into them, searching for . . . something.

"Isn't it? When she has asked me not to, and for good reason? Isn't it selfish of me to expose them to all my shit?"

"But you're not. You come here to see them while they play. You aren't taking them to bars, Jet."

"No. I'm not that bad."

"That's not what I meant."

"I know," he says, his smile small and sad. "I never felt bad about it before. Not until recently."

"Why now? What happened?"

"I met you. You make me want to *be* the kind of person they can look up to, that my mother would be proud to have in their lives. Not the kind that lives like hell and then sneaks around to see them anyway. The selfish kind. The kind I've always been."

"Jet, you make it sound like you're a monster. I think it's wonderful that you want to be a better person. We should *all* strive to be better. Every day. Everyone could use some improvement. But wanting to see your brothers doesn't make you a selfish asshole. You're not a bad person just because you've got a few problems, Jet. We've all got problems. Even your mom."

Jet's eyes bore into mine. Something in them pains me. "You wouldn't say that if you knew all the things I've done. If you knew what kind of person I *really* am."

"I'm not stupid, Jet. I know who you are. I know about your problems. But, despite them, you're here. With me. Feeling guilty for the things you've done, for the way you live your life. That hardly sounds like a person beyond redemption."

"But Violet, you don't know . . ."

"And I don't have to. Because I don't care. It doesn't matter. What matters is what you do from here on. What matters are the things you can control, like the future and what choices you make today and tomorrow. You can't fix yesterday."

Jet reaches for the chains to my swing. He turns me toward him and pulls me close, his face set and his eyes desperate. "Do you really believe that? Could you really overlook every bad thing I've done? Are you *that* forgiving?"

I get the feeling he's asking me about much more, but I don't know what. And I don't know how else to respond. So I tell him what I *hope* I'd have the personal strength to do. "Yes, I am *that* forgiving."

I can hear his breathing. It seems that he's fighting some internal battle and the situation with his brothers is only scratching the surface. If I didn't know any better, I'd say he was feeling guilty over something he'd done *to me*. But that's impossible. He hasn't *done* anything to me.

"I hope that means you'll start now."

Before I can ask what I need to forgive him for, Jet shows me, crushing his lips to mine. They're heated. Hungry. Urgent.

They're soft yet firm, just like I remember. And the flavor of Jet is the same. Heady. Seductive. Male. But there's something in the kiss that feels different. Like he's taking off the gloves. Tonight marks a change, and I'm not sure what it means for me.

I just know it means something.

Jet tilts his head and deepens the kiss. I don't resist. It doesn't even occur to me to try. I'm only feeling. Not thinking.

His tongue slips between my lips to tease mine, to stroke it, to entice a response. Without conscious thought, my body gives it. I slide mine along his, reveling in the taste of him, in the smooth warm feel of his flesh.

And then he's dragging me out of my swing, pulling me to my feet, hauling me against him. His hands are in my hair, on my back, at the base of my spine. They're holding and begging, pressing and demanding.

He's hard where I'm soft. Unyielding where I give. Alluring where I drift.

I melt into him, unable to do anything else. I let my fingers slide into his hair. I grab fistfuls of it, holding him to me even though I know I should be pushing him away.

He moans into my mouth. I breathe it in. I feel it like warm caramel oozing through my veins, drowning me in sugary desire, in the heady power of our attraction.

When Jet pulls away to look down into my face, his breathing as hard as mine, his eyes are ablaze. But among the flames, I can see concern.

"Can you forgive me for that?"

"Yes," I say without hesitation, wondering if I could forgive him if he *hadn't* kissed me.

"Can you forgive me if I can't be *just* your project? If I can't leave this alone?"

"Jet, I . . ." I don't know what to say. I know what I feel, but I know that I should keep that to myself.

"Because I can't stay away from you, Violet. I don't want to. I know I should. But I need you. I need to have you, to be with you. I need to see if I can be the man you make me want to be."

"Jet, I can't make you someone else. I'll help you in any way I can, but I can't change who you are."

"Then can you accept me like I am?"

Like a snowball tossed right into the center of my face, I feel his words like ice, cooling the fires of my passion.

"Can't we just keep doing what we're doing? See how it goes?"

He sighs. I can see the disappointment in his eyes. I know what he *wanted* me to say, but I can't lie to him. I can't tell him something that I know would be a lie. I've been dishonest enough for a lifetime. I can't add to it with more half-truths.

Jet loosens his hold on me and steps back to give me room. An opaque curtain drops down over his face. While a casual glance shows no change in his expression, there's a shadow of something else lurking just beyond that which is clear.

"Then I'll do my best to honor that, for as long as I can. Just know that we can't stay here forever."

"Where is here?"

Jet doesn't answer me. He simply reaches for my hand, curls my fingers over his, and kisses my knuckles.

Then, with a disheartened curve of his lips, he turns and leads me back the way we came. Back to where we started.

TWENTY-TWO: *Jet*

For the first time in forever, it seems, the words just flow. As I sit here in the parking lot, outside the SAA meeting, song lyrics pour out in an unstoppable symphony. I've written dozens of songs in my life. Some are even pretty damn good ones. Fewer since Mom and Dad split and my life turned to shit, though.

But this one is different. This one is gold. I can feel it. In my soul, I can feel it. This song is going to *mean* something. And not just to me.

I'm staring through the windshield, hearing the notes in my head, when I see her car pull up. Her name floats through my mind. Drifts almost, like a vibrant fog. It's more than that, though. More than a name. It's a color and a person and a beauty that I've never seen before in life.

Violet.

I put my head down and scribble more words. I should go inside, but I need to get this down before I forget. I can't stop writing. Not now.

I glance back up and watch her walk in with her friend. I know I should go in, too, but I can't. Not yet. Not until I get this out.

I get a heavy feeling in my chest when I pen the next words. It's guilt. And dread.

Will she hate me when she knows? Will she take her love and go?

I look up again, and she's gone. I wonder how long it will be until she really *is* gone.

TWENTY-THREE: *Violet*

I'm more than a little disappointed when I scan the crowd and don't find Jet anywhere. He didn't say he was coming, but he didn't say he wasn't either. I guess I just assumed.

"What's the matter?" Tia asks as we take seats in the nearly empty row at the back.

I give her my brightest, most carefree smile. "Not a thing. I'm just glad you came tonight."

She rolls her eyes. "Of course I came. I'm more dependable than *that*."

"Since when?"

"Since always."

"Sure. And monkeys might fly out of my butt," I tell her derisively.

"Not with *that* attitude they won't," she sniffs haughtily.

I chuckle, and we turn our attention to Lyle when he starts the meeting. After several minutes of forcing myself *not* to continue to look around for Jet every four seconds, it has finally gotten a little easier, but then I hear a noise at the back of the room. I make myself stay facing forward. I refuse to look.

It irritates me that I expected him to come, that I wanted him to. That I so wanted to believe he was doing better. And that he was right in that I am making a positive difference in his life. Then I chastise myself, reiterating that *this* is exactly why I don't get too involved. There is nothing but disappointment and heartbreak to be had. Nothing else.

All that resolution is wiped away—again—the instant I feel someone slide into the seat beside me and drape an arm casually across the back of my chair. Even before I turn my head to look, I smell him. Even before I confirm with my eyes, I feel him. I feel Jet in the way my pulse speeds up. I feel him in the way my lungs get tight. I feel him in the way my blood sings.

I steal a glance over at him. He's watching me. When my eyes meet his, he winks and rubs the back of my shoulder with his thumb. And for the first time since all this began, I realize that, as much as I've tried to avoid it and outsmart it, I've still managed to get myself into trouble. With an addict. A hot rocker who has an impulse control problem and a small portion of the world at his feet.

But I feel something more in him. I feel the soul of someone better, someone who wants to *be* better. And I feel hope. Whether mine or his, I feel it. And maybe that's the reason I can't walk away.

Maybe . . .

Throughout the entire meeting, Jet teases my shoulder and my neck and my hair. With the tips of his fingers, he pulls every ounce of my focus toward him. Inescapably. In a room full of sex addicts, I can think of nothing more than what Jet's fingers would feel like on my naked skin, in a dark room, with no one around but us.

My cheeks are warm and flushed by the time Lyle breaks. I stand, ready to excuse myself to the restroom, when Jet takes my arm. He holds me still and studies my face as I look at him. In the harsh overhead lights, I see his pupils dilate and I know *he* knows why I'm excusing myself.

He leans closer to me, so close I can feel his breath, but not so close that I can no longer see his eyes. I see the bright white flecks that shoot out from his pupils like starbursts.

He speaks to me, so softly only I can hear. "You know I can take care of that for you. Only you. You have my word."

I feel short of breath. He doesn't have to explain further what he means because I already know. I know *exactly* what he means. And I want to say yes. More than I've ever wanted to say yes to anything.

The muted ring of my phone shatters the moment, giving me a reprieve I know I need, but I'm not sure I want.

"Crap! I forgot to turn off my ringer," I say, pulling away from his eyes and searching for my phone. When I find it and take it out, my heart sinks at the number displayed on it.

"Hi, Stan," I answer, much more brightly than I feel.

"Looks like Thursdays just aren't his night, Violet. He's out early again."

I smother a sigh. "I'll be there as soon as I can."

"Take your time. He's not bothering anybody yet."

Yet, I think with dread. That must mean he's having a rough go of it tonight.

I hit end and throw my phone back in my purse. Tia speaks from behind me. "Your dad?"

"Close enough. It was Stan." I meet Jet's eyes again. "I need to go."

"Wait. What about me?" Tia says, coming around in front of me. "I had Dennis drop me off, remember?"

"Crap!" I say again, feeling my level of frustration escalate. This night has not turned out *at all* the way I'd hoped.

"What's the problem?" Jet asks.

I feel embarrassment well up inside me. I know I shouldn't. It's not *my* problem; it's my father's. But still . . . it's kind of humiliating.

"It's, uh, it's my dad. I need to go pick him up."

"Well, why don't you let Tia take your car? I can take you to get your father and then we can pick it up later."

I'm torn between that *awww* feeling that comes from an unexpectedly kind offer and stuttering over an excuse to get out of it.

"Well, he, um, there's not really . . . I mean, I . . ."

"Stop trying to make excuses. Tia," he says, handing her his keys, "you can take my car to your house. I'll pick it up later. I'll go with Violet."

I want to ask why he doesn't just offer to give Tia a ride home, but I already know the answer. And by the smile she's wearing, so does Tia.

She snatches the keys from Jet's fingers, glancing down at the key ring. "BMW? Nice," she appreciates with a grin.

"Please don't make me regret trusting you," Jet adds as Tia bolts past him.

"I won't. You two have fun." And with that, she's gone in a blur.

"You really didn't have to do that," I say.

His smile is sincere. "I know. But I don't mind helping you. It's the least I can do."

Something about his face tells me he's being truthful.

I sigh. "Well, then I should probably tell you that my father's at a bar. Drunk."

Jet dismisses my concerns with a wave of his hand. "Do you remember what my band is like? Do you *know* how many of these calls I've gotten? And how many of them have been *placed* on *my* behalf?" He laughs, taking me by the hand and leading me to the door. "There might not be a person alive who's better equipped to help him than me."

I smile, feeling better about the evening already.

TWENTY-FOUR: *Jet*

When we reach our destination, we're at an old-people hangout called the Teak Tavern. I've been in it once or twice years ago. To me, it's always seemed like a place where dreams and men go to die. It's a shame this is where Violet's dad comes. It tells me all I need to know about the situation.

I open the door for Violet and let her precede me. I see the bartender glance up and smile. And not just any smile. It's a look I recognize. One that pisses me off a little.

I lean forward just enough to speak into Violet's ear. "He looks like he wants to take you to the beer cooler and show you his longneck bottle collection."

Violet glances at me over her shoulder and giggles. "Stop!"

"Just sayin'," I tell her as we start across the room toward a guy laid out in a corner booth. As we get closer, I recognize him as the man I met at my father's house. Violet's dad.

She bends to gently tap his leg. "Dad, you ready to go home?"

He rolls his head to one side and murmurs something. Even though I don't know him, I can tell that his tone is sharp. It seems like he might be a mean drunk.

"Come on, Dad," Violet urges quietly, her voice calm and even. "Let's get you home. You have work tomorrow."

"I don't give a damn," he moans hatefully. "Why should I work and keep a house waiting for her if she's never coming home?"

Violet glances at me and quickly away, like she's embarrassed. "You keep your house for *you*, Dad, not for her."

"No, it's *all* for her. She's all I ever wanted. And she's gone. How am I supposed to live without her?"

"You've been doing just fine without her, Dad."

Violet's father struggles to sit up, his face contorted in an angry scowl. "How would you know? You're too cold to fall in love. You have no idea what this feels like."

His expression crumbles into one where his chin is trembling and he's fighting tears.

"I love *you*, Dad. Isn't that enough?"

"You must not love me *that* much. You left me just like she did."

Violet sighs. "I didn't leave you. I moved a couple of miles away."

"You abandoned me, just like she did. If you ever cared one bit about me, you wouldn't have left. You *knew* how lonely I'd be. But you left anyway."

"I'll come by more often, Dad. And I'll stay tonight so I can make you breakfast in the morning. I'll make all your favorites."

Like an overgrown kid, Violet's dad looks up at her with hopeful, watery eyes. "You promise?" he slurs.

"I promise."

"And you'll come this weekend for supper?"

"I'll come for supper, too."

Her father scoots to the end of the booth and reaches for her hand, now all sappy and sweet. "You know I love you, right, Vi?"

Violet's voice is as soft as her expression. "Of course I do, Dad."

He holds her hand to his cheek and then comes to a shaky stand. When he's wobbling unsteadily in front of her, he looks at me, as though he just now noticed that Violet isn't alone.

"Where do I know you from?"

"You do some work at my father's place."

His eyes are blank for several seconds before it clicks. I see the change instantly. "Oh, right. Beautiful place you've got there."

"Thank you, sir."

"I'm thinking of planting some azaleas along that fence toward the back of the property."

"That'll look great, sir."

He reaches up to clap me on the back, and I ease him toward the door as he chatters. "Needs some color back there. And they'll be green all winter. Perfect for detracting from that house behind you."

I nod and agree with everything he says, steadily getting closer to the door. He stumbles once and grabs onto me. He's a hefty guy, but I still catch him easily. The thing is, I bet he's hard as hell for Violet to handle. I glance back at her. She's walking behind us, just watching and listening, her expression clouded and unreadable.

I realize two things as I make my way to Violet's car, towing her dad along. Number one, I see why she parked near the front door. And number two, she's a saint. And if she's not, she's got the *patience* of a saint.

He nearly falls twice. Once while attempting to bend and speak to someone we pass, and a second time at the curb. I feel more sympathy for Violet with every minute that passes.

When I have him tucked into Violet's passenger seat, I climb into the backseat. She's already inside. I can see her watching me through the rearview mirror, her expression still visibly unsettled. She says nothing on the way to her father's house, so I don't either. He fell asleep within a minute or two of getting on the road. I figure she's trying not to wake him.

She turns onto a quiet street lined with small, square brick houses and drives all the way to the end. At the bend of the cul-de-sac, she pulls into a driveway and cuts the engine. Without a word, I get out and open the passenger door, ready to help her dad out.

"Wait until I can get the door open, then bring him," she instructs. I nod, watching her scramble up the cracked sidewalk to the plain white front door.

She digs something out of a bush (a spare key, I presume) before she opens the door, cuts on a light, and then hurries back down the walk to the car. "Dad, we're home," she says, jostling his shoulder to stir him. He doesn't even break stride in his snoring. "Dad," she whispers more sharply. More snoring. "Dad, wake up. You need to come inside." Violet shakes his arm again, a little harder this time, but he just snores that much louder. Finally she turns to me, the pink spots on her cheeks visible even in the low light from the streetlamp that sits at the curb two houses down. "Guess he'll be sleeping out here tonight." Her smile says she's not happy about it, but that it's nothing new. And I hate it for her. I hate that this is what her life has been filled with for who knows how long now.

"Do you mind?" I ask as I nod toward him.

"I don't want you to hurt yourself. He'll be fine out here. It's not supposed to be very cold tonight."

"I can get him inside. Just back up." Her mouth opens and she starts to argue. I put my finger over them. "Not a word," I tell her. "Let me help you."

I see both the gratitude and the humiliation in her eyes. But she gives in, taking a few steps back and gesturing for me to have at it.

I grab her father's legs and turn him in the seat, setting his feet out of the car and onto the ground. I take one of his arms and pull his upper body forward, enough so that I can get my shoulder into the meat of his belly. I pull on him and lean back to stand at the same time, hauling him up in a modified fireman's carry.

I hear his grunt when the pressure hits his stomach. I just stay still until he can adjust. When I hear his breathing return to that deep, even cadence it had before, I walk slowly up the walk, carrying him through the front door and into the small living room. I turn to get further direction from Violet. She's right on my heels, scrambling to shut the door and then get ahead of me. She leads me down a short hall to another small room. A bedroom this time, one dominated by a queen-sized bed and a dresser that sits against one wall under a window. She pulls back the covers and pats the mattress. I bend, gently depositing her father a few inches from the edge. I hold on to his hand as I move away so that he doesn't flop back before Violet can get his shoes off.

Once they're tossed onto the floor, I ease him down on his back and then pick up his legs and put them up on the bed, straight out from his body while Violet adjusts his pillow then tugs the covers up over him.

Quietly, we make our way out of the room. I hear her sigh as soon as she shuts the door behind us. She doesn't look at me, but keeps her eyes facing forward as she leads me back out into the living room.

Finally, nervously, she turns and asks, "Do you want something to drink?"

"Violet," I begin.

She hikes a thumb over her shoulder, indicating the kitchen. "There's beer or soda. Or water, if you'd rather have that."

"Violet," I begin again.

"Or if you're hungry, I'm sure there are still some snacks in there. Or I could fix you something."

"Violet!" I say more sternly, taking hold of her shoulders. She stops and stares up at me with her wide, innocent eyes.

"What?"

"Stop. I don't need anything. I don't need you to take care of me. Why don't you sit down and let *me* get *you* something to drink, okay?"

"It's no trouble. I can—"

"Violet, sit. And that's not a request," I say as gently as I can.

Her eyebrows shoot up, but she doesn't look mad. Just surprised.

"You don't know where anything is," she argues.

"I'll find it. Now sit," I repeat, pointing toward the sagging old sofa.

I make my way through the house into the galley-style kitchen. I find glasses and the fridge easily enough, of course. There's a case of Sprite in the bottom of the pantry, so I take a can and crack it open. I open the freezer for ice and find a bottle of vodka stuffed in on its side by the frozen dinners. I get some ice for each glass, add a splash of vodka, and fill the rest with Sprite. I figure Violet could use a little calming, whether she knows it or not.

I carry the glasses into the living room, cutting off the kitchen light with my elbow. Violet is sitting on the couch, her bent arm on the back of the cushion, her head resting in her palm. When she looks up at me, I notice that she seems tired. More so than she had at the meeting.

I sit beside her, handing her a drink. "This has just enough of a kick to relax you."

She sniffs the glass and then frowns. "Thanks, but I don't need anything."

"Maybe not, but trust me, you look like you could use it."

"Are you saying I look bad?"

I give her a derisive smirk. "You could *never* look bad. I just mean you look tired. This will help you relax and sleep."

"But I don't want anything to help me relax."

"You don't have to forego every little thing in life, on the off chance you could get addicted, Violet. For most people, it doesn't work that way. *One* drink, *one* time isn't going to kill you."

"I know that. It's the circumstances. If I just *wanted* one that would be different. I don't want to *need* one. Becoming dependent on it is the problem."

"So you steer clear of everything that you feel like you need?"

"Of course not. I mean, there are necessities in life. But there's a danger in wanting something *too* much or liking it so much you feel like you *need* it."

"Is that what happened to bring you to the meetings?"

Her expression totally shuts down. "I'd rather not talk about that right now, if you don't mind."

"Fair enough," I say agreeably, taking a sip of my own drink.

After a long, tense silence, Violet speaks. "Thank you for tonight."

"Nothing to it. No thanks necessary."

"You were really good with him."

"I was thinking the same thing about you."

She smiles. "Sometimes it works better than others."

"Was tonight a bad night?"

"No. He settled down pretty easily. This has been a great night compared to some."

"How often do you have to do this?"

"Now? Maybe a couple of times a month. Thursdays seem to be his magical night these days."

"Is that because you are gone to meetings on Thursday nights?"

Violet shoots me a strange look. "You know, I haven't thought of it that way, but I guess it could be. I've only been attending these for a few weeks."

"Where did you go before?" She gives me a withering look, and I put up my hands in surrender. "Sorry. Retracted."

"I thought it would get easier for him, but sometimes I think he'll never get over her."

"Is that why he drinks?"

"It's why he drinks *in excess*. He never went on benders when she was here. He just can't handle life without her sometimes."

I finally realize what I see on her face. It's pity. And frustration. And disgust. "You think he's weak."

"What?"

"I just realized that you think addiction makes you weak. You think that *having* a weakness makes you *weak*." For some reason, I'm stung by this insight into her.

"I . . . I . . ." she stammers, her expression that of a cornered animal.

"Is that how you see me? Like I'm some kind of weak person who can't control himself?"

Her cheeks burn bright pink and her mouth opens and closes around words she can't say. Because any explanation she gives won't be true.

"Having *a weakness* doesn't mean a person *is* weak. I would have thought you, of all people, would understand that."

"It's not . . . I just . . ."

I stand, feeling increasingly pissed off and knowing there's not a good, rational reason to be. I just am.

"You know, Violet," I say, setting my glass down on a coaster on the banged-up coffee table, "maybe one day you'll come across someone or something that will make you see the difference."

With that, I turn and walk to the door. When I look back, Violet is standing, watching me.

"What about your car?"

"I have a friend that lives near here. I'll get him to take me to Tia's. It's not far."

She says nothing as I open the door and step out into the night, and I'm glad. I don't want her excuses. Or her sympathy. And I sure as hell don't want her pity.

I take deep, calming breaths as I strike out down the street. I have no intention of stopping by anyone's house. I'll walk the whole damn way.

I don't know what pisses me off more—that she has such a shitty opinion of me, or that I give a rat's ass.

I remind myself why I'm even in this. I bet she wouldn't think so little of me if she knew what kind of an asshole I really am. She'd probably hate me, but she sure as hell wouldn't think I'm weak.

Not that I care *what* she thinks of me. I can do this no matter what her personal thoughts and feelings toward me are.

And I remind myself of that all the way to Tia's house. Every time I see that look of disgust on Violet's face.

TWENTY-FIVE: *Violet*

After the world's worst night's sleep, all I can think about is Jet. Just like he was all I thought about last night.

Growing up surrounded by addiction in one form or another has made me a little bit jaded about both the addiction *and* the addict. Jet's bitter words made me realize that I *do* see people with weakness as weak. Maybe because I've watched them hurt themselves and others without being able to stop, or maybe because they just can't stop *period*. I don't know, but Jet is right. And the way I feel is wrong.

And Jet makes me see that.

There is nothing weak about him. Although he has some issues with self-control, not once has he given me the impression that he is anything but strong. Maybe a little hedonistic, but not weak. Never weak.

I don't consider myself weak, but as much trouble as I've had staying detached from Jet, as much difficulty as I've had keeping my rational thought processes intact, I can see how weakness might come about. And how it doesn't make you weak. It just makes you vulnerable. And there *is* a difference.

I roll off the couch, ignoring the creak of my muscles. I sit up and determine that, even though Jet probably doesn't want me around tonight, I'm going to go and watch him, I'm going to support him anyway. I need him to see that I don't think he's weak. I need him to see that I'm not going anywhere, that I want to help him.

Even though a big part of it *now* is that I just want to be with him.

Period.

After fixing Dad breakfast, heading home for a shower, cleaning my house like I'm expecting the Queen of England, and then taking another shower, I find that waiting might not be the easiest thing. So I call. Not because I'm weak, but because I need him to know how I see him.

"Yeah," Jet answers abruptly after four rings.

"Hi, Jet. It's Violet. Do you have a minute?"

There's a long pause, during which I manage to convince myself that he will never want to see me or talk to me again.

But he does.

"Actually, I was just heading out."

Or maybe he doesn't.

"Oh. Okay. Well, I . . . uh . . . I'll—"

"Are you busy right now?"

"No, I just . . . no."

"I'll be by to get you in ten minutes. Okay?"

I should probably ask why or where we're going. But I don't. Because I don't care.

"Okay."

With a click, he's gone and my nerves are at fever pitch.

Not knowing how to dress, I choose jeans and a cap-sleeved peasant shirt in sage green. According to Tia, it makes my eyes look smoky and sexy. Why I should care whether I look sexy is not something I dwell on. I just know that I'm pleased with my reflection when I shut off the bathroom light to head for the living room to await Jet.

When I hear the engine of his car come to a purring stop at the curb, I lock up and leave, walking to meet him before he can come to me. I smile shyly. He returns it in a casual and polite way before he opens the passenger door to help me into his car.

He doesn't say much, so I'm forced to ask him, "So, where are we going?"

"To my mother's house."

I feel like doing a double take. "What?"

Jet looks over at me and grins. A real grin. And it makes me feel much better about things. Just like that. Just that easily. I didn't realize how much I would've missed it if I'd never gotten to see it again.

But I would've. I would've missed it a lot. I would've missed *him* a lot.

"She called. Right out of the blue. She needs to go to Summerton and doesn't want to leave the boys by themselves."

"I thought the oldest was fourteen."

"He is. She's just crazy overprotective—thinks they'll get into trouble if she leaves them alone for ten seconds. But I don't really care what her reasons are. I'm just happy she called me. That she'll trust me at least this much. It's been a while since she would."

I can feel his pleasure like a tangible thing, flavoring even the air in the car. And it makes my heart ache for him. "Then that's good enough for me."

We fall silent again. Part of me is hesitant to bring up last night, just in case it damages the fragile peace that we've struck for the moment. But it's too important for me *not* to mention it.

"Jet, about last night . . ." I pause to gauge his reaction. I see his jaw flex as though he's gritting his teeth, but it's too late for me to stop now. "After thinking about it for quite a while, I realized that you were right. Well, at least partially."

I see one dark brow arch. His voice is droll when he says, "Partially, huh?"

"Yes, partially. I think that I *do* view many people in my life as weak because of their weakness. And although I can appreciate that you do have some . . . issues to work through, I can honestly say that I've never once considered you or thought of you as weak."

He says nothing, just nods.

I turn in my seat to more fully face him, desperate to make him see my view. "Jet, whatever kinds of habits or addictions you have, for whatever kinds of reasons you do what you do, there is nothing weak about you. You are strong. In every way. But even strong people have chinks in their armor. That doesn't make you weak. It only makes you human."

This time, Jet glances over at me, his eyes narrowing on mine, searching them. "And what makes you human?" he asks quietly.

Even *I* am surprised by the words that spill out. I'm surprised by the truth in them. "My aversion to weakness. I think that, in and of itself, makes me human. It's like a phobia almost. I've seen it destroy the happy parts of so many of my loved ones that I despise it. I avoid it at all costs. But it's for that reason that I think weakness is my weakness. Not wanting to feel it. Avoiding it. I've always considered it a strength, but I'm beginning to think I've hidden from it for so long, looked down on it for so long, that when I come across something that tempts me . . ." I can't help but think of Jet as I speak. "It will turn my world upside down. And I won't be prepared for that at all."

"You mean when you find something *else* that tempts you."

It takes me several puzzled seconds to figure out what Jet is referring to. Once again, I'm forced to acknowledge how little he knows of me. And how much of what he *thinks* he knows is a lie. He's referring to my supposed sex addiction.

"Right. Something *else*."

Even saying the words feels treacherous. Maintaining the lie, even though I'm trying to convince myself it's for good reason—to help him, to help Tia—still feels . . . wretched.

"Well, if my opinion matters, I don't see you as weak either. I think you're probably one of the strongest people I've ever known. I guess that's why I don't want you thinking that *I'm* weak. I would hate to disappoint you."

Jet turns his eyes back to the road. I see his brow wrinkle as though his own words hurt him, a testament to the veracity of them.

"I could never be disappointed in you," I tell Jet softly.

He doesn't look at me when he answers. "Don't be too sure of that."

Before I can think of the best way to respond, Jet is pulling into the driveway of a nice brick split-level house in an upper-middle-class neighborhood. Although it's nice—far nicer than the one I grew up in—it's a ghetto compared to where his father lives now. It's already easy for me to sympathize with his mother's bitterness.

Jet cuts the engine and comes around to open my door. He doesn't hold my hand going up the walk. Not that he's supposed to. Or that I expected him to. But I am certainly noticing (and missing) that he's not. It seems he's held it more often than not lately. Until today.

When we reach the front door, he surprises me by knocking. Within seconds, the door is wrenched open and an exuberant little boy is flinging himself into Jet's arms.

I watch as Jet gently roughhouses with the boy, flinging him around like a rag doll, something both of them seem to enjoy. Then, with the child squealing and giggling, Jet announces "Back breaker!" and turns the kid belly-up and pretends to bend him over his knee.

Then, breathing heavily, Jet rights him and squats to introduce us. "Todd, this is my friend, Violet."

Shyly, Todd looks up at me with eyes that are the exact shade as his older brother's and says a short, "Hi." And then he disappears back into the house.

When Jet glances over at me, his eyes are shiny and happy. I'm relieved and equally happy when he reaches for my hand and nods toward the door. "Come on. Let's go get mauled."

I don't ask what he means by that. Because I don't care. I'm game as long as I get to be with Jet.

TWENTY-SIX: *Jet*

The living room is empty when we walk in, so Violet and I follow Todd to the kitchen. Chad is sitting at the small table that's pushed into one corner and Mom is standing by the stove, leaning against the counter. Her arms are crossed over her chest defensively and she's facing the doorway like she was just waiting for me. To pounce.

Her eyes are sparkling and her chin is lifted, which makes me brace for a fight. That's the look she gets when she's ready to tear into somebody. Like me.

She straightens, and I think to myself, *Here it comes!* But then she surprises me. She stops, mouth open like she's going to speak, but she says nothing when her eyes settle on Violet.

Stunned, she asks in a small voice, "You brought a girl?"

"No, I brought Violet. She's my friend."

"Friend, huh?"

It hadn't occurred to me that she might not want Violet here, but now that I see her, I realize that it was a huge mistake on my part to bring her.

"Yes, ma'am. I'm Violet Wilson. I live on the other side of town. I went to school right here in Greenfield. Graduated a few years after Jet. Now I'm a social worker," Violet blurts, stepping forward to offer her hand to my mother.

I'm a little shocked by her forwardness. She's normally so shy, even around me sometimes. Still. But not now. It seems that my mother has brought out the professional side of Violet, a side I've never seen before. She appears friendly, down to earth, and competent. Nothing like the women I normally consort with. Not that my mother has met any of them since I was a teenager. But still, she has to know. It's a small town.

I see the frown flicker between my mother's eyebrows. "Gail. Gail Blevins. It's nice to meet you, Violet."

Violet's smile is wide and genuine. "You have a beautiful home. And a beautiful family, too," she says, glancing over at Chad. "You must be Chad." I watch as she walks over and bends just enough to put her closer to Chad's level where he's sitting. She offers her hand to him as well. "I'm Violet."

Chad gives her a small smile and shakes her hand, but when she walks away, he looks at me and gives me a *real* smile. Like any other hot-blooded teenage boy would give when a gorgeous woman pays him some attention.

Mom is still frowning as her eyes dart from Chad to Violet to me, then back to Chad. "Homework first, you hear me, young man?"

"I know," Chad answers, rolling his eyes.

Mom looks to me. "Make sure his homework is done before you leave, Jet."

"Yes, ma'am."

I know she wants to say more, but she doesn't want to do it in front of Violet, which is unlike her. Normally she doesn't hold her tongue in front of anyone.

"I'll be back by eight at the latest," she says as she walks past me to grab her purse from the table near the door. I follow her, leaving Violet and the boys in the kitchen.

"Take your time."

"Don't you have plans tonight?"

Shit. I hope this doesn't start a fight.

"I do, but I can have them stall if I need to. I'm here until you get back. Don't worry."

She eyes me warily. "I'm trusting you . . ."

"I know, Mom. And I appreciate it. Really. I do."

"I thought maybe you could come over here and sit with the boys for a while rather than sneaking around to see them at the park."

Busted!

"You know about that?"

"Of course I know about that." I brace for what I thought was coming the second I walked in. But it *still* doesn't come, which surprises the shit out of me. "Let's try it this way and see how it goes."

"I won't disappoint you. I promise."

She grunts, glancing over my shoulder toward the kitchen. "I like her. Where'd you find her?"

"At the very bottom, Mom," I tell her meaningfully.

Her eyes lock on mine and I see her looking for more. But she doesn't find it. She finds the truth. Because it *is* the truth. I don't think I realized how low I'd gotten until this very minute. How low I'd gotten until I found Violet.

"See that you stay on top then, son."

"I'm trying."

With a ghost of a smile, Mom pats my arm and grabs her car keys.

"You boys be good. I'll be back soon," she calls, looking over my shoulder at my brothers, and then she's gone.

TWENTY-SEVEN: *Violet*

Watching Jet with his brothers is unlike anything I've ever experienced. I've never felt so overcome with so many emotions. It's like seeing a totally different side of Jet. It's a side I like very much. And I didn't need anything else to like about him.

I played chess with Todd while Jet helped Chad with his algebra homework. Just listening to them, it was easy to ascertain that Jet is very intelligent. Even the way he explained it to his brother was brilliant.

After they finished, Jet made popcorn with the intention of the four of us watching a movie, but the boys then insisted on a wrestling match. Everyone had to wrestle each other at least once. The two who won the most matches would then have a face-off for the illustrious title of *winner.*

I was skeptical at first, but it didn't take me long to see the fun in it, especially when it came time for me to wrestle Jet.

As all previous matches had, we started the bout on our knees, facing one another. Jet had a sexy, playful curve to his lips and a gleam in his eye that made my stomach flutter.

"You'd better not hurt me," I said, trying not to grin as I edge away from him.

"I promise not to do anything you won't like," he replied suggestively, one brow rising the tiniest bit.

And then he lunged for me. With a squeal, I tried to get away, but he was far too big, too strong and too long of limb. Within a few seconds, he had me half on my side, half on my belly, and he was stretched out on top of me, holding me down.

"Oh, wait! My hip," I complained primly. Immediately, Jet rolled slightly, moving most of his weight off me. I took advantage of his momentary lapse and levered myself up onto my elbows and rolled over on top of him instead.

I pinned his arms above his head and leaned down into his face. "Hah! Gotcha."

Jet was looking up at me, his eyes as intense as I'd ever seen them, and he murmured, "Maybe you do."

His voice was low and silky. His belly was hard and warm. My heart leapt, my stomach clenched, and every place his body touched mine went up in flames.

But then, so fast I could barely react, he flipped me over to pin me beneath him. His body was stretched full length along mine. I could feel every prominence and hollow. And, like I had done to him, he held my arms above my head, leaving me helpless against him.

"Or maybe *I've* got *you*."

For a moment, I'd forgotten we weren't alone. All I could think about was how much I wanted Jet to kiss me, how much I wanted him to run his hands down my arms, down my sides. How much I wanted him to touch me everywhere, all at once.

But then his rambunctious brother interrupted, reminding me that we did, in fact, have an audience.

"Get a room," Chad snickered.

With his eyes fixed on mine, Jet bent his head forward just enough to bite my chin. I felt the brush of his tongue for just a second before he leaned away and then rolled off me.

He didn't take his eyes off me, though. And I could see that he was as . . . bothered by the encounter as I was. And that it was a good thing we weren't alone.

We finally settled down to at least start the movie before Jet's mom got home, but even that did nothing to alleviate the tension between us. Every second that his side is pressed against mine on the sofa feels like a special kind of torture. I've ached the entire twenty-two minutes that I've been feigning interest in the show.

I'm both relieved and nervous when I hear the door open. All heads turn to find Gail dragging some bags through the door. The boys get up and run to see what she's got.

"Ah, ah, ah! You just stay right there. This is birthday stuff. Nothing you need to be nosing around in," she declares, holding the bags behind her and out of sight.

"Aw, Mom," Todd says, but it's easy to see that they're both pleased and excited about whatever she bought.

Gail directs her next words to Jet. "Let me get these put away and you two can go."

Jet stands, holding out his hand for me. I slide my fingers across his palm and he squeezes them, pulling me to my feet. When I stand, he doesn't back away. He just stares down into my face, his body so close I can still feel the heat of it.

"Since we're only playing Lucky's tonight, do you want to just ride over with me?"

Lucky's is a local bar, one of the only places the younger crowd can go. I know about it, even though I've never been. The party atmosphere was never my scene, for obvious reasons.

"Ummm, am I dressed okay? I mean, I didn't—"

"You look mouthwatering. You don't need to change anything," he replies softly.

I feel the flush of pleasure rise from my belly to my chest and into my face. "Then yes, I'll just ride with you. If you don't mind taking me home afterward."

Jet's thumb is rubbing slowly back and forth over the top of my hand. "I don't mind at all."

Gail comes back out and walks to the couch, grabbing a few remaining popcorn kernels. "Thanks for coming. I appreciate you two."

Jet nods. "Anytime. I'm glad you called."

I watch the uncomfortable interaction, wishing I could just melt away and leave them alone in the moment. It seems there is so much more being said between them than just words.

"You still writing?" she asks, making her way slowly to the door.

"Hadn't been until the last little while. I think it's coming back, though."

Gail's eyes flicker to me and then quickly move away. She nods. "Good. Don't give up on that. It'll make all this band nonsense worth it if you make it."

I'm sure Jet would like to comment, but he does the right thing and just lets it ride. No reason to leave on a bad note or being argumentative.

"I'm trying."

"Good for you," she says, swinging the door open, a not-so-subtle hint that it's time for us to go. I suppose her tolerance is at an end. At least for the moment.

"Call me if you need me."

"Maybe I will," she says noncommittally. And just when I think that she's so cool and casual that I want to slap her, she pleasantly surprises me. "Love you, Jethro."

I can almost feel the exhale in Jet. And his fingers actually get tighter around mine as he leans forward to kiss his mother on the cheek. "Love you, too, Mom."

She gives him a warm smile then turns it on me before she shoos us out the door and locks up behind us. Jet seems to walk a bit lighter down the walk than he walked up it a few hours earlier. I know this was huge for him. For his mother, too, I'm sure. But probably more for Jet.

I want to take him in my arms and hold him, but I know I can't. I shouldn't. So I just hold on to his hand a little tighter, hoping he'll get what I'm saying without me having to open my mouth. And when he looks down at me as he's opening the passenger side door, I know that he got it. Loud and clear.

Lucky's is quite a bit different than the other venues where I've seen Jet play. There's no backstage area for them to dress and await their show time. There's no big crew of people there to coordinate everything. In fact, this is more like a few members of the crowd who just hop up on the small stage and sing to a bunch of their friends.

And I like it much better.

I can see a happiness in Jet that hasn't been there at the other places. I can hear an ease in his voice, see a comfort in his body language, all telling me that he feels safe when he's among friends.

And it probably doesn't hurt that he had a good evening with his family. That seems to taint everything, for better or for worse.

Jet sat me at a table near the stage, telling me to stay put, that some friends of his would be joining me. But the show just started, and I'm still sitting alone.

Until the blonde shows up.

"You must be Violet," the beautiful woman says.

"I am," I reply, waiting for her to introduce herself.

She pulls up the chair closest to me and plunks down, glancing over her shoulder at someone. Finally, she turns her attention back to me. "Sorry. How rude of me! I'm Laney. Laney Theopolis."

"Hi, Laney. It's nice to meet you."

"I hear you got to witness the heathens at play at my husband's bachelor party." She's smiling like there's an inside joke.

"Well, I was there. I don't know how much I witnessed, though."

"Oh, girl, don't you worry about spilling the beans. Jake told me as soon as he got home." She waves it off like no big deal. "Men!"

I only vaguely remember the others from that night. The one that hit on Tia is pretty clear in my head, but I can't seem to recall Jake. Probably because all I could concentrate on was Jet.

It's when Jake makes his way to the table and sits down that I very clearly remember him. He's absolutely gorgeous!

"Nice to see you again," he says, winking one amber eye and flashing me a breathtaking smile before he turns to kiss his wife on the lips. "They're out of Sprite, but they're sending someone across the street for a few."

"Babe, you didn't have to have them go out for some! I can drink something else."

"Nope. Only the best for my wife," he teases.

Laney beams at him. "Say it again."

"Nope."

She slaps his arm playfully. "Not that! The other part."

"Only the best," he says.

Laney eyes him in a mock threat. Finally he gives in with a look that could melt the coldest of hearts. "My wife."

She sinks into him, and I think, for the moment, they have no idea who else is in the world with them, and I envy them their easy love. I don't know exactly how long they've been married, but it couldn't have been that long. A couple of weeks, maybe. But it's plain to see that they are very much in love and destined to be together.

I turn my attention back to Jet where he's finishing up a song. My heart does a little flip when his eyes meet mine and he winks at me. As handsome as Jake Theopolis is, he doesn't hold a candle to Jet's amazing good looks. In fact, he just doesn't hold a candle to Jet, period.

When the stage lights dim and the music slows, I feel a flutter in my stomach. I love it when he sings the slow songs. In a way, it feels like he's singing to me. Only to me. I know that's hardly the case, but it's easy to pretend.

As is his custom, Jet sits on the edge of the stage with his legs dangling over, his acoustic guitar cradled against his body. When he begins picking the notes to the song, I search for it somewhere in my memory, but it doesn't even sound familiar. It's beautiful, though. I'm sucked into it within a few bars.

When he begins to sing, his eyes find mine again and, once more, I feel as though he's singing for me, *to* me. Only to me.

> She crept in with the night, violet streaks on the wind.
> She saw my soul, stole my heart, found the place where I'm a better man.
>
> If I cared enough, I think I'd let her go.
> Or do I care too much to ever leave her alone? (To leave her alone, leave her alone, leave her alo-one.)

It's when he gets to the chorus that I realize that he *is* singing to me. And that he's singing *about me*.

> She pulls me down, takes me under, makes the noise of the world seem softer.
> Touch her body, feel her lips, lose myself in her sweet, sweet kiss.
> Drowning in violet, drowning in violet. Don't pull me out, because I'm drowning in violet.

My heart is beating so heavily, I wonder that my chest hasn't exploded from the pressure. And when the second verse begins, and I see the pain and worry in Jet's eyes, I feel sure my ribs can't take it.

Will she hate me when she knows?
Will she take her love and go?

But they do. As much as my heart swells and throbs and aches, it's safe inside me. But how long can I keep it that way? How long before it's no longer mine to keep safe, mine to keep at all?

I know the answer to that when the song ends and Jake leans forward in his seat, putting his head in my line of sight. "So you're the one, huh?"

"Pardon?" I ask, still feeling dazed.

"You're the one that finally got her claws in."

I struggle to wrap my head around what he's saying, what he means.

"You're the one who finally got Jet Blevins's heart. Sounds to me like that boy's in love with you."

And just like that, everything changes.

TWENTY-EIGHT: *Jet*

I sit with the phone in my lap, shocked and satisfied and excited as hell. I rerun the last ten minutes over in my head, like pinching myself to make sure I'm not dreaming.

The call came in as I was onstage. When the show ended, I came into the back room to listen to the message.

Back here, it's basically just a lounge area for Lucky's employees and the few bands that they ever host here. It's nothing more than a bathroom, a small kitchenette, and a lunchroom-style table littered with packets of salt and sugar substitute and half-full ashtrays.

But all I needed was a chair and some quiet. To sit in while I listened to the message of a lifetime. Even as I digest what I heard, I feel the urge to replay it. Just to make sure I wasn't dreaming.

I know I won't be able to hang out for the rest of the night, acting casual around the other members of the band and some of my friends. No, I need to get the hell out of here and find a place to think. Really think.

After taking a couple of deep breaths, I make my way back out to the main bar area, to Violet where she's sitting with Jake and Laney. The three of them have their heads together, talking about something, until one of them says something funny and they all laugh. Laney is facing me. It's not hard to see why Jake fell for her. She's a classically beautiful blonde. But when Violet turns in her chair, presumably to look for me, and her eyes stop on mine, I can barely remember what Laney looks like. And that scares the shit out of me. For several reasons, not the least of which is the way I've misled Violet. If she ever finds out, she'll be out of my life so fast my head will spin. And I'm not ready to let her go just yet.

But that doesn't make me feel any less shitty about the whole thing.

What the hell were you thinking, brother?

When I stop at the table, I hold her gaze for several seconds, enjoying the way she licks her lips nervously, and the way she seems like she wants to look shyly away, but can't. Finally, I look up at Jake.

"Thanks for coming, man."

"My pleasure. Laney hated every minute of it, though," he teases.

Laney slaps his arm and smiles kindly up at me. "He's lying through his pearly white teeth, Jet. Don't you believe a word he says. You were amazing! And that slow song . . . what was that called? I don't think I've ever heard it before," she says.

"You haven't," is my only response.

"Oh," is *her* only response, although the glance she sends Jake tells me that she suspects she knows what's behind it. Or, rather, *who.*

"I'd love to stay, but I promised this beautiful woman a ride home," I say, referring to Violet.

"We can stay as long as you want," Violet says kindly.

"I'm ready if you are." I don't want to give some half-assed excuse or explanation in front of my friends. I respect them too much to treat them like they're stupid.

"Well then, we can go. I just thought . . ." Violet trails off and, when I don't offer to stay, she stands, grabbing her purse from the back of the chair and saying her good-byes to Jake and Laney. "It was so nice to meet you, Laney. And congratulations to you both on your wedding."

"I wish we'd met you a little sooner and you could've come. We'd have made Jet here bring you," Laney says, winking at me.

"I doubt any force would've been necessary," Jake says, sliding me a knowing look.

I grunt and put my hand on the small of Violet's back, giving Jake a nod before I go. "Talk to you next week, man."

Jake nods back before he gives his new wife his full attention. I'm glad he moved back to Greenfield. I missed that crazy, firefighting bastard and I'm pleased to see him happy.

When we get to the car and Violet climbs inside, she looks up at me from the passenger seat. "We could've stayed, Jet. Really. I didn't mind."

"I know," I tell her, bending down to whisper to her, "but there's something I have to tell you."

I see her mouth drop open and her eyes get wide. I wonder if she thinks I'm about to confess my undying love or something. I wink at her, not yet putting her out of her misery. A laugh bubbles in my chest as I walk around the front of the car.

I slide in behind the wheel, but I don't move to start the car yet. I turn to face Violet.

"I just got a call from Kick Records. They want to hear some of my songs."

"What?" she asks, surprised but visibly excited. "Jet, are you serious? What did they say?"

"They're interested in a couple of my songs. They want to hear more. Said they're looking for something fresh and they want me to give them a private demo."

"Oh my gosh! When? Where?"

"Well, they're out of California, which would be a bitch of a trip, but they're opening an office down in New Orleans, so they're willing to meet me there."

"When?"

"This weekend."

Even if I couldn't see the pleasure on her face, I could tell she's enthused. I can hear it in the pitch of her voice. "I'm so, so happy for you. Oh my gosh!" she says again, cupping her hands over her mouth.

Then she surprises me. With a shrill squeak, she flings herself against me, wrapping her arms around my neck and squeezing.

I hug her back, careful not to put my hands on her too much. At this point, that could be dangerous. This isn't the place.

When she leans back, her face is shining. It looks like she's every bit as happy for me as I am.

I can't stop my own smile. "I knew I couldn't stay in there one minute longer. I was about to bust, and I don't want anyone to know yet."

"I won't say a word," she promises, zipping her lips and pretending to throw away the key.

"Don't lock 'em down yet," I say, unable to keep my eyes from taking in her lush lips and remembering the way they taste. "I need them for a little while longer."

Her face is serious now. Serious and hot.

"You do?"

I grit my teeth. I do, but not for what she's thinking. Damn it! At least, not tonight.

"I do. I need an answer."

"To what?"

"Look, I know it's short notice, but would you want to come with me? I could really use the support."

My conscience needles me a little. That's not the real reason I'm asking. Well, maybe a small, microscopic portion of it. It *will* be nice to have her there. But there's so much more to it than something professional. No, I want Violet to go for a whole laundry list of personal reasons, the biggest one being that I just can't wait any longer to get her alone. Really alone. And all to myself.

"I'd love to," she says, her smile tentative. Her response is quiet and shy, which makes the blood rush to my dick. It's that whole hot librarian thing again. If I closed my eyes, I could easily picture her standing in her panties and a pair of chaste glasses, biting her fingertip, looking up at me with those incredible eyes, pretending to be all innocent, coy. Sexy as hell.

I smile. "Good. Can you be ready to leave by six in the morning? That way, we'll get there in enough time to clean up before I have to meet them at night."

"I can be ready. Should I bring anything specific?"

"Something kinda hip and sexy maybe." I give her my most lascivious grin. "But not for me. For these record execs. I figure bringing some eye candy can't hurt my chances."

"So I'm eye candy? Is that it?"

"Oh you're eye candy, all right. But, to me, you're mouthwatering in a lot of other ways, too."

I see the color hit her cheeks. And I feel it, all the way to my groin where it's making my pants tight.

"I'll see what I can find," she says, still holding my eyes.

"Then let me get you home. Tomorrow will be a long day. But I hope to make it up to you tomorrow night."

Her smile says she's down with that. I just wonder if she'd be as agreeable if she knew exactly what I have in mind.

TWENTY-NINE: *Violet*

I don't know what I expected a long car ride with Jet to be like. Quiet. Brooding. Introspective. Whatever I imagined, I was wrong.

Although the trip did *start* a little more sedate, it quickly picked up after some breakfast and coffee on the go. Jet treated me to a musical montage of some of his favorite songs, as well as some of *his* songs, all of which show me what I already knew—Jet has some major talent.

I don't ask and he doesn't mention the song he sang last night. It gives me a little thrill, a little jitter in the pit of my stomach just to think about it. Even though I only heard it the one time, I can't forget the words. I probably never will.

About halfway there, we stop for lunch.

"So tell me," he begins, turning down the volume on the stereo, "what does a beautiful woman such as yourself like to eat? I know you must get hungry."

He's not looking at me, so I can't tell if he's taunting me or not. It sure *feels* like it, but that could just be my mind, my body, and my imagination, all working overtime.

"I like all sorts of things. Depends on what I'm in the mood for, what I'm craving."

"And what are you craving today?"

An ache, one that's becoming all too familiar, is forming in the lowest part of my belly, making my appetite for *real* food take a backseat to my desire for . . . something else.

"I'm open to suggestions. I'll go along with whatever you want."

Now Jet looks at me. And I see that it wasn't just *my* imagination that took off in the wrong direction. Or maybe it's the *right* direction.

"I was hoping you'd say that," he admits, his eyes dark and steamy.

He says nothing else, just leaves me to my thoughts as he steers the car off the highway and onto a secondary road that's lined with restaurants.

When he stops in front of a seafood place with an outdoor patio that overlooks a stretch of river, I have to wonder why he chose it. He answers my question before I can ask it, though. "Since we're on a pretty strict timetable, we need to be quick." He cuts the engine and removes the key from the ignition. Before he climbs out of the car, he turns those hot eyes to me and says, "Just so you know, though, 'quick' doesn't mean 'less satisfying' when you're with me."

He leaves me with that sentiment as he gets out and walks around to open my door. When I slide my fingers into his, I feel the friction in every nerve of my body, like his touch is rasping along each one, bringing them to screaming life. He says nothing more as he closes my door and places his hand at my lower back to guide me inside.

And I'm glad. With Jet touching me, I don't think I could concentrate on what he was saying right now anyway.

Jet requests the outdoor area, so the hostess leads us to a table in the corner of the patio. The day is already very warm, but the ceiling fan helps keep the area cool.

Our waitress brings some water and two menus. I look at mine with unseeing eyes, every bit of my attention focused on Jet's knees where they're brushing mine under the table.

"Have you ever had raw oysters?"

"Like on the half shell?"

"Yeah."

"Ummm, once."

"And?"

I shrug. "They were okay."

Jet grins. "Well, today they're going to be delicious. Because I'm going to show you how to eat them the right way."

"I'm game," I reply, still feeling a bit dumbstruck by the increasing tension that seems to permeate our every look and word.

"I was hoping you'd say that," he says again, his grin devilish.

Since they don't have to be cooked, the waitress returns with our food within minutes of Jet placing the order. She sets two flat platters on the table, each filled with ice and topped with oysters sitting prettily inside the bottom half of their shell.

I watch as Jet loosens each of the two dozen oysters from its shell and then grabs the hot sauce. It's sitting on the table with the salt and pepper, like it's a normal condiment. Of course, in a place that serves raw food, it might *be* a normal condiment.

He sprinkles a few drops on one of the oysters and then looks up at me to ask, "Would you rather eat it out of the shell or with a fork? If you eat it from the shell, don't be surprised if you get a little bit of grit from it. But don't worry, it's nothing that will hurt you."

I don't know how, but I manage to keep my top lip from curling up in a sneer of distaste. Proud of my self-control, I give him my answer calmly. "Fork please."

Jet uses his fork to stab the oyster and then hold it out to me. "Come here," he says huskily, his smoky eyes telling me that he's looking forward to putting something in my mouth. And, if I'm being honest, *now* I'm looking forward to it just as much.

I rise a little from my chair and lean forward, just enough that I can easily take the food from his fork. I watch his eyes as I do. They are dark and sensuous, and glued to my mouth.

I'm barely aware of the salty, spicy, slimy oyster sliding down my throat. All I feel is the heat of Jet's gaze. I lick my lips and Jet does the same, as though he's wishing he could taste mine instead.

Finally his eyes rise to mine. "Good?"

"Delicious," I respond, not in any way referring to the oyster.

Jet lowers his fork as I resume my seat. He says nothing for a few seconds as he watches me. "As much as I would love to feed you every oyster on this damn table, I'm not sure we'd make it out of the parking lot before sunset if I do."

"Why is that?" If I weren't so entranced by him, I would be surprised at my curiously brazen question.

"Because," he says, reaching across the table to wipe my bottom lip with the pad of his thumb, "I can't watch your lips close around my fork or watch your tongue lick them without remembering what you taste like. And then *wondering* what you taste like *everywhere else*." Suddenly, the air seems warmer, thicker than it was a few seconds ago, and I feel a flush flood me from my cheeks to my core. "I hope you don't mind."

I'm breathless and completely mesmerized by his words and the images they bring to mind. "No, of course not," I say automatically.

"That's kind of a shame, because if you really, *really* wanted me to continue putting things in your mouth, *you* are the one thing I'd miss this meeting for."

Pleasure races behind the gush of heat that moved through me, pleasure that he'd blow off something so important to be with me.

"I couldn't let you do that, not even if I wanted to."

Jet's grin is devilish. "The fact that you might want to gives me something to look forward to."

I say nothing. I can't admit that I would even consider it—but I am. Not only am I *considering it*, but I doubt I'll be able to stop thinking about it for the rest of the trip.

Finally, when the silence drags on and the tension is nearly unbearable, Jet speaks. "Eat," he says. "You'll need your strength."

It's a promise. Not only the words, but the look in his eyes. And as often as I've told myself that this is a mistake and that I shouldn't get involved, I know there's no going back now. It seems that as much as I tried to avoid it, as much as I've tried to explain it away and lie to myself about it—just like an addict would—I've finally found my weakness.

It's Jet.

THIRTY: *Jet*

I don't know how the hell I've made it this far without putting my hands on Violet. It has to be the anticipation of tonight. It's keeping me going. That *has to be* it. If I didn't believe relief was right around the corner, I don't think I'd have made it this far.

But here I am. Standing in the lobby of a posh, historic hotel in the heart of New Orleans, waiting to get checked in.

After watching the clerk frown and tap furiously at his computer before picking up his phone and speaking softly into it, I'm not surprised when I see the concierge approach, wearing a smile that says he's ready to kiss ass.

It doesn't take a rocket scientist to figure out that something's wrong.

"Mr. Blevins, while the suite that Kick Records reserved for you is prepared for your arrival, there was a problem with the second room.

Since it was reserved in your name and not associated with the suite, the dates were entered incorrectly, showing a vacancy when, in fact, we have none. I apologize for the inconvenience. I would be happy to make arrangements for another room, upgraded to a suite, at one of our other hotels, if that would be suitable for you and your guest."

"So you're saying you'd find *her* a room at *another hotel*?"

"Yes, sir. I'd be happy to."

I look over at Violet. "It was *not* my intention to bring you here and leave you at another hotel all by yourself. I hope you know that."

She wrinkles her brow. "Of course I know that."

I turn back to the concierge. "Just cancel my suite here. I'll get a room wherever she'll be staying."

"Yes, sir," the concierge nods.

"Wait," Violet says, putting her hand on my arm. "Don't do that just because of me. I don't mind staying somewhere else. Kick put you *here*, so you should stay *here*."

"Absolutely not. If you can't stay here, then I won't stay here either. We *will* be staying at the same hotel."

"Well . . . you have a suite. How many rooms does it have? I mean, how many beds?"

I look to the concierge, who is discreetly observing our interaction. He glances at the computer screen. "Sir, the suite reserved for you is a two-bedroom."

"Great!" Violet exclaims. "If you don't mind I'll just take the other bedroom. Unless you were expecting company."

Her eyes sparkle with mischief and her grin says she's teasing. God, how I'd love to cart her upstairs and watch that grin turn into a soft smile followed by a long, luxurious moan.

"Are you sure?" I ask. "I mean, *are you sure*?" I wonder if she gets that my question is about *so much more*.

She meets my eyes, hers smoky and sexy, and she holds them. Calm. Steady. Resolute. "Yes, I'm sure."

She doesn't look away. She just watches me. I can see that she knows exactly what she's signing up for. She's ready. And so am I, as witnessed by the blood that rushes south. I grit my teeth against the sensation.

Hating to look away, but needing to, I glance back to the concierge and nod. He smiles and taps furiously on the keyboard. A minute later, something is printing and he's slipping two credit card-looking room keys into an envelope with the hotel logo on the front and our suite number scribbled on the flap.

"The elevators are directly behind you. Insert your card and press the S1 button. That will give you access to the suite's floor. I'll have your bags sent up straight away, sir."

"Thank you," I tell him.

"If there is anything else we can assist you with, please don't hesitate to ask. We are here to serve your needs."

I smile and nod, thinking to myself as I guide Violet to the elevators that the only thing I need right now is the girl at my side. Naked. And wet. And begging for me.

I try to focus on mundane things as the elevator rises. Neither Violet nor I speak until I am unlocking the door to our room and holding it open for her. Although she doesn't say much, I can tell that she's impressed.

"This is . . . this is very nice," she remarks. I smile from behind her. It *is* a very nice suite, which is great. But I'm a guy. This is hardly the kind of thing I get excited about. Seeing Violet's reaction, however, pleases me. I like seeing pleasure on her face—*any* kind of pleasure, although I'm very much looking forward to seeing a *better* kind of pleasure there. But for now, I'll take this.

We stroll through the expensive accommodations. From the lavishly appointed living room and dining room combination to the master bedrooms on either end, this unit oozes quiet money.

"Which is which?" she asks as she comes out of the en suite bathroom of the room to the right of the foyer.

"I don't think it really matters. You can take whichever one you like best."

She smiles up at me. "Are you always this agreeable?"

"I can be. I can be even more agreeable than this in the right circumstances."

Her laugh is light and airy, like she's a little breathless. That, along with practically everything else she has said and done since lunch, is tearing me up inside.

"In that case, I'll take the other one. I think I like the colors in there better."

"Whatever makes you feel good," I reply. I'm a fraction of a second away from giving in to my urge to touch her when a knock sounds at the door.

With a sigh of frustration, I clench my fingers into fists. Rather than putting my hands on Violet, like I was about to, I move to open the door.

It's the bellhop, bringing our two bags. "Where would you like them, sir?"

"I'll take this one," I state, lifting my duffel from the hook of his fingers. "The other one goes in there," I explain, tipping my head toward the first bedroom.

He nods, taking Violet's bag into the room she chose. I wait for him to reemerge so that I can tip him and send him on his way.

"Thank you, sir," he says with a nod as he accepts my folded bill. I nod in return and shut the door behind him.

The unwelcome interruption was exactly what I needed to get my head back in the right place.

I glance at my watch and turn to Violet.

"I guess it's about time for me to leave you to get ready. We've got about forty-five minutes before we need to head downstairs."

I don't know if Violet's eyes actually show me that she's disappointed, too, or if it's just my imagination. "I guess I need to head for the shower then," she says, swinging her arms like she's waiting on something.

I can't resist one more poke. "Unless you need some help in there. I'd gladly put them off for a couple of hours if your back needs washing."

Violet's smile is slow and sexy as hell. "I think I can manage this one by myself."

She keeps her eyes on mine as she backs away. In my head, her expression is filling in what was left unsaid.

But maybe later.

Later can't come soon enough.

THIRTY-ONE: *Violet*

It's unnerving, knowing that Jet is just a few feet away while I'm standing under the spray of warm water, completely naked. Every inch of my skin is super sensitive. It's not hard for me to close my eyes and imagine his soapy hands on me, gliding smoothly all over my body. In fact, I'm so involved in those thoughts as I wash with *my own* lathered hands that I jump guiltily when Jet knocks at the bathroom door.

"Violet, are you all right in there?"

Even behind a closed door where no one can see me, I feel the blush sting my cheeks. "Yes. I'm nearly done."

"Okay, well they just called and want me to meet them in the hotel bar for a drink first. Do you mind just coming down there when you're ready?"

"No, not at all. I won't be long."

"Take your time. I'm sure we'll just talk business until then."

"Okay. Good luck!"

"Thanks," he replies, and then I hear nothing but silence.

Even though I didn't actually *see* him, it makes going back to my bathing all the more disconcerting. I know I can't linger much longer, though. I need to be ready so they don't have to wait on me.

Quickly finishing up my shower, I get out and towel off before smearing on a nice, thick coat of scented lotion. After I dress, I blow out my hair and heat up the curling iron as I put on my makeup. Twenty-two minutes later, I'm surveying my reflection, hoping that I made all the right choices for this thing. I'm technically here to support Jet, so I need to make a good impression on the execs, but what feels more important at the moment is looking nice for *him*. And that should worry me.

I drop a lipstick, a compact, some mints, and my room key into a clutch that matches my dress and head for the elevator. Once in the lobby, I glance left and right, looking for the bar. The lobby bends around a corner on both sides, so it's impossible for me to tell in which direction my destination lies. I take a few steps forward, craning my neck to see beyond the curve. It's as I'm straightening that my eyes pass the front desk and I notice that the young man behind the counter is watching me. I smile politely and he does the same. Then, oddly, he points to his right, my left. I feel myself frown in confusion, and he points again. I look to my left, wondering what he's indicating. Is someone looking for me?

I see no familiar faces, so I look back to the clerk. He motions me over to him. Reluctantly, I go.

"The bar is that way," he says, pointing to his right again.

"How did you know that's what I was looking for?"

His smile gets wider. "The gentleman that came down a little while ago told me that a beautiful woman might need directions to the bar."

"How did you know it was me?"

"He told me I'd know you when I saw you. And he was right."

His eyes are glowing with masculine appreciation. My face warms happily as I nod. "Well, thank you very much." I start to walk off, but before I do, I turn to add, "Thank you for the directions, too."

The clerk winks at me and I smile. I'm pretty sure he's watching me walk away. This couldn't have happened at a better time, of course. My confidence is nicely boosted as I make my way into the bar.

I stop just inside the wide doorway and scan the faces for Jet's handsome one. He's easy to spot, as he's by far the most gorgeous man in the room. His eyes flicker up and stop on me just as I find him, and he stands.

My breath catches in my throat. I'm not sure if I'm breathless from seeing him in the black suit, cut perfectly to hug his wide shoulders and trim waist, or if I'm breathless from the way he's looking at me.

His eyes travel slowly down my body, so slowly I feel the heat of them as though they were his hands instead. I try to move toward him as naturally as I can, willing my feet not to tangle from his heated perusal.

When I stop at the table, Jet continues to watch me. Wordlessly. There's absolute silence around us, and, for a few seconds, it's easy to forget that we aren't the only two people in the room. In the world.

THIRTY-TWO: *Jet*

I've thought Violet was hot from the first time I ever laid eyes on her, but I swear to God she gets hotter every time I see her. And tonight? She makes me ache. I would almost walk away from this meeting if it meant taking her back up to our room and licking every square inch of that beautiful skin.

I move to pull out the chair next to mine, indicating with a nod that it's for her. She rounds the table and stops in front of me, looking up into my eyes. Her lips are curved in the barest hint of a smile. I bend to whisper into her ear, "You look amazing."

And she does. She picked the perfect dress. Not just for here, but for *her.* It's a form-fitting sparkly silver dress that clasps over one shoulder and stops about midthigh. Every lush curve is highlighted without looking trashy, and the color makes her eyes look like pewter. It doesn't hurt that her lips are a dark, suckable red and her smooth skin has a sheen to it that makes my fingers itch to touch it.

I push her chair in when she's seated then take my place beside her.

"So, this must be your associate, Violet," Rand says from across the table. As hard as it is to tear my eyes away from Violet, I do, looking to Rand to reply to him. But he continues before I can, addressing Violet instead. "Jet didn't tell us what beautiful people he has on his team."

The big, toothy smile that Rand gives Violet pisses me off, but I figure he's trying to schmooze. To a large degree, that's what some of these guys do—they kiss ass. I'm not sure which act throws gasoline on my temper—the next comment he makes or the way he's looking at Violet like he was wishing *she* was on the menu—but one of them definitely does. It's all I can do not to stick my foot in his ass and stomp the shit out of him.

"I thought tonight was going to be all business and no pleasure, but I can see that there is *plenty* of pleasure to be had. Thank you for coming, Violet."

Violet smiles prettily. "Thank you. And you are . . . ?"

"Randall Gregory, but I'd love it if you called me Rand."

Violet nods. "It's nice to meet you, Rand."

I don't think she's flirting with him. She's just being polite and charming and gorgeous because she can't help it. But still, it aggravates the hell out of me.

Violet's hand is resting at the edge of the table, so I reach over to take it. "I'm glad she could come. I can't imagine being here without her."

Violet turns a dazzling smile on me, which makes me feel a little better until Rand starts talking again and she looks back at him. It's like her attention feels warm and the minute she turns it elsewhere, I feel nothing but cold air and the sting of jealousy.

"We know what Jet does, but we know nothing about what a stunning woman such as yourself does with her time. Tell me, Violet, do you model? Because I have a friend who is always on the lookout for talent. And he knows I have a great . . . eye."

It's all I can do to hold my tongue. What the hell kind of an asshole would hit on Violet when she's clearly with me?

"Oh gosh no! I'm too short to model, but I appreciate the compliment," Violet replies.

"Even without the height, your face and your figure are so beautiful, so perfectly proportioned, any man in his right mind would snatch you up. I mean any *business*," he says with a wink and a laugh.

Violet laughs, too, and it kills me to see her cheeks bloom with color. It eats at me that *anyone* else can make her blush, much less this useless douche.

"Violet is a social worker. She's one of the kindest people I've ever met," I interrupt, regaining Violet's attention and hoping that Rand will shut his mouth before I have to shut it for him. No doubt that would totally blow my chance of giving my songs a shot at the big time. I raise her hand to my lips, brushing them over her knuckles.

Her eyes take on a sharp, confused look that I ignore. She might not get what's going on, but I sure as hell do. And I don't like it one bit.

"Well, it's our pleasure to have you, Violet. Can I offer you a drink or an appetizer?" Paul, the most important of the three execs, asks. I'm relieved to see him taking over the conversation.

"Thank you," Violet says, reaching for a chicken firecracker to put on her bread plate. "I'd love a ginger ale."

Paul nods, signaling the waitress who shows up within seconds, taking Violet's drink order and returning with the soda a short time later.

I feel better about everything as the night wears on. Rand keeps his comments to himself, although it chaps my ass every time I look at him and he's staring at Violet or smiling at her, trying to engage her. For the most part, though, the conversation stays firmly in the realm of business.

At one point, I see him at it again so I lean in closer to Violet, draping my arm over the back of her chair as I give Rand my biggest smile, all but daring him to take it one step further. He returns my tight smile and cocks one eyebrow at me. A challenge?

If it is, all I can say is that he's on!

I nod at him, brushing my fingertips over Violet's silky shoulder. I see Rand's lips thin, and I have to fight the urge not to laugh in his smug face.

After Violet finishes her drink, when I assumed we'd be heading to the "private" room, Paul surprises me with his suggestion. "Since we're all pretty comfortable, why don't you just sing us a couple of your songs right here, Jet?"

I glance around the table, wondering if this was the plan all along, like a test. But I quickly discard the notion. There's no reason for them to test me. This is about my songs, not about my ability to perform.

For that reason, I agree without hesitation. Not only do I not give a shit where they want me to sing, but at this point, I want to get this over with so I can get Violet the hell away from Rand.

I scoot back my chair and grab my guitar from under the table. I look around and see that there's a booth behind us that's empty. I get up and put my guitar case onto the table, take out my instrument, and then slide the case onto one of the padded seats. Turning to face Violet and the Kick execs, I lean against the edge of the table and pick out a few notes as I tune my guitar.

I sing "Every Time I Close My Eyes" first, a song I wrote three years ago. I believed in it then, but now? Now I love it even more. It takes on a whole new meaning since I met Violet. Just like the song suggests, she has gotten under my skin.

She didn't do it on purpose, of course. She didn't plan for me to need her like I do—to *need* to feel her body beneath mine, to *need* to taste her soft recesses, to *need* to be inside her more and more with every day that passes. It's not her fault that I see her face every time I close my eyes. And it won't be her fault when I dip my tongue into that hollow at the base of her throat tonight, and then lick every sensitive spot below it before the break of dawn. It's just something I have to do now, consequences be damned.

When I finish it, Paul claps. "One more, Jet. Let's hear something new and fresh."

I had hoped to do a few and end with "Drowning," but it looks like I won't get that chance. I clear my throat and strum the strings, feeling the music all the way into my soul, just like I did when I wrote it.

And when I first sang it.

To Violet.

I look up to find her eyes on me. It's as easy to sing it to her this time as it was the last. It comes to me like I've sang it a thousand times, the notes and the words as familiar to me as songs I've known for years. She watches me the whole time, never taking her eyes off of me. I know this because I never take my eyes off of her.

When I pick out the final three notes, letting the last one hang in the air until it fades completely, there's absolute silence in the bar. For a few seconds, it's like the world is breathing it in—my music, my words, my soul.

After that reverent pause, Paul starts to clap. Then others do, too. Quite a few others—people I hadn't even been aware of before. But now, as I look around, I can see that I've drawn a small crowd.

I nod and smile, turning to pack up my guitar. When it's lying safely against the velvet inside the case, I walk back to the table and sit back down beside Violet. I notice that she's unnaturally stiff, but I can't question her about it. Instead, I turn my attention to Paul. "So, what do you think?"

His smile is big and encouraging. "We'll need to discuss it, of course, but I'm optimistic," he says with a nod. "I'll give you a call before you check out tomorrow."

"Sounds good," I say, trying to be nonchalant, trying to hide the frustration that I feel.

More waiting.

"Maybe you two should spend the rest of the night out celebrating," Paul adds, nodding to Violet. His grin is reassuring. And he used the word *celebrate*, which is encouraging as hell.

I nod, feeling better about things.

I turn to smile down at Violet, anxious to see the excitement in her eyes, but her head is tipped down. I watch her for several seconds, but she doesn't glance up. She seems inordinately interested in the beads on her purse. "That sounds like a great idea."

I run the backs of my fingers down her upper arm. I feel her flinch. It's barely perceptible—certainly not visible—but I feel it nonetheless.

She doesn't look at me when she says, "It's been a pleasure meeting you gentlemen. If you'll excuse me, I need to run up to my room."

She smiles politely and stands. We all stand with her. "The pleasure was ours," Paul says.

Rand is the only one dim-witted enough to give her his card in front of me. "If you're ever in L.A., give me a call. I'd love to show you around."

I have to flex my fingers to keep from snatching the card out of his fingers and throwing it in his face.

"Thank you," Violet says simply, nodding at the trio before she turns to ease away from the table.

I reach across the table to shake the hands of the Kick Records people. "Thanks for meeting with me. I'll look forward to hearing from you tomorrow."

Paul nods, as does Gene, who hasn't said a word since introductions were made. Rand just gives me a tight smile, which makes me want to break the fingers that I'm still gripping in mine.

I grab my guitar and take off after Violet. I catch her just as the elevator doors are closing.

"Are you all right?" I ask.

At first she says nothing. She just taps her purse against her thigh. But after a few seconds, as though she can't contain it anymore, she turns furious gray eyes on me.

"What *was* all that?"

"What was what?"

"All that posturing down there? Is that why you brought me? To have your own groupie?"

"What? What the hell are you talking about?"

"All the special attention, all the sweet touching and singing to me like that. I've never felt more used."

"I wasn't using you, Violet."

"Then what were you doing? You've never acted like that before."

"I didn't realize it would bother you."

"It bothers me because you did it as part of your show."

"Trust me. That had absolutely nothing to do with my show."

"Of course it did! Why else would you act like that?"

Thoughts of the way Rand was looking at her, of the ways I *know* he was thinking of touching her, gets my anger fired back up again.

I turn toward Violet, stepping in closer, my face inches from hers.

"You wanna know why? I'll tell you why. It had nothing to do with me putting on a show. It had *everything* to do with that slimy asshole hitting on you. It was pissing me off."

"What? Because some random guy was flirting with me? That's ridiculous!"

"Is it? Is it ridiculous that I hated the way he talked to you? Is it ridiculous that it made me want to rip out his eyes out every time he looked at you? Is it ridiculous that I wanted to kill him when you smiled at him?"

Violet shrinks back, away from my anger. "Jet, I'm sure that was just part of the way he does business."

"The hell it was! He wanted you, and it was eating me up inside. *That* is why I was touching you. I wanted him to know that you are mine."

Violet's voice is soft. "But I'm not yours."

I take a few long, deep, ragged breaths. "But that doesn't mean I don't want you to be."

THIRTY-THREE: *Violet*

His confession takes all of the winds of humiliation and indignation out of my sails.

"All of that because you were jealous?"

Jet sighs and hangs his head. "Yes. Damn it." When he lifts it, there is nothing but miserable sincerity in his eyes. "It makes me furious to think of another man putting his hands on you. Of another man even *thinking* about putting his hands on you. And you might not have seen that he was doing more than flirting, but I sure as hell did." He takes another deep breath and sighs again. "But I didn't mean to make you uncomfortable."

I want to reach out and touch him, to smooth the wrinkle from his brow. And, for the first time, I don't stop myself. I just do what I feel like doing. What I *need* to do. And I touch Jet.

"There's no reason to feel that way. I would never in a million years let him touch me, no matter how much he wanted to, or how rich and powerful he thinks he is." One corner of Jet's mouth tips up in an attempt at a grin. "But I love that you didn't like it. No one has ever been jealous over me before."

"That just shows me you've only known complete imbeciles. But I hope that works in my favor." His smile is hopeful, which makes me giggle.

"It seems like it might be."

"Does that mean you forgive me for acting like a Neanderthal?"

"Well, since you didn't pee on me *or* club me over the head and drag me off to your cave, I think I can forgive you."

Jet grabs my wrist and pulls my hand, which still cups his face, toward his mouth where he takes one finger between his teeth and bites down lightly. "Does that mean me dragging you off to my cave *later* is out of the question?"

The opening of the elevator doors alleviates some of the rising tension that has once again erupted between us. With a smile, I step away from Jet, backing out of the car.

"I thought we were supposed to be celebrating or something?"

"I can't think of *any* better way to celebrate . . ."

With a light laugh, I walk across the hall to slide my key into the door. "You promised me New Orleans. Let me use the bathroom and then you can show me."

A little tingle ripples through me at the suggestive sound of not only my ending statement, but the timbre of my voice. Even to my ears, it seems provocative. Hoarse. Sexy.

"I'd be happy to show you anything you'd like to learn."

I give him a smile and rush off to the bathroom where I can collect myself enough to go back out there.

After I freshen my makeup, I nearly swallow my tongue when I step out to find Jet stretched out on his side on my bed. He ditched his jacket and loosened his tie, making him look like a delicious businessman who's ready for a good time.

With me.

"Ready?" I ask, aware of the thick crackle of electricity in the air between us.

"Very."

Jet slides off the bed and takes my hand. Neither of us says anything all the way down to the lobby. And it's a good thing. The way he keeps looking at me and smiling has every nerve in my body on high alert, making it hard to focus on anything. Speech included.

With Jet's warm body pressed against my side, we exit the hotel onto the lively streets of the French Quarter. We walk slowly, leisurely, Jet pointing out interesting places and trivia as we go. Every time he leans in to speak near my ear, chills shoot down my arm. And every time his eyes meet mine, I'm more and more convinced that he knows it.

We stop at a quaint café for a beignet, which is a delicious little pastry. I tear off a bite and let it melt on my tongue, resisting the urge to let my eyes roll back in my head. But I'm glad I did. I wouldn't want to have missed the sight of Jet watching me eat. His heavy-lidded eyes are trained on my mouth. As I watch him watch me, he licks his lips, sending a pang of desire shooting into my stomach. It's a sweetness that even the delicate pastry can't match.

I find myself warm and disconcerted after only one bite. Watching Jet watch me is incredibly erotic, something I'm far from accustomed to. But it's heady and exciting in a way that makes me feel more alive than I've ever felt before.

A few doors down from that, Jet stops to order us both a drink from a bar that has a walk-up window, a fact that I find amusing for some reason.

"The fast food of alcohol on Bourbon Street," I say as I put my lips to the straw in the LED-lit collectible glass. The drink is fruity and a little bit salty, and it tastes like heaven in my dry mouth. I take a few more sips.

"Go easy on that. It's definitely not a Coke, fast food-like or not."

Over the top of my cup, I smile happily at him, thrilled with the way he watches me and the way it makes me feel. "This is New Orleans," I finally say. "I'm supposed to loosen up and drink like the natives, right?"

Jet grins. "You can get as loose as you want to with me."

I laugh and suggest impulsively, "Let's find one of those little hole-in-the-wall clubs like they show on TV and dance until we're hot and sweaty."

"One of those places that are so crowded everybody is smashed together?"

"Exactly!"

"As long as I'm the only one you're planning to plaster that body against."

Spontaneously, I stretch up on my tiptoes and brush my lips over Jet's. "I can't think of anyone else I'd rather be up against."

"Then let's get the woman what she wants."

Jet guides me along the street to a little bar that's just off the main drag. The door is open, and both music and people are spilling out into the street. Jet shoulders his way through the crowd, tugging me along behind him. Once inside, I look around at the hazy interior. Smoke hangs low and thick in the air, adding a shroud of sultry mystery to the writhing mass of bodies packed into the tight space in front of the band.

This is precisely what I had in mind.

Jet pulls me to one of the few empty places along the wall. "Finish that, and then we'll dance."

I glance down at my drink, ready to argue. But much to my surprise, I see that I only have a small amount remaining in the bottom of the glass. I must've sipped a lot more than I thought I did along the way. I haven't been paying much attention. I didn't even notice Jet finishing his and dumping it in the trash.

Pushing the straw to the side, I tip up the drink and let it pour into my mouth, cool and refreshing. When I hit bottom, I lower it and grin at Jet. "Ahhh, delicious."

He takes it from my fingers and sets it on the corner of the bar behind us. "Then let's go."

The band is finishing up their set as we make our way into the middle of the dense crowd. They play one more song, something steamy and sensual, like the atmosphere itself. Jet moves in behind me, plastering his body to mine, as promised. I can feel every hard inch of him, dipping and swaying to the beat of the music. The heat of him at my back and the crowd on every other side makes me feel warm and relaxed.

When the band puts down their instruments to take a break, regular music is piped in overhead. The change does nothing to diminish the enthusiasm of the crowd, though.

I recognize the unique and soulful voice of Joss Stone. Effortlessly, her sultry voice and the sexy notes seep into my limbs and set my body into motion.

I lean back into Jet, letting my head fall onto his shoulder. I feel his hands come to my hips, his fingertips brushing my stomach. They tug me in closer to him. Every movement his body makes against me creates a sweet friction that I feel all the way into my core.

I arch my back and raise my arm to wind it around his neck. I tilt my head to the side when his lips tease the tender skin just beneath my ear, giving him better access. Against my butt, I feel his hardness. Gripping me with his hands, he holds me tight as he grinds against me, sending a shower of chills down my back and an ache into the V of my legs.

Instinctively, I move my hips back and forth against him. Above the music, I hear his groan at my ear as his fingers bite into my flesh.

"Don't do that," he murmurs.

"Don't do what?" I ask coyly, breathlessly.

"Don't tease me with that delicious ass and that short skirt. You may care that we're in public, but *I* do not."

"Don't do *this* you mean?" I ask, unable to keep the naughty smile off my face as I arch farther and rub him with my backside.

"Violet," Jet warns gruffly, his teeth visibly gritted. "You're playing with fire. Are you sure you wanna do that?" As he speaks, he lets one of his hands trail down my hip to the front of my thigh where he sweeps it in toward the inside of my leg and drags it up toward my center. I gasp, feeling an almost painful sense of frustration when he stops just short of where I need his touch most.

"Are you sure you want to talk me out of it?" I ask, closing my eyes against all the people around us. No one is paying us any attention anyway. No one cares how Jet is touching me.

I could almost pretend we are alone . . . with just the music . . .

"The only thing I want to talk you out of right now are these," he says, running his palm up to the bend of my leg, his fingertips just grazing the edge of my panties.

"You wouldn't," I taunt, giving myself up to the night, to the music, and to Jet.

"Wouldn't what?"

"Wouldn't do something like that in here."

"Is that a dare?"

I smile, knowing I'm safe to tease him. There's no way he would . . .

"No, it's a fact."

Jet slides his hand around my thigh to the outside of it, raising it to my hip and dragging the hem of my dress with it. I feel his fingers slipping under the thin band of my panties and clenching into a fist. With one quick jerk, I feel the snap of elastic. I gasp again, in desire as much as surprise.

"Still think I won't?" he breathes against my neck.

I gave in to whatever this is between me and Jet hours ago. Now, there's no going back. This time, I don't want to.

"No."

Still swaying to the intense beat of the music, my arm still wrapped around his neck, my body still pressed to his, Jet reaches up under the opposite edge of my skirt and quickly tears the other side of my panties. I feel them drop slightly away from my body.

My pulse is thumping in my ears, louder than any music in this whole town, as Jet pushes my hips away from his just enough that he can reach up the back of my skirt and tug my panties from between my legs. Slowly, he pulls on the material, the slight friction of the silk over my sensitive flesh making my insides clench in the most delicious way.

When there is nothing under my skirt but the warm New Orleans air, I hear Jet whisper in my ear. "Now you can walk around all night knowing that your damp panties are in my pocket."

"They weren't damp," I deny, ignoring the warmth that suffuses my face.

"You're so wet for me, baby, I can almost smell that delectable body of yours. Mmm, so sweet."

"You're lying," I breathe, trapped in the honey of his words.

"Am I?"

Bending me sharply forward, his body folding over mine from behind, Jet runs his hand up the inside of my thigh and eases his thumb into me. I can't stop the moan that bubbles up in my chest and spills from my lips.

My heart is pounding. My blood is on fire. When Jet straightens, I can feel my body squeezing, begging for more. The ache is almost more than I can withstand. I say his name. It's the only other sound that will make it through my parted lips. "Jet."

When he whirls me to face him, wrapping one arm around my waist and holding me tight against him, I nearly crumble at the heated look on his face.

With his eyes on mine, Jet brings his thumb to my mouth and drags it along my lower lip before sliding it inside to rake it over my tongue.

"Still think you're not wet for me?"

I swirl my tongue over his skin, loving the way he sucks in a breath, the way his pupils get even bigger.

"I don't know. You tell me."

Jet pulls his thumb from between my lips. I watch as he brings it to his mouth and slowly licks the moisture from it.

Inching his face toward mine, Jet asks softly, "Do you know what that tastes like?"

"What?" I manage.

"More."

His hands move down to the base of my spine, pressing me into him, pressing my softness into his powerful hardness.

"Tell me yes, Violet," Jet says, his lips so close to mine I can feel his warm breath on them.

"Yes to what?" I ask, feeling dazed in the face of such overwhelming attraction and desire.

"Yes to everything." Jet flicks his tongue over the corner of my mouth. "Please," he adds, licking at my bottom lip before pulling it between his teeth to suck on it.

I feel a tight, throbbing sensation in the lowest part of my stomach, a throb I know won't go away until I can feel Jet touching every part of me.

"Yes," I whisper.

Jet's lips take mine in a kiss that leaves my head spinning. The world is a blur of light and color and sound and heat by the time he leads me back out into the street.

I lose count of how many times he stops, right in the middle of the sidewalk, right in the middle of the teeming street, to kiss me. My whole being is on fire for him. Every touch of his hands, every brush of his lips, every look that he sends me makes me melt on the inside.

In the elevator at the hotel, Jet is pushing me into the corner the instant the doors close. Kissing and touching, biting and sucking, he throws gasoline on an already raging inferno. When he reaches under the short hem of my dress and pushes one long finger into me, I do the only thing I can. I hang on, tight. To his shoulders, to my sanity, to the feeling that bliss is just around the corner, I hang on.

"This is all for me," he moans, thrusting another finger into me, deeper than the first. He pulls them out and rubs the slick tips over my clitoris, pinching it lightly. I cry out, unable to help myself. "I don't think I can wait to taste you, Violet," he says, dropping to his knees in front of me and pushing my legs apart.

I look down, both astounded and more aroused than I've ever been. Jet is watching me, his eyes never leaving mine as he leans forward and buries his tongue inside me.

I throw my head back and grip the rail with all my might, determined not to melt into a heap. Jet swirls his tongue over me before he stands again, just in time to nudge my dress down and turn to face the doors. Seconds later, they slide open.

I walk on rubbery legs to our room. Once inside, where the world is quiet and the air is cool, Jet sweeps me into his arms and carries me to my bed. Gently, he sets me on my feet at one corner of the mattress.

"Do you know how much I want you, Violet?" he asks, his lips teasing my chin and my throat while his hands roam my back. "Do you know what kinds of things I've dreamed of doing to you?"

His words are an aphrodisiac unto themselves. I close my eyes, concentrating on his hands and his mouth.

"Tell me."

"I've dreamed of what your face would look like the first time I take one of your nipples into my mouth." As he speaks, his fingers nimbly work the clasp at my shoulder, loosening it and letting the bodice fall away from my chest. I feel the pucker of my nipples against the cool air when he leans back. "God, they're even more perfect than I imagined," he says, cupping my breasts in his palms. "Now I'll know just what it feels like to slide my tongue between them." As he speaks, I feel his lips move against me and then the wet heat of his tongue as he traces my cleavage. "And if your face looks like I imagined." My knees nearly buckle at the first touch of his tongue to me. He laves my nipple before pulling it into his mouth to suck on it. I thread my fingers into his hair, holding him to me. "Even better than I imagined," he declares, moving his attention to my other side, to toy with the other one. "Mmm, you like that don't you, baby?"

"Yes," I answer.

"Just wait," he murmurs against me, his hands pushing my dress down over my hips. When I'm standing before him in nothing but my heels, Jet urges me to sit on the corner of the mattress. He nudges my knees apart, my legs dropping over either side of the firm surface. "I'm gonna make you come, Violet. So hard that your body goes limp. So hard that I can feel it when I stick my tongue inside you."

Again, Jet kneels between my legs, placing his palms against the inside of either thigh and pushing them farther apart. As I watch, he presses kisses from my knee to my groin, growing ever closer to the throb that he alone put in me. When he leans slightly forward to run his tongue down my crease, I jerk, unable to control the contraction of my muscles. I gasp, and Jet pulls me toward him, sliding his tongue inside me, licking me from the inside. I throw my head back, resting my weight on my hands behind me, lest I fall back on the bed.

Jet moves his hands under my butt and grips me tight, picking me up and holding me up to his mouth, open and ready. With his lips and his tongue, he savors every inch of me, inside and out. When the tension in me builds so high it takes my breath, Jet seems to sense it, quickening his movements, flicking his tongue over me until something inside me bursts and I come apart in shards of sparkling glass and light.

As if he knows exactly what I need, Jet moves me against his face as wave after wave washes over me. I feel him in all the right places, licking and sucking, nibbling and biting. I don't know when my arms gave up, but when my body settles back down to earth, I'm lying flat on my back and Jet is kissing the insides of my thighs.

"I could eat you for breakfast every day and never get tired of it," he says, dragging his tongue up the crease of my leg where it joins my hip. Tentatively, he eases the tip of one finger into me. "I could feast on your body, every juicy part of it, until you begged me to stop." I feel my muscles sucking at him, already ready for him to fill me up, to bring me to the edge again and push me over. "Mmm, that's what I like to feel. I want you sucking my cock from the inside. I want you squeezing it so tight, you can feel me throb when I come inside you."

Already, my body is getting tight again, tense. Ready. I feel the gush of warmth when he moves his finger in deeper, eliciting a moan from me. "You'd like that, wouldn't you? To feel me coming inside you?"

"Yes," I breathe, my eyes still closed, oblivious to everything except Jet's hands and voice.

"To feel the hot gush of it, way up in you?"

"Yes," I say again, getting more excited by the moment.

"Are you on the pill?"

"No," I answer reflexively, feeling a bit confused as my muddled brain tries to make sense of anything other than what I'm feeling.

"It's okay," he says, his touch leaving me briefly as he searches for something. I can hear the shift of cloth, so I lift my head and open my eyes.

Jet is pulling a condom from his pocket. I watch as he stands to unbutton his slacks and push them down his legs. His boxer briefs follow, leaving him naked to my eyes. The tails of his shirt fall to the tops of his thighs, but it doesn't hide anything. As big around as my wrist, I can see his hard length rising up from between the two halves of his shirt, standing strong and long, making me ache for him all the more.

I can't take my eyes off him as he unwraps the condom and rolls it from tip to base. I know this is going to hurt. He's huge! But it will be a good hurt, one my body is more than ready for.

When Jet's movements still, my eyes flicker up to his. He winks at me. "Don't worry. I won't hurt you unless you ask me to."

"How can you be sure?"

Jet drops to his knees again, sitting back on his haunches. "Come here," he says, opening his arms. I sit up and start to slide off the bed. "Stand up first," he instructs, so I do, unwittingly putting the apex of my thighs right at the level of his mouth. "Just like that," he says. "Now spread your legs." Heart beating faster again, I do as he asks. I resist the urge to throw back my head again when I feel his fingers teasing me farther apart. "Do you know what I love to hear?" he asks.

"What?"

"That little noise you made when I sucked you into my mouth." He's looking up at me, his fingers teasing me, making me want to grind my hips against them for more pressure. "My cock throbbed to be inside you at that exact moment." I feel myself falling under his spell again, unable to think past what he's saying, what he's doing. "Bend your knees," he whispers. I don't question him. I just do as he asks, bending my knees. I feel his hands slide up the outsides of my thighs, guiding me over his legs until I'm straddling him. I can feel his length pressing against me.

"Now I can touch you as much as I want," he says, teasing my clit with the pad of his thumb. "And I get to watch your beautiful lips tremble when you come. Because you will," he whispers, his mouth finding one aching nipple to suck as his fingers bring me to the brink.

I'm barely aware of it when Jet winds one arm around my waist and lifts me. I only know that when he eases me back down, I feel the most delicious fullness at my entrance. I gasp, my body once again begging him for more. When I hear the air hiss through his gritted teeth, it only makes me throb all the more.

A little farther, he moves me down over him, his thumb still playing between my folds, his tongue still teasing my nipple.

"God, you are so wet," Jet groans. "And so hot." He eases me down even farther. "And so . . . oh God! So tight." He pants, his hand moving around from my front to my backside. He reaches between my legs and spreads me from behind. The action tilts me forward on him, bringing my most sensitive part in contact with his body as he rocks me on top of him.

The more he moves me, the more friction he causes, the more I *want* to move on him. And the less control I feel like I have over my hips. I'm gyrating against him, the tension ratcheting ever higher, when I hear Jet growl. Lifting me, I feel him bite my nipple as he drops me down onto him.

The world stops spinning. The air stops flowing. I'm invaded by him. Completely. And he's wrapped in me. Completely. I cry out in the most exquisite pleasure I've ever experienced.

Jet goes perfectly still. "Did I hurt you?" he asks, his voice strained.

"No. Oh God, no!" I moan.

"Good," he says, withdrawing and thrusting again, going a little deeper.

I arch my back, taking in more of him, wondering how much is left. Jet's hands find my hips and guide me up on him, almost completely off, and then pull me back down, impaling me on him again.

My head spins with the intense pleasure of it as Jet urges me into a rhythm, long, deep strokes up and down. His hands are touching everywhere. His lips are kissing everywhere. His tongue is teasing everywhere. I move on him faster and faster, harder and harder, inflamed by the sound of his voice as he whispers dirty things to me, dark and naughty things, thrilling me with each one.

Needing to do something with my hands, needing to feel every inch of him against me, I reach for Jet's shirt, my fingers fumbling with the tiny buttons. Jet murmurs against my breast, "Tear it."

Some small part of me questions the wisdom of it, but not enough to stop. With a freedom I don't often feel, I fist my fingers in the smooth cotton of his shirt and jerk, laughing as the buttons pop off.

"Oh, God," Jet groans, his fingers biting into the meat of my hips, making me swallow my laugh on a moan.

"Did you like that?" I ask, feeling him grow even harder inside me.

"Yes."

I see the low light glimmer in the gold hoop at his nipple, drawing my attention and my hand. I reach for it, tugging gently. I hear his hiss, I feel his pulse as he grinds my hips onto his.

Leaning down, I flick his nipple ring with my tongue as I tease the other one with my fingers, pulling and nibbling, reveling in the way Jet reacts. It makes me feel sexy and powerful and wanted.

He increases his tempo and I straighten, moving harder and harder on top of him. I feel his fingers back between us, playing with me, torturing me, until I feel like I'm losing my mind.

All at once, Jet sucks my nipple hard into his mouth, holds me tight and flexes his hips, driving his body deeper into me than I thought possible. I move on him, crying his name.

"God, yes," he moans, "ride me. Take every inch of it. Come all over me."

Sliding up on him, I fall back down hard, another orgasm tearing through me like a runaway freight train.

Jet holds me down on him, grinding his hips up into mine, increasing the friction and driving me wild. I feel him stiffen a fraction of a second before I feel the first throb. Jet wraps me tighter and jams his body into mine once, twice, and then for a third time, holding me against him as he gives in to his own release.

THIRTY-FOUR: *Jet*

I'm in the floor, flat on my back, staring at the ceiling. Violet is stretched out on top of me, having collapsed onto my chest after we both came. Neither of us are ready to move yet.

I don't know if it was all the anticipation or the fact that she was a little hard to get, or if it's because I haven't had sex in a few weeks, but that shit rocked me. You'd think after amazing sex with a hot woman, I'd be feeling sublime. And I am—mostly.

Part of me is pissed, though. Pissed at myself, for what I've done and the pretenses under which I've done them. Again, I'm reminded that Violet would hate me—even more so now—if she knew what I'm capable of.

When she finally stirs, leaning up to look down at me, her flowery-smelling hair falls to one side, tickling my face. Her eyes are soft and dreamy, her lips are slightly curved. She looks happy. Satisfied.

I smile up at her, running my palms down the smooth skin of her back and over the round globes of her ass.

"That was incredible," I tell her.

She smiles and her cheeks take on that rosy hue I love to see. "Really?"

"You didn't think so?"

"Well, yeah. I thought it was awesome, but . . ."

"But what?"

She shrugs one shoulder. "I didn't know how it would seem to you. I mean, it's been a while for me."

"It has for me, too."

As I watch, like clouds rolling in over a turbulent sea, her eyes darken and her expression sobers. She doesn't say anything, just closes her eyes and leans her forehead against my chin. I reach up to stroke the silky hair at the back of her head.

"What's the matter?"

She waits for a couple of really long, uncomfortable minutes before she speaks. And when she does, she looks up at me with tears in her eyes.

"This was so selfish of me."

"What? What are you talking about?"

"You needed my help, and this is what I give you. A setback."

"This is not a setback, Violet. This was . . . different."

She rolls off me and stands, holding her hands to either side of her head. "Oh God, what have I done? What have I done?" she says quietly, over and over.

I get up, walking to where she's pacing, and I stop her, taking her face in my hands.

"*You* haven't done anything. We did this together. We're both consenting adults. We both know the score."

Words that were meant to calm her only seem to worsen whatever bullshit guilt she's feeling.

"No, we don't. You don't know the score," she groans, turning away from me. There is misery in her voice, and I have no idea why.

"Of course I do. We both wanted this, Violet."

"Yes, but you . . . you . . . of course *you* wanted it."

"What's *that* supposed to mean?"

She finally turns back to face me. Her eyes are as miserable as her voice. She's torturing herself over something.

"Jet, there's something I have to tell you," she begins, wringing her hands.

"What is it? You can tell me anything."

Her chin trembles at my words and she looks up at the ceiling. "Oh, God! Please don't be so nice. I don't deserve it."

"Violet, you're being ridiculous. Of course you deserve someone to be nice to you."

She squeezes her eyes shut, like it hurts to look at me. "Jet, I'm not a sex addict," she mumbles. Her voice is so low and quiet, I'm not sure I heard her correctly.

"Say that again."

When she opens her eyes and they meet mine, they are shiny pools of tears and anguish. "I'm not a sex addict."

I shake my head, trying to understand what she might mean by that. "What? What are you talking about?"

"I went there for Tia. She's my best friend, not just someone I sort of sponsored. She has a problem, but she doesn't think so. She would never go unless I went, and she was getting ready to lose the trust of a really good man. So I went to support her. Only she never showed up that first time."

I take a step away, my mind scrambling to catch up. "So you lied about being a sex addict?"

She nods once. "I didn't want to just . . . just . . . *leave*, so I stood up and said the same thing everyone else was saying."

"So all the . . . everything you said . . ."

"Was a lie."

It's hypocritical as hell for *me* of all people to be pissed off by her confession, but I am. All this time, I'd thought . . .

"Why didn't you just tell me?" I ask, feeling betrayed, which is a load of shit.

"I didn't want to hurt you. I didn't want you to feel like the one place you went for help, the place that should be a sanctuary, was anything less than that. I knew how damaging it would be if anyone ever found out. I swear I didn't do it maliciously. I was just trying to help my friend."

"And were you trying to help her when you made up that crap about being a sponsor?"

"I didn't say that," she defends. "Tia made that up. Not me."

"And why the hell would she do that?"

Violet casts her eyes down, tucking her chin against her chest. "She thought you were hot, and she thought I needed a social life."

"You're shitting me?"

She looks up at me and somberly shakes her head. "No, unfortunately, I'm not. This is the God's honest truth."

My laugh is bitter, even though I have no room to be anything less than forgiving. But I don't feel forgiving. I feel deceived. And angry.

"How am I supposed to believe anything you say?"

"Why would I lie *now*? There's no point. The damage is done. Ask me anything and I'll tell you the truth. Anything."

"Why?"

"I told you why."

"Then tell me again," I snap.

"I help people, Jet. It's what I do. It's *who I am*. My friend needed my help, even if she didn't know it herself. And I wanted to give it to her." Her voice breaks as she continues. "And then I met you. And you needed help, too. I knew that telling the truth would hurt so many people, including you and Tia. But keeping the secret would only hurt me. So I chose to keep it to myself so that I could do more good than harm."

"So how does it feel? Does it *feel like* you've done more good than harm? Because I sure as hell don't think so."

With a sob, Violet buries her face in her hands. "I'm so sorry, Jet. I never meant to hurt you."

A wave of sympathy is overwhelmed by bitterness when I think of the full implications of what she's done, even though *she* doesn't have all the facts either. "So you slept with me tonight, knowing that you could just get up and go on with life in the morning like nothing happened, while *I* . . . the addict . . . might suffer a huge setback because of it?"

She crumbles onto the bed like her legs just stopped holding her up. "Oh God, oh God, oh God!"

"Miss High and Mighty, looking down on the rest of us for our weaknesses. But not because you *overcame* yours like the paragon of strength you pretended to be. No, you've never even *felt* weakness. You have no idea what it's like . . ."

"But I do," she moans. "Now, I *do*. I've never wanted something so bad that it has had control over me. Never. I've seen it so much, all my life, I avoided anything that could be dangerous. Until you. Don't you understand, Jet? *You* were my weakness. You *are* my weakness. I did horrible things to be with you. I told myself horrible lies, too. Just to be with you. Just to let myself think, even for a minute, that it was okay to be with you. Please don't hate me, Jet. It was selfish and cruel, but I swear on my life that I never meant to hurt you." She drops her head again. Her last words are so soft, I barely hear them. And I'm not sure she wanted me to. "I never meant to fall in love with you."

THIRTY-FIVE: *Violet*

My heart is being ripped apart! I should've told him sooner. Certainly before we had sex. I kept telling myself that I was doing it all to help him, but now I see that I was just afraid.

Afraid of losing him.

But by waiting, that's exactly what I've precipitated. That's exactly what is happening. And I deserve it. God help me, I deserve it.

I feel like the lowest of the low. Who would *lie* to a person with a true addiction? Someone seeking help? Someone who trusted you with his secrets? What kind of person does that?

An awful one.

I flinch when I feel Jet's hands. They settle on my shoulders and are still for a few seconds before they travel down my arms, tightening at my elbows. Gently, he pulls me to my feet.

I can't look up. I can't face him and the heartbreaking betrayal I know I'll see in his eyes. When he puts a finger under my chin and lifts, I keep my lids squeezed shut. I can't take the sight of what I've done. I can't bear the wreckage.

"Violet, look at me," Jet demands, his voice not as harsh as it was.

Against my better judgment, I slowly open them, focusing on his face. I don't see the hatred I expected. Or the disgust. Or the devastation. I see a quiet, hesitant tenderness.

"Thank you for telling me."

"I'm so sorry I waited so long," I blubber.

He places a finger over my lips. "No more apologies."

"Please forgive me. I—"

"There's nothing to forgive. I know you didn't do it on purpose. That's not the kind of person you are. And I know that. I was just . . ." Jet sighs. "I was just a little hurt. And surprised. Even though, in retrospect, I think I should've guessed."

I frown. "Why do you say that?" I ask.

Jet's lips curve into a small smile, and he brushes away the strands of hair that have stuck to my wet cheeks. "You don't look anything like a sex addict."

"What does a sex addict look like?"

"Not like a librarian. Even if it's a sexy as hell librarian. The first time I saw you, I thought you looked innocent. It was hard for me to picture you being some uncontrollable sex fiend."

I know it's insane that I might take offense at that, but still, his words sting. "I've never even *enjoyed* sex before. I can't help it if that shows."

"Never really enjoyed it? You mean . . . have you never had an—"

I feel humiliation roll up from my stomach to choke me. "No. And I'd rather not talk about it."

I start to turn away from him, but Jet stops me. "That's not your fault, Violet. It's nothing for you to be ashamed of. That's strictly your partners' shortcoming."

"That should be singular."

"What should be?"

"Partner. Only one."

"You've only been with one other man?"

I nod, feeling worse about this entire trip by the second.

"God, what a stupid asshole he must've been to give you up."

"I doubt he'd agree."

"That's why he's stupid. You're smart, witty, gracious, kind. Gorgeous. And your body . . ." Jet trails off, stepping away from me so that he can see me more clearly, an action that has my cheeks flaming up within seconds. "How responsive it is to touch." I gasp, in both surprise and a little bit of arousal, when he drags the backs of his fingers over one nipple. I feel it come to a firm, tingling point. "I've never been with a woman like you. I've never felt with someone else what I felt just now."

His voice is low. When I look up at him, his eyes are dark and heavy.

"Jet, I—"

"Don't ever sell yourself short, Violet. Any man would die to have this just once."

He rolls my nipple between his fingers. I hold my breath, willing my body not to respond, wishing I could just disappear.

"You weren't fighting it earlier. Don't start now," he says, bringing the tip of one of his fingers to his lips, wetting it with his tongue, then drawing a damp circle around my other nipple with it. "There is nothing sexier than a woman who just lets go. Watching your reaction, knowing how much you like what I'm doing to you is the most intoxicating thing in the world." Jet leans in to whisper in my ear. "Don't fight it, Violet. Don't fight *me*."

He skims his lips along my jaw, bending to press them to my throat before dropping to his knees in front of me.

"*This* is beautiful," he murmurs, tweaking one nipple and making it furl into an even tighter bud. "God, that makes me ravenous. For you, Violet. Just you."

In his eyes, I see the truth of his words. And in my body, I feel them. I can't fight him. Because I don't want to. I stopped wanting to a long time ago. I just never admitted it to myself.

"Let me have it, baby," he says, leaning forward to trace one aching peak with the tip of his tongue. "Let me have it all."

When he draws my nipple into his mouth, his eyes still holding mine, I know it's pointless to fight it. Whatever is between us, however we arrived here, it's consuming. And I want to be consumed.

Jet lets one hand slide down my stomach to the increasing ache between my legs. I feel him slide a finger down my crease and back up again to massage my most sensitive part. Air sticks in my chest. Time stops on the movement of his hand. When he pushes that finger into me, I exhale a shaky breath. Jet closes his eyes, groaning as he lets my nipple pop out of his mouth. "That's it, baby. Just let go."

So I do.

* * *

My head is filled with junk on the trip home. After a night, morning, and part of the afternoon full of the most fulfilling, creative lovemaking I've ever heard of, I thought I would feel more . . . connected. And I did. Right up until a few minutes before we left.

I glance over at Jet again, still mourning the loss of what we had in New Orleans. "Is everything all right?" I ask for the thousandth time.

And for the thousandth time, he replies, "Of course."

There have been variations to the dialogue—yep, everything is fine, why wouldn't it be—but essentially both the question and the response have been the same. Yet, my feelings of unease are only getting worse.

I want to ask him specifics, but I'm afraid to. I've searched every corner of my mind trying to figure out what happened. Whatever it was, it had to have happened right before we left, but I just can't think of what that might've been.

I think back, once more, looking for the trigger.

After having some marathon sex followed by a very late breakfast, I decided to take a shower, the first half of which was deliciously interrupted by Jet. It was when I got out that I noticed he just seemed . . . off. I asked him then if something was wrong. He denied it with a faint smile and a kiss to my forehead.

My *forehead.*

I wondered if it was because he hadn't heard from the guys with Kick Records, but I didn't want to bring it up in case it made things worse. So here we are. Hours later, and I've made zero progress on discerning what is wrong. I just know that something *is.*

I don't want to pry when he seems reluctant to tell me what's going on. And I don't want to push, because I feel like I'd be digging my own grave if he's feeling a relapse of hurt or aggravation over my deception.

So, in the absence of pushing him, I just keep asking. And he just keeps denying.

"Are you hungry?" he asks when it's close to suppertime.

I shrug, food not the least bit appealing since my emotions are so up in the air. "If you want to stop, that's fine. I can do whatever," I answer agreeably.

Jet's quiet for a few seconds before he declares, "Let's just drive on through. I'm anxious to get home."

I give him the brightest smile that I can, which isn't very bright at all, I'm sure. I turn to look out the window, wishing now that this uncomfortable ride could just be over. I need time to *feel* in private. I suspect that there might even be tears in my future.

By the time the headlights of Jet's car are illuminating the signs for Summerton, I'm emotionally exhausted. I've known a lot of people who have gotten inside their own heads and turned completely manageable situations into train wrecks, so I know the danger of thinking too much, in overanalyzing. But I've never been prone to doing it. I've always been able to let things go, just put them out of my mind until they can be resolved in a pragmatic way.

Until now. Until Jet. Until I came face-to-face with my one weakness. And now it's tearing me apart, turning me into the very kind of person I've secretly abhorred all this time.

Maybe this is just desserts. Maybe this is what I get for looking down my nose at people who can't control themselves. Maybe this is life's way of making me better able to relate to my clients, my friends, my family. I'm getting a little taste of what it feels like to want something so much it hurts, to obsess about it and not be able to stop. And to feel the agony of having it slip right through my fingers, to feel the frustration of driving myself crazy trying to figure out what went wrong and how to go back.

I relax my head against the seat, trying to clear my mind and lose myself in the melancholy notes of the song on the radio. But that doesn't help. It seems only to underscore my misery, making it feel nearly unbearable.

Jet's phone rings and I'm grateful for the interruption. The tension in the car is driving me bonkers.

I only hear Jet's end of the conversation, but I can still make out the gist of the call.

"Hey, man, what's up?"

"Yeah, I'll tell you all about it."

"On my way back now. Why?"

"Nah, my schedule's clear Wednesday. Where is it?"

"Is that the club right down from Brass?"

"Yeah, yeah. I know the place. So what time? Seven?"

"Cool. Let's get together sometime tomorrow. I wanna practice something new to add to the first set."

"You'll let 'em know?"

"All right, man. See you tomorrow."

When he hangs up, he glances over at me and smiles a crooked smile, but says nothing. I return the gesture the best that I can before, once more, turning to look out the window at the dead, lifeless night passing me by.

Less than an hour later, Jet is pulling up at the curb in front of my tiny house. I don't know why it feels so depressing when he shifts into park, but it does. It tells me that he's not planning on staying. Or even coming inside. It tells me that he's anxious to get away.

I don't wait for him to come around and open my door. I get out quickly, reaching into the backseat for my overnight bag and my purse. When I straighten, Jet is there beside me, closing the door and taking the bag from my shoulder.

He walks me up the steps and takes my keys from me to unlock my front door. As I turn on the entry light, he leans in to set my bag in the floor by the console table against the wall. When he straightens, he's still on the outside looking in.

From less than a foot away, I look up at Jet, watching him, trying to figure out what went wrong, and feeling heartbroken over the fact that it did. My chest gets tight and I feel tears threaten as my eyes scan his handsome face and his politely interested expression. Even though I've only ever had it happen once, I know when I'm getting ready to be gently dumped.

My smile is tremulous and my voice unsteady when I speak, facts that I wish more than anything that I could take away.

"Thank you for showing me New Orleans," I say simply.

Jet is silent for well over a minute. Then he surprises me by stepping forward. Cupping my face in his hands, he bends to brush his lips over mine. My heart, my soul, everything that I am melts into a puddle like butter on a hot stove.

When he raises his head to look down at me, I'm certain I've never seen something more beautiful—and more gut-wrenching—than his face.

"Thank you for coming with me. I had an amazing time."

He smiles down at me. In the gesture, I read the words THE END.

I swallow my emotions in one difficult gulp.

"I did, too."

"I'll call you," he says, already backing away.

I nod, unable to force one more syllable past the lump in my throat.

Jet taps the doorjamb, near the dead bolt, as he pulls my door shut. "Lock up."

Again, I nod, determined to keep my smile in place until he's out of sight.

Out of sight, out of mind, I think wistfully.

Unfortunately, I know deep down that the age old adage will not apply to me. Jet will never be out of my mind.

Never.

THIRTY-SIX: *Jet*

As many shitty days as I've had, I can't think of a time when I've felt worse. About everything.

Looking back over the last couple of days, I can pinpoint several great things. But now, less than forty-eight hours later, every single one of them has gone to hell.

I got a call from Kick Records on Friday, a call that I knew might change my life. This afternoon, I got another call from them, letting me down easy.

I had just gotten out of the shower with Violet, which was a helluva good thing, when I saw the message light blinking on my phone. It was that asshole Rand telling me that, although I have some talent, I'm just not what they're looking for.

That started a cascade of other shitty things, the first of which was the realization that I'll have to either play more gigs with the band until I can get some interest elsewhere, or I'll have to give up music altogether and finish school. I don't like either of those options.

But that wasn't even the worst part of it. As I stared at the closed bathroom door and listened to Violet humming happily in the shower, I thought back to her confession. I wasn't even mad about it anymore, which is good because I had no right to be. No, I thought about how brave she was for telling me, about what a good person she is. Deep down, she's a really good person—unlike me. I've done some pretty despicable things, and I don't even have the decency to confess them to her. Because I'm a bastard and I don't deserve her. I can't bring one good thing to her life. Not one. I'm a piece of crap for messing around with her to begin with.

But the worst part was how I felt about my decision to go forward. Rather than doing the decent thing and leaving her the hell alone, or doing the conscionable thing and telling her what she deserves to know, I decided I'm going to keep seeing her. I'm going to keep my secrets, because she'd hate me if she knew. And, in the end, I'd rather risk hiding things from her than giving her up. I can't let her go.

Because I'm a bastard.

Still, it's a jagged pill, and I found myself choking on it more and more as the day wore on. So here I am, walking away from Violet, yet promising her I'll call. Which I shouldn't do. But I know I will.

Because I'm a bastard. And I want her. More than anything, including my soul, which will surely burn for doing this to her.

But will it stop me? *No.*

Why? Because I'm a bastard.

THIRTY-SEVEN: *Violet*

"Are you kidding me? What an asshole!" Tia blusters.

"I should've seen it coming. I mean, how stupid am I? He's a twenty-six-year-old playboy. He's even in a rock band. And he's a sex addict, for God's sake!"

"But he seemed like such a nice guy . . ."

"I should've known better."

"Violet, you can't refuse to take any kind of risk on the *off chance* you might get hurt. That's ridiculous! You can't live like that."

"Why not? I've gotten along just fine for twenty-two years."

"Oh, yeah right. And what a spectacular life you've led."

"There's nothing wrong with my life, Tia."

"Of course there's not. It's perfectly normal to have only one friend. It's perfectly normal to surround yourself with broken people that eat up your time being unfixable. It's perfectly normal to have *zero* social life to speak of."

"You make it sound like I'm some kind of freak. I've dated. I've gone to bars. I've done things. But it's never worth the aggravation. Avoiding it isn't pathetic, Tia. It's prudent."

"I didn't say you were pathetic, Vi," she says, her tone rife with regret. "You're far from pathetic. But I know you well enough to know that you're miserable."

I feel my chin tremble. "I didn't used to be."

"Maybe you *think* you weren't, but you were. Violet, you watched everyone else live and you stood on the sidelines, waiting for your chance to pick up the pieces when things fell apart for them. Myself included. But that's no way to live. You *have to have* something for yourself. You *have to have* something else to live for."

"And risk feeling like this?" I murmur woefully. "No thank you."

"What I don't understand is why you're just letting it end this way. Why don't you confront him? Ask him what the hell?"

"Now *that* would be pathetic!"

"That's not pathetic. That's strong. That would be you taking charge and letting him know you're not some piece of garbage that he can so blithely toss aside. Because you're *not*, Vi! You're the best thing that has ever happened to him, and if he can't see that, he's not just an asshole. He's a frickin' *stupid* asshole."

"No, I refuse to give him the satisfaction."

"Don't look at it that way. Look at it as you taking charge, growing a pair, taking life by the horns."

"I already do that."

"No, you don't. You hide."

"I don't hide."

"Yes, you do. Can't you just trust me on this?"

"Ummm, no. I don't need to feel *any* worse than I do right now."

"I bet you a Sherpa that you'd feel better afterward, regardless of what he says."

"Tia, you don't *have* a Sherpa."

"But if I did, I'd bet that woolly, mountain bastard that you'd thank me later."

I shake my head, even though Tia can't see it over the phone.

"I think you're nuts."

"So what's new?" Tia sighs. "At least tell me you'll think about it."

"Fine," I say, giving in just to shut her up. "I'll think about it."

"Good God, Vi, for once in your life, don't think so much."

"You just told me to think about it."

"But what I meant was for you to just do it. Can't you just 'do'? Just this once?"

"It's not that easy, Tia."

"It's *exactly* that easy, Violet."

I sigh again. I foresee this conversation being repeated again and again until I give up or stick hot pokers into my eardrums.

"Just go by one night before he has a gig or something. You know where he'll be. You'll surprise the shit out of him. And maybe you'll even get an answer. But if not, you'll walk away, and he'll be thinking, 'Damn! That bitch has some balls!' And he'll respect you for it. Any wuss can let herself be treated this way and say nothing about it. Only a woman with a strong sense of self-worth will call a guy on his crap. To his face. Don't be the wuss, Vi!"

I say nothing for a few seconds. For once, I can actually kinda see her point.

As I sit in the quickly filling parking lot of a club in Summerton, the only one across from Brass that boasts a sign saying that Saltwater Creek is playing tonight, I replay the conversation with Tia in my head. She had me feeling convinced she was right at the time. But now, now that I'm staring at the place where this showdown will actually occur, I'm wondering how in the world I ever saw wisdom in Tia's advice.

But I know I did. And that my reluctance now is probably just nerves.

I haven't heard a word from Jet since he dropped me off on Sunday night. It's Wednesday, which is only a few days later, but when our last run-in involved a weekend of sex followed by his quick emotional withdrawal, it might as well have been a month. To my heart, it feels like it. And I need to know why. I need this for myself. So I can get over it and move on.

Even though I know that will likely be a process that could take months or maybe years, if it ever even happens.

Minutes tick by until they become an hour. Then two. I know my window of opportunity is closing quickly. I missed my chance to talk to him before the show. Now my only option is to wait until after. Or don't do it at all. This is the only place I know of that I can ambush him, because I'm sure as heck not going back to a meeting!

Taking a deep breath, I get out of my car and close and lock the door. Boldly, I walk into the club, paying the cover charge to hear only a couple of songs. I know the set will soon be over since I waited so long.

I go to the bar and order myself a Coke, finding a nice dark corner to stand in and watch Jet perform. He's amazing, as usual. Something about watching him, watching him work the crowd, and listening to him, listening to the rough rasp of his voice, is mesmerizing. I can completely understand why the women in the crowd want to touch him, to get close to him, why they'd risk getting thrown out just for a moment onstage with him.

But how many of them get thrown out? How many of them just end up backstage, as toys for the band?

My stomach roils and I close my eyes against the ache in my chest, against the knowledge that maybe I was just one of these girls. Maybe I was just one of many who couldn't stay away from the flame. And got burned. And now he's up there, wings spread, shining brightly, while I'm down here, hurt and alone.

Determination wells inside me. I'm *not* just like them. And I'm not going to let him treat me as if I am. I won't let him just discard me without so much as a by-your-leave. It's with that in mind that, when Jet finishes the last song, I skirt the crowd and make my way to the door that leads backstage.

Thankfully Trent is there, guarding the entrance. Thankfully, Trent remembers me. He smiles and opens the door to let me go back.

The hall is empty but for a few random people. I smile, holding my head high like I'm supposed to be here, and I aim for the door marked AUTHORIZED PERSONNEL ONLY. This one isn't guarded, so I turn the knob and slip through. There's a small anteroom, furnished with a thin couch and coffee table. Both are empty. Beyond the tiny room, I can see light, and I can hear the rowdy voices of the band.

I make my way slowly forward, listening.

"Hell yeah it was! And dude, you were definitely on with your vocals tonight. We might just have to kick Jet to the curb and put you up front instead."

There is laughter.

"God no! We can't get rid of him. Nobody brings the women like him, man."

More laughter and agreement.

"At least he *could*. He's off his game since he started attending those bullshit meetings."

"I am not," I hear Jet's familiar voice say.

"Actually, bro, you are. Who would've thought one simple bet could bring a bucking bronco like you down?"

"Nothing has—"

"Look," the strange voice continues, "you made your point. We thought even *you* weren't *that* bad. None of us thought you'd *actually* go to one of those meetings and pick up a sex addict. I mean, shit, dude! That's cold! But damn if you didn't prove us wrong. You won the bet. You bedded a damn nympho. You're the king of all players, the big dick around here. We bow down to you and shit. Blah, blah, blah. Now stop pretending you're pussy-whipped and get back to bringing the strange."

My feet weigh a million pounds as I drag them around the corner to look at the band members sprawled about the room. They're all here—laughing at my expense—but for Jet, who must be in the bathroom.

You won the bet.

I see them with perfect clarity, but I no longer hear them. I hear only the words they've already said, ringing through my head, an unstoppable noise. An earsplitting scream.

You bedded a damn nympho.

Stop pretending.

I hear only the beating of my heart and the tearing of my soul. I'm in a daze of pure agony as I look from one laughing man to another. No one notices I'm here. No one bothers to look around, until the drummer throws his head back to laugh at something and happens to glance in my direction. His expression falls and he whips his head around, surprised and sheepish.

I stare blankly at him. I feel nothing. Not even humiliation. I'm numb. Completely and utterly numb.

I watch him throw whatever is in his hand at the guy in front of me. He's sitting with his back to me, but I recognize him when he turns. It's Sam, the bass player. Both of them just watch me, like they're watching a car accident unfold right before their eyes.

And I *feel* like that car accident. I feel the metal of my world caving in around me. I sense the devastating injuries. But I don't feel their pain. I'm still in shock. The hurt will come later.

I see their mouths moving, but I don't hear anything more than the gush of blood as it pulses through my veins. The whole scene is surreal. And devastating.

On stiff legs, I pivot to walk back the way I came. Just before I round to the anteroom, from the corner of my eye I see Jet step back into the room.

Quickly, I turn away, holding tight to the fragile pieces bound by nothing more than a delicate thread, and I run. I run as fast as I can.

THIRTY-EIGHT: *Jet*

Holy mother of shit!

"Was that . . . ?" I ask Sam as I catch a glimpse of dark hair and see a familiar profile disappear around the corner. I'd recognize that beautiful face anywhere, but I'm hoping for all I'm worth that it didn't belong to who I think it did.

Sam is grinning and nodding. "Sure was."

"Why the hell are you laughing?"

Sam shrugs. "I don't know. It just seems funny that you got busted. What difference does it make?"

"Are you kidding me? She's gonna hate me, damn you!"

"So? Like you care." He laughs again.

"Sam, I'd shut that hole right now before I come over there and beat your ass."

Sam holds up his hands in surrender, but I can still see that shitty smirk around his mouth.

As I stand in the doorway, astounded, looking around at the other members of the band, I realize something that's pretty damn sad. They're all good guys, deep down. They like their fun and they like their women, but basically they're all decent people. They would never have done what I did. Not one of them would ever have *dreamed* of attending a sex addicts meeting to prove a point, or to tap some nympho ass just to win some stupid, thoughtless bet. None of them believed that *even I* could be that cold. Because it's the shittiest thing in the world to do.

And I did it.

Because, in a room full of decent people, I'm the only real asshole here.

I take off after Violet. For a million reasons, the first of which being that I can't picture my life without her in it. And I have no desire to try.

THIRTY-NINE: *Violet*

I keep my head down and move as quickly as I can back through the crowd and out the front doors. When the night air slaps me in the face, the dam bursts and I feel the tears come. And in the quiet privacy of the deserted parking lot, I let them fall.

I thought I'd been hurt when Jet had cooled so much on the trip back from New Orleans, but that is nothing compared to this. These feelings of betrayal and humiliation and devastating heartbreak are enough to steal my breath. It's because I'm gasping and trying to choke back sobs that I don't hear my name at first.

I don't know how many times he calls before I hear him, but finally, I do. And I recognize the voice. Sometimes I think I'll never be able to forget it.

"Violet! Violet, wait!"

My heart lurches in my chest. I don't want to talk to Jet right now. Maybe not ever again. I feel so stupid and so embarrassed and so deceived that I want to crawl in a hole and die.

I pick up the pace and run for my car.

His voice gets louder and louder, closer and closer, his longer legs eating up the distance between us.

"Violet, stop! Wait."

When I reach my car, I pause, fumbling in my pocket for my keys. I tug them out and notice that my hand is shaking as I depress the remote unlock button. But I'm not fast enough. Before I can wrench open the car door, Jet is grabbing my arm.

"Violet, please. Let me explain."

He turns me toward him. I keep my head down. I don't want him to see that I've been crying.

He's breathing heavily, and so am I. "Let me go, Jet," I say quietly.

"Not until you let me explain."

"I don't need an explanation. I heard all I needed to hear."

"But it's not what you think."

I flinch at the sudden burst of hope that blooms in my chest like a rose. I hate that I want so much to feel it, for it to be real. But something inside warns me not to trust it.

"So there was no bet?"

Jet's pause tells me all that I need to know. "It's not what you think," he repeats vaguely.

My sorrow and humiliation give way to fury, fury that he's trying to weasel his way out of this.

"Oh, really?" I ask, finally looking up, anger spitting from my eyes. I feel it like the snap of firecrackers. Jerking my arms free, I cross them over my chest, eyeing him sharply. "So you *are* a sex addict, and you *were* at those meetings legitimately?"

Jet watches me closely, likely weighing the benefits of being honest. "No, I'm not a sex addict. And no, I wasn't at those meetings legitimately."

Hearing him admit it, even though I already knew the answers, is like a broadsword to the sternum.

"Oh, God! How could I have been so stupid? How could I have trusted you? Of all people, why you? Why did I pick you to trust?"

Jet grabs my arms again, hauling me in close to him. "Because you knew that, deep down, I'm a man that you *can* trust."

His eyes are pleading with me, but I don't care. All I see is a liar and the man who betrayed the only trust I've ever given.

"Well, now I can see that I was wrong. You're nothing like the person I thought you were. And now, you're nothing to me *at all*."

I twist my arms free, pushing against his chest until he lets me go. In his face, I see pain and disappointment and shame, but my heart is hard. Right now, there is nothing he could say or do to penetrate the iron shell around it.

I turn back to my car, angrily snatching open the door. I barely hear his voice before I slam it shut.

"I guess you really didn't love me after all."

His words barrel into me like a train going a thousand miles per hour. I actually gasp in the quiet and squeeze my eyes shut, praying that he'll just go away and not make things worse. But when I look up to start my vehicle, I see that he's still standing at my window, still and silent. I don't look at him as I shift gears. And I don't look back as I drive away.

FORTY: *Jet*

I never knew words could hurt so much, and I've heard some pretty shitty ones. My mom. My dad. A few other people I've cared about. They might've bothered me. But hurt? Nah. Not really.

Not until now.

Violet's words hurt. Hearing her say that I'm nothing to her was like being run over by a '54 Buick.

I watch her drive away, holding my breath until I see her taillights disappear, hoping she'll stop. Or turn around. Or come back to me. But knowing she won't.

And she doesn't. She just keeps going. Driving out of my life. Probably never planning to come back.

I wish she'd given me a chance to explain. Not that it would've made any difference. I knew that if she ever found out she would hate me. I guess that's why I never wanted her to know, why I didn't have the balls to tell her. I could've confessed when she did, but even then, I didn't have the courage. Not like she did. That's what separates us. She's a good person, a strong person, and I'm an asshole. Just like I've always been. Just like everybody knew I was. Even my own mother.

As I stand staring at the empty parking spot, my mind wanders, wanders to the what ifs and the if onlys. If only things had been different . . . but not so different that I wouldn't have really *seen* her. But what if I'd met Violet under different circumstances and I *hadn't* really seen her? What if I hadn't been able to appreciate her? Or what if I wouldn't have been attracted to her?

I know the answer to one of those. I know I would've been attracted to her. She's hot, plain and simple, regardless of the situation. But would I have taken the time to get to know how kind and beautiful her soul is? Would I have recognized her strength? Or would I have hit on her, been rejected, and then moved on to another?

It's hard to say. I imagine I'd have moved on, but it's impossible to know for sure. Right now, it seems like the guy I was a couple of months ago is a complete stranger. Somehow, while I thought I was just enjoying myself, Violet was making me a better person. Not because she was trying to or because she didn't think I was good enough. She did it through no fault or effort of her own. It's just who she is. Being with her made me the man that my mother could let back into my brothers' lives. Being with her made me see what a dickhole I've been, and how I don't want to be that guy anymore. And being with her made me realize that I'm an addict. Maybe not in the traditional sense, but I'm an addict nonetheless. Addicted to feeling good. To hiding from anything slightly uncomfortable or unpleasant.

At least I *was* an addict. I don't know what I am now, other than lost. Without her, I'm just lost.

Needing her, wanting to be with her snuck up on me. Loving her came too easy, too naturally. I hadn't even gotten used to it and now it's gone. *She's* gone. And I don't know what I'll ever be without her.

Other than less. A lot less.

That I know for sure.

FORTY-ONE: *Violet*

My anger only lasts a few miles. It only burned hot enough to withstand the hurricane of my anguish for a short while. Now it's gone, leaving me with devastation again. Cold, miserable, hopeless devastation. Nothing more.

When I've stopped sniffling enough to speak coherently, I dial Tia's number. She answers with a question.

"Please tell me you went. Did you go?"

"Oh, I went all right," I reply.

"And?"

Just like that, the flood starts up again, as if there is an endless supply of tears locked away somewhere deep inside me.

"Oh, God, Tia! I was part of a bet!"

There's a short, tense pause and then, "Say what?"

I snort and hiccup. "Th-the other guys in h-his band bet him that even he wa-wasn't such a playboy that he'd bed a sex addict. And-and he did it. He t-took the bet and I was the . . . I was the pawn." The last word is virtually drowned out by the sob torn from my chest.

"Are you shittin' me?" Tia says, her voice dangerously calm.

I can't even collect myself enough to answer her right away. "Of course not," I finally manage.

"Tell me where to find him, Vi. I'll pull that bastard's dick off with a pair of pliers and shove it so far up his ass he won't be hungry for a week!"

Normally, a comment like that would elicit some kind of reaction in me—laughter, chagrin—but not tonight. Tonight, I don't want her anger, even though it's on my behalf. Tonight, I need something else from her.

"Tia, tell me how to fix this. Tell me how to make this go away."

"Make what go away, honey?"

"The pain. It hurts so bad," I cry. "I feel like I'm dying inside. Please. Help me."

"I wish I could, Vi. But the only thing that takes away the pain is time. It will, though. I promise. It goes away. Eventually."

As fun and free as Tia is, I've seen her with a broken heart before. It was one of those times that I was glad to be the way I am. Or the way I *was*. I wanted nothing to do with pain like that. I'm not sure she ever recovered. Not fully. Her wild ways seemed to get wilder and then never completely go away after that. Ryan was his name, and he damaged Tia. Maybe permanently.

Just like Jet probably damaged me—permanently. With no hope of ever being repaired.

Unfixable.

Unhelpable.

Hopeless.

"Do you need me to come over? Because I will."

I'm sure she would, but this isn't exactly Tia's strong suit. If I were in need of a night out, she'd be my girl. But this? I think this puts her in a place where she's not comfortable, a place where she doesn't want to go again. So I won't ask her to.

"No, I'm fine. I think I'd rather just be alone anyway. But thank you."

"If you change your mind, call. Or send up the Bat Signal. Or smoke signal. Whatever you can find and I'll be there."

"I will," I say, even though I won't.

"I love you, Vi."

"I love you, too."

"You're too good for him anyway. You know that, right?"

"Yeah," I reply, wishing I really thought that was true. But even now, even after everything, I can't forget the tenderness I saw in him, the brokenness. That might've been a lie, too, but right now I can't bear to think of it that way. Losing that might just be more than I can take.

FORTY-TWO: *Jet*

I have no idea how long I've been outside. More importantly, I don't give a shit. I've lost enthusiasm for anything but figuring out a way to get Violet back, to at least talk to her and make her see . . . make her see . . .

I stomp back inside. I'm angry. At myself. At my band. At everybody. Except Violet. She's the one innocent person in all this. But everyone else can suck my dick!

I fling open the door and shoulder my way through the crowd. I ignore the girls who try to talk to me, who get in my way and put their hands on me. I'd just as soon they all go to hell. Everybody.

I barely take notice of the complete *lack* of women backstage when I walk through the door. I just want to get my shit and leave. It's the quiet that really gets my attention. Everyone, from Sam to Trent, is standing or sitting in the small room, just watching me.

I glance from face to face. "What?" I snap.

It's Sam who speaks. "You all right, man?"

I clench my hands into tight fists. I'd love to punch him right in the face. For laughing earlier. For not caring earlier. For daring me to do something so twisted. For just being around on a night when I don't want to see anybody. Except Violet.

But I bite it all back. I don't even want to waste my time fighting. As good as it would feel, I'd rather just be alone.

Or with Violet.

"Hey," Sam repeats. "You all right?"

"What the hell do you care?" I yell. "This is *your* fault!"

"How is it *my* fault?" he asks indignantly.

"What kind of shit do you have in your soul, man? Who would even *think* to dare someone to do a sick thing like that?"

"Dude, I was just yanking your chain. Nobody actually thought you'd *do it*. You can't blame me for sick, man. That's all on you."

I know he's right, but that doesn't stifle my fury one bit. With a growl, I lunge at Sam. I have every intention of breaking his arrogant jaw. With as many punches as it takes.

But the others are between us before I can get close enough to touch him.

"You're an asshole, Sam! Did it ever occur to you that people could get hurt?"

"Of course it did, you idiot. But I never thought it would be you."

That sobers me—that Sam thinks I'm so hard and twisted that it wouldn't bother me. It's not lost on me that he would care so little about hurting *someone else* either. The whole thing is just disgusting.

And it's nothing worse than what I was doing. In fact, I'm the *real* villain here. All the disdain I feel for him is being directed at the wrong person. It belongs on me. Like the blame and the shame and the fallout. It all belongs on me.

Furious, with myself and with everyone else in the room, I grab my stuff and head right back out the door. I'm ready for this night to be over.

FORTY-THREE: *Violet*

It's finally Friday, the end of one of the worst weeks of my life.

It began with the "Monday of Puzzled Devastation," as I like to call it. After the disheartening trip home from New Orleans, I woke feeling unsettled and . . . raw. Little did I know what tsunami of sadness was headed my way.

Wednesday. I might forever look back on it as the day my heart was permanently broken. And then encased in a fragile box of glass just behind my ribs. I've never felt more emotional agony or hopelessness in my life. And it seems that all it has taken to bring me to tears since that night is a sharp word or a stern look. The glass case is cracked on every surface, and ready to crumble at a moment's notice. It's all I can do to hold it together.

For today. Friday. When I can fall apart and no one will care. No one is depending on me to be at my job, to be focused on helping them. I get to be selfish for forty-eight hours. I get to tend to the ever-bleeding wounds that lie just beneath the surface.

I unlock my front door and step inside the dark, quiet interior of my sanctuary. Quickly, I shut it behind me, like I'm running from something that's hot on my heels.

Which I am. I'm running from the truth. From reality. From the realization that I fell. And I landed flat on my face. On a bed of nails.

I throw my purse on the entry table and kick off my shoes, pushing them haphazardly out of the way. Out of habit, I glance down at my phone. It's still silent. Like it has been since the last time I talked to Tia.

It kills me that I keep waiting for Jet to call—and that he doesn't. And that it even bothers me, which it shouldn't. I should be glad he's not calling me. I should be relieved. But I'm not. It hurts every time I look at my phone. Maybe more each time.

Deep down, I wanted him to beg. To grovel. To plead with me to listen to him, to give him one more chance. Maybe I thought that would mean that he actually *did* care. Which he didn't. That much is obvious.

I throw my phone onto the couch. It's that or throw it onto the floor and dance on it until it's nothing more than black powder.

Dejectedly, I make my way back to my bedroom to change into suitable hibernation clothes. Obviously, that means finding the ugliest, rattiest, holiest items that I own. In this case, a pair of blue sweats that have a huge tear in the leg and a white, threadbare T-shirt that's spattered with every color of paint under the sun. It also sports a tear. Right in the middle of my stomach. I've had both the pants and the shirt since high school and it shows. But they're comfortable and soft, and right now it's like slipping on a better time of life. And *that's* what I need more than anything.

I make a pass by the kitchen for some hot cocoa before I swipe three of my favorite heartbreaking romance movies from the closet. Might as well wallow in it while I have the chance. Most of the time, I have to hide what I'm feeling and put on a strong, happy face. But not tonight. Tonight, I can let it flow—the misery and the pain, the disillusionment and the grief.

I'm less than twenty minutes into movie number one and I'm already crying like a baby. Not because anything sad has happened yet, but because I know it will. I know it's coming. And I feel the pain of it more than ever. Before Jet, I'd always sympathized with these characters in a detached, clinical sort of way. I had never felt such intense emotion, nor did I really want to. I saw it as something that made a person weak. And, sure enough, it does. Finally experiencing it feels like it's killing me in slow degrees.

I'm sniffling and wiping streaks of mascara off my cheeks when the doorbell rings. I look around for my phone, finding it wedged between the cushions of my couch. The screen shows no missed calls or texts, which confuses more than reassures me. I hope nothing is wrong . . .

Without so much as checking my reflection, I rush to the door and fling it open.

To find Jet on the stoop.

My heart slams to a stop before it starts back up at runaway train speed.

A kaleidoscope of emotions melt and swirl and shift inside me. Pleasure at seeing him. Anger that it took him so long. Disgust over what he did to me. Humiliation that I let him.

Those are the biggest ones, but there are more. Smaller, underlying feelings. A desire for him that never ceases, and regret that things ended the way they did.

Once my inner turbulence settles down, I react. I start to slam the door right in his face, but Jet's arm shoots out too fast, stopping me before I can physically shut him out.

"Wait! Violet, please. Just give me five minutes."

"I gave you five minutes. I gave you more than that, and you wasted it."

"I know I did, and I'm sorrier about that than you'll ever know."

His eyes, gorgeous and sparkling blue, are pleading with me. And for a second, I feel a softening. But I steel myself against it and push on the door again.

But, again, he stops me.

"You don't owe me even five more *seconds*, but I'm hoping that what I did hasn't affected the amazing, understanding person that you were before I came into your life. And that *she* will give me a few minutes."

I reach deep for my anger, pulling it to the surface to wear like protective chain mail. It's not as bulletproof as what it should be, though. I feel the chinks in it, the holes of uncertainty and the gaps of hope. Whether it's that I wanted him to call so badly, or that I want to believe him so badly, whether it's that I've been wallowing in misery for so long that the anger has taken a backseat to every other emotion, I don't know. Whatever the reason, and against my better judgment, I open the door a little farther and lean against it, crossing my arms over my chest.

"Five minutes."

"Thank you," he says sincerely. Jet clears his throat, reaching into the pocket of his leather jacket for a small flash drive. "Before I forget, I want you to have this."

I take the tiny rectangle from him. "What is it?"

"Some songs. Some new material I've been working on. Kick has even bought a few of them."

I straighten. Despite my determination to hold on to anger and to keep a canyon of distance between us, I'm immediately interested. "What? They decided to buy them?"

Jet smiles, but it's not as bright as it should be, considering that his dreams are coming true. "Yeah. I didn't think they were going to."

"Why? You're very talented."

His expression softens even more. "Thank you. But while we were in the shower on Sunday afternoon, Rand had called and left a message saying that they were going to pass. That's why I was a little . . . distant on the ride back. I had hoped I wouldn't have to play with the band anymore, that I'd finally be able to take my career in the direction that I want it to go, but . . ."

His words, his unwitting explanation, wash over me, run through me. An overwhelming sense of relief floods me, and I actually let out a deep breath, a breath that I think I've been holding all week.

I close my eyes against pleasure, pleasure that there was a rational explanation for the way he acted on the trip home, one that had nothing to do with me. But then, before I can take a step toward forgiving him, I remind myself that his actions that afternoon aren't the only reason we are where we are tonight. In fact, *now*, they have nothing to do with it.

Jet being a deceitful, heartless bastard does.

"Someone must've called back then," I say mildly, settling back against the door. "Good for you."

"Yeah. I got the call from Paul on Monday morning. Rand had made the decision unilaterally. Evidently, he has a problem with me *personally*. But he was wrong, and they *do* want me. I spent most of the day in talks with them, and then they flew me out to California to sign the paperwork and go over all the particulars. It was so nuts, I really didn't get back and settled in until Wednesday afternoon. I slept for a couple hours, met with my lawyer, and then had that gig Wednesday night. I didn't want to call and tell you all of this until I knew it was concrete. By Wednesday night, I knew. That's why it was my last night with the band. I'd made reservations at La Petite Maison that night. I was going to surprise you. I wanted to take you out so we could celebrate, and I could tell you everything."

It feels like my heart is flopping around inside my chest like a fish out of water. He's saying all the things that I wanted to hear, all the things that I *needed* to hear.

But that was *before*. Before I found out that I was part of a bet.

"That's great, Jet. I'm really happy for you. Now if that's all . . ." I say, curling my fingers around the cool doorknob.

"Will you at least listen to them?" he asks, nodding toward the flash drive in my hand.

With my eyes on his, I give his request genuine consideration before I answer. "Yes, I'll listen."

"Good. Because they're all for you. I wrote every one of the songs on there for you. With you in mind. Since you came into my life."

Jet might as well have handed me a knife and then asked me to drive it into my own chest. That's how the songs will feel now—like finding the most amazing life and love in the world, and then watching it drift away. Destroyed. By Jet.

"I'm glad I could help you," I say quietly.

With his cerulean eyes searching mine, Jet sighs. "I know I'm too late, but I want you to know that I was a different person when I took that bet. I'm not proud of who I was. In fact, I'm pretty disgusted. And I didn't know it at the time, but I changed from the moment I first laid eyes on you. Every day after, I became a better person. Just for knowing you. You told me that you help people, that it's who you are. And you were right. You helped me in more ways than I could ever tell you."

"I'm glad," I repeat, holding on to the reins of my heart as tightly as I can.

"I know it was never your intention to get involved with me. Definitely not to make me fall in love with you. So I can't blame you for any of this. Or for being mad and hurt when you found out what I'd done. I'd hate me, too. But it *kills me* to think of you walking away from us thinking that everything that happened was just a part of some stupid, sick, juvenile bet. Because it wasn't. When I made love to you, I did it loving you with the heart that *you* changed. Not the one who sang in a band and went through women like water.

"I like to think that I won't be drowning my problems in every convenient person and substance now. The last thing I hid from, which was the truth of what I'd done, is a regret I'll have to live with for the rest of my life. I'll go to my grave knowing that I lost the best thing that ever happened to me because I was so afraid of losing her that I lied to her.

"So don't think I don't blame you for not being able to forgive me. I'll never be able to forgive myself."

His last words ring between us like a death knell, one that echoes in the silence for several seconds after he stops talking. For a heartbeat, I wonder if he's waiting for me to say I forgive him or to throw myself into his arms, which would seem incredibly manipulative on his part. But I can barely finish the thought before he's leaning in to kiss my cheek, whispering, "Good-bye, Violet." And then he turns to leave, the black night folding in around him, swallowing him up as he walks out of my life.

But the night isn't the only thing folding in. As I stand watching the last place I saw Jet, my chest aches with a pain so deep, it feels as though my ribs might implode. But as much as I wanted a future with him, as much as I'd love to call him back, I can't think of a way to forgive him. I can't think of a way to go forward after everything that has happened.

It's with an abyss forming in the empty place where my heart used to be that I close the door and lock it behind me before I fall to pieces on my entryway floor.

FORTY-FOUR: *Jet*

There's a burn behind my eyes as I slide behind the wheel of my car. I knew there was a good chance she wouldn't even talk to me, hear me out. And, although she did, I can see that she can't forgive me. At least not now. Just the thought of her *never* forgiving me is what's making my gut churn, my heart ache, and my eyes burn. It's eating me up inside, not being with her, thinking that I'll *never* be with her.

But what are my choices? I can't really see that I have any. I've told her the facts, apologized to her, and asked for her forgiveness. Even told her that I loved her in a roundabout way. But none of it mattered. I didn't know if it would. I had *hoped*, but I knew it was a long shot.

Now, I should just walk away. She's made her choice, and I ought to respect it.

Only I can't.

I can't live with her choice. I can't live with her unforgiveness. I can't live *without* her.

So what the hell am I supposed to do?

That question rings through my head all the way back to my father's place in Summerton where I have to go to pick up some stuff I'd left there.

It's when I pull into the driveway, thinking of Violet when I see the place where she was dropping off her dad that day, that I realize there *is* something I can do. I can love her from a distance. I can do things for her, make her life better and happier, without her ever having to know. But *I'll* know. I'll know that, somewhere, she's smiling and feeling a little happier, and that I might've had a small hand in it.

And as long as I can make her happy, make her life better (even without me in it), that'll have to be enough.

FORTY-FIVE: *Violet*

It's been three weeks since the night Jet came to my house to apologize. I haven't heard a word from him since. No calls, no impromptu visits, nothing overt. But he's been around—at least I think he has.

Odd things have happened for weeks. They could be coincidence, of course. But they could *not* be coincidence, too. Maybe I just *want* them to be Jet-related. Or maybe they really *are*.

One morning, a few days after he'd visited me, I was walking to my car before work and noticed that there was a single rose on the ground in the grass. Had it been on my windshield, I would've been more suspicious, but it was just lying there, as though it might've fallen or even been blown over by the wind. Anything is possible, of course. But something inside me wants to believe that Jet put it there. To say what, I don't know. That he's thinking of me? That he wishes me a good day? That he's sorry? Again, it could be anything. *If* it's even him.

Other things have been more blatant. One night, I got a knock at the door and my favorite pizza was being delivered to me. Anonymously, of course. That following Friday afternoon, a week from the night Jet visited me, I got a call confirming my appointment for a full spa treatment the next morning. It was scheduled and paid for anonymously, of course. One night, I even came home and found my yard mowed. It could've been Dad, but he wouldn't give me a straight answer, so I can't be sure.

Chocolates in the mail, flower petals in front of my door, to me it all points to Jet. But does it change anything?

No.

Every day I keep hoping for it to hurt a little less, but it doesn't. I only seem to miss him more and more. I only seem to be getting lonelier and lonelier, no matter how many other people I fill my time with. But I'm not going to stop trying. I can't give up. I just can't. And I can't dwell on it. I have to keep busy. I'm afraid what little piece of sanity I've managed to retain will disappear completely if I give myself too much time to think.

Even now, I find myself looking forward to SAA with Tia, just as an escape, despite the fact that it only brings up painful memories.

That is until she calls and jerks the rug out from under me.

"You busy?" she asks when I answer.

"Just pulling the brush through my hair before I head out. You running late or something?"

"No. Ummm, I, uh, I'm not going."

"What?" I ask, brush in midair, hovering over my head. "Why?"

There's a long pause that makes me distinctly uneasy. "Please don't take this the wrong way, Vi, but seeing what you've been going through has made me realize that I need to make some changes. If I don't, I'll lose Dennis, and then I really *will* be miserable. It's time for me to grow up and stop letting my past cripple me. You know, be a victor not a victim. All that shit." I hear the smile in her voice at the last.

"Oh. Well, that's good. That's a good thing, Tia." It's all I can think to say.

"Please don't take that the wrong way."

"I'm not."

"I think you are."

"I'm not. How can I take it the wrong way? You've turned a corner. That's great." And it is. I have no idea why it doesn't exactly *feel* that way.

"I just . . . well, I'm not cutting on you. And I don't want you to think I've somehow benefited from your pain. At least not in the bad way like it sounds."

"I know you don't mean it that way, Tia. But the truth is, you *have* benefited from it. And honestly, that makes it a little easier—knowing that at least one of us has gotten something good from it. It makes what happened less of a waste."

"Well, it helped me to see that Dennis is good to me. He's good *for* me. And he really loves me. He forgave me when he didn't have to. I know it wasn't easy for him, but he loved me enough to look past my betrayal and see it for what it was. And he stuck with me until I could fix myself. I can't risk losing that."

Finally, I feel a genuine smile. "Tia, that's awesome. I agree with all that, and I couldn't be happier for you."

"You're not mad?"

"Of course I'm not mad! Don't be crazy."

"I know you think I needed those meetings."

"I did. But that's because I wanted you to get some help. Now, it sounds like you've finally got a handle on things."

"I do. I just hate it had to come this way."

"Tia, as much as I wish I could erase everything that happened, I can't. But it makes it more . . . tolerable to know that it helped someone I love."

"I wish it hadn't happened either. I always wanted you to fall in love, not be alone, but I never would've wanted you to go through something like this. Not even for me and Dennis."

"Well, I brought it on myself. I'm a victim of my own poor decision making. No one else to blame. Now, I just have to move forward and be smarter."

"Do you really think we can be smart when it comes to love, Vi?"

A knee-jerk answer pops into my mind—YES—but I hesitate to speak it aloud, mainly because I really don't believe it anymore. So I give her the truth instead.

"I used to think so, but now I'm not so sure."

"I think the only thing we can control in love is how we act. I think the rest is all left up to the heart. Like Dennis. He chose to forgive me. Over and over and over because he loved me. And it paid off because his heart was in it. I think as long as your heart's in it, everything will turn out just fine."

"I wish I believed that, Tia."

"Maybe one day you can," she says simply. I don't know what to say to that, so I say nothing. When the silence stretches on, Tia continues. "Well, at least now you don't have to worry about going to those awful meetings. You are officially free on Thursday nights."

That sounds like a good thing unless, as in my case, you avoid free time like the plague.

"Yep. Free as a bird."

After we hang up, I feel that freedom like a thousand-pound weight dragging at my feet, threatening to pull me under. Already this week, I've cleaned the house, washed all the curtains, rearranged the pantry, organized my shoes, and cleaned out the fridge. And I'm going to clean and polish my floors this weekend because I'll have to move the furniture.

I look around my house and realize I have nothing to do. I can't even *invent* something to do. It's all been done. The only place I haven't torn through like a tornado is Dad's. But maybe it's high time I take some of my constructive energy over to his place. That would benefit us both.

Without even stopping to give it more thought, I rush to my bedroom, change into cleaning clothes, and hit the door at a run. Free time is the enemy!

I hit the road as soon as I load the backseat of my car with chemicals, gloves, and brushes. It's as I'm driving the couple of miles to Dad's that I happen to think about how long it's been since I've had a call from the tavern. I'm about due, it seems like. Maybe I can be there to keep him company and dissuade him from drowning his woes in a bottle tonight.

Because of my load of cleaning paraphernalia, I pull around back so I can go in the laundry room door. I cut the engine and grab an armful of supplies and haul them up the steps to Dad's back door. I use my elbow to bang on the screen. I listen for the telltale sound of his heavy footsteps trudging to answer. Only the trudging never happens. My father never comes to the door.

Setting down my chemical arsenal, I go back down the steps and around to the front of the house. I had been so preoccupied upon arrival, I hadn't even noticed that my father's truck is nowhere to be found. With a deep sigh, I walk to the dying shrub to the left of the front door, fish out the spare key that's tied to a string that dangles inside it, and open the front door.

I replace the key before closing the front door and walking through to let myself in the back, my enthusiasm dampened considerably by the likelihood that this night will end with me going to fetch my obliterated father from his favorite dive. With a sigh, I tell myself to buck up. I wanted something to keep me busy—well, I've got it. Between cleaning this giant man cave and then babysitting for the remainder of the night, I should have zero time to think about Jet.

I'm elbow deep in bleach when I realize fate had a different plan for the evening. I hear banging from the other room. That *has to be* my father.

Men are so noisy!

Holding my dripping hands up, I walk from the kitchen into the living room to greet Dad. He's standing at the front door, banging dirt off his shoes, sending little particles of caked clay all over the tile of the entryway.

"Dad! Don't do that in here! Do it in the grass," I fuss good-naturedly.

"Oh, sorry sweetheart," he says sheepishly, setting his shoes to the side and tiptoeing away from the dirty zone, completely ignoring my suggestion. “What are you doing here?” he asks, walking past me to grab the broom and dustpan from the tiny closet just inside the kitchen.

“Cleaning. I hope that’s okay. I figured you’d be here.”

He doesn’t offer any kind of explanation, doesn’t tell me where he’s been, nothing. He just smiles.

“I guess I should’ve called,” I say, trying a different tack.

“You never have to call, Vi. You’re always welcome in this house, whether you’re cleaning it or not.”

I swallow my *humph*.

Mindful of my wet, gloved hands, I turn to head back into the kitchen, throwing casually over my shoulder, “What have you been into tonight?”

“Ummm, not much. Just . . . you know, a little of this, a little of that.”

I frown. That’s very vague. Not like my father at all.

“What’s *this* and *that*?”

“Oh, nothing you’d be interested in,” he says cryptically.

“Of course I’m interested, Dad,” I reply, even more curious now.

“I hate to bore you. Hey, have you had dinner?” he asks, quickly changing the subject.

I glance at the clock on the wall. It’s nearly eight, and he knows I never eat after seven thirty. Peeling off my gloves and tossing them onto the counter, I head back into the living room. I stop beside the sofa, crossing my arms over my chest.

“All right. What’s going on?”

My father looks up at me, his most innocuous expression in place. “What do you mean?”

"You're acting all . . . sneaky. What have you been up to?"

"I told you—"

"You told me exactly nothing. Now what gives?"

"Vi, I—"

I gasp, something just having occurred to me. "Oh my gosh! Dad! Were you on a *date*?"

His laugh is genuine, which gives me my answer before he speaks. "No, Violet. I was not on a date."

"Why is that funny?"

"It just is."

"Then where were you? Why the secrecy?"

I watch his smile die. "I don't know if you're ready for my answer yet, hon."

My frown deepens. "What's that supposed to mean? What could you possibly have been doing that I wouldn't be ready for?"

"It's not so much *what* I was doing as much as *who* I was with."

A million scenarios run through my mind, only one of which is even slightly bothersome. "As long as it wasn't a hooker, I don't think I'll care, Dad. Just tell me." After a heartbeat, I add, "Unless it *was* a hooker."

"Violet Leigh, what's the matter with you?"

"What? It's a legitimate . . . fear."

Dad shakes his head and walks past me toward his bedroom.

"Seriously?" I say.

"What is it now?" he calls from what sounds like his closet.

"You're just gonna walk away like we were done?"

"Is that a problem?"

"Yes, as a matter of fact it is," I snap, becoming as aggravated as I am curious.

A knock at the door interrupts our discussion, and since Dad's in his bedroom, I go to answer it. I yank open the door in agitation, not even pausing to look through the peephole.

But I wish I had.

Although I doubt it would've prepared me.

Standing on the doorstep, looking as surprised as I feel, is Jet.

We stare at each other for at least a full minute before speaking. And then, when we do, we both speak at the same time.

"What are you doing here?" we ask simultaneously.

Neither of us bothers to answer; we simply resume staring quietly at each other. Then finally, after such a long pause that my nerves begin to jangle, I break the silence and ask again, "What are you doing here?"

"Ummm, I . . . your father left this in my car." Jet hands me a cell phone that I recognize as my father's. I'm pretty sure no one else in the history of the world has a plastic iPhone cover that looks and feels like Astroturf. Leave it to a landscaper . . .

I take the phone from his fingers, even more confused. "Why was my father in your car?" Jet doesn't answer. He just watches me. Cautiously. I prompt him, "It's not a trick question."

"I know it's not. I just . . . I didn't . . ." Jet stammers.

I feel like strangling him when he just trails off and doesn't continue. "You didn't what?"

Jet sighs. "I didn't want you to know."

"Know what?" I ask, taking a step back, my defenses suddenly on high alert.

"It's nothing bad, Violet," Jet explains, his tone making me feel like a silly girl.

But then I get a little defensive. How dare he act like I have no reason to be skeptical. Once burned . . .

"Don't pretend like that's a foregone conclusion. You don't exactly have a sterling record of full disclosure."

He has the good grace to look sheepish. "You're right. And I deserve that."

I feel guilty for my dig, even though I really shouldn't. "I'm sorry," I offer, closing my eyes and rubbing the back of my hand over my forehead. "It's been . . . I'm a little . . ."

I don't finish. I don't know how to explain to him that he turned my life upside down. Twice. And that I've been a mess for weeks.

"Don't apologize," Jet says softly. "You have nothing to apologize for." I glance back up at him. His eyes are a deep, soulful blue that makes me ache right behind my ribs, all the way through to my back, like I've been shot. His lips pull up into a sad smile, and he continues. "Just let him know I dropped it off."

With that, as if no other explanation is required, he turns and walks away.

I watch Jet until I can no longer see him. I feel torn. Part of me wants to go after him, to call out to him and ask him to come back. Or at least to wait. For what, I don't know.

Another part of me, however, is still stinging. And still hopeful that one day . . . one day . . . I might be able to get over him.

Maybe . . .

When I hear an engine start somewhere down the street out of my line of sight, I close the door on the night. And on Jet.

Rubbing my thumb back and forth over my father's phone, I'm still standing at the door, lost in thought, when he comes out of his bedroom.

"Who was that?"

I look up to meet his puzzled green eyes.

"Jet."

He doesn't look surprised or worried or . . . anything really, he just asks, "What did he want?"

I hold up his phone. "He said you left this in his car."

Dad pats his right leg, as if automatically feeling for it in his pocket. "I hadn't even realized I dropped it."

I don't move, so my father walks to me and takes the phone from my fingers, sliding it into place in his pocket. We stand, staring silently at each other for a couple of minutes before I speak.

"Do you have something that you want to tell me, Dad?"

He shrugs. "Not really."

"Well then maybe you've got something that *I* want you to tell me."

"Maybe I do, maybe I don't."

"When were you with Jet, Dad? And why?"

"I was with him tonight, not that it's any of your business."

My mouth drops open. I'm incredulous. "Are you kidding me? How is it *not* my business?"

"Since when is every friend I have *your* business?"

"Since that 'friend' is a guy I used to . . . to . . ."

Dad holds his hand up. "Stop right there," he says, closing his eyes and cringing. "I don't want you to finish that sentence."

"I wasn't going to say *that*, Dad!" I feel my face flame. "I just don't quite know how to characterize our relationship."

"Good. I might have to kill him if you'd said—"

It's my turn to stop *him*. "Don't say it, Dad. Why don't you just tell me what you were doing with Jet so we can put this whole conversation behind us?"

"What if he doesn't want you to know?"

Again, my mouth drops open. "Why would that matter? I'm your daughter!"

"I know that, hon," he says kindly. "But I know how you are. I know how hard you can be sometimes."

"What? When am I ever hard?"

"I'm not complaining, Vi. I'm just saying that you've had a lot of years of bad examples and it's understandable that you'd have a tough shell by now. But sometimes, a parent has to do what he thinks is best for his daughter. Whether she approves or not."

"And just what is it you think you're doing for me?"

"Not *me,* per se."

"Dad, just cut to the chase. Tell me what's going on before I get mad."

He watches me for several seconds, his eyes searching mine. "He's been taking me to AA meetings for the past few weeks."

Of all the things I might have dreamed, imagined, or even guessed that my father might say, his answer was nowhere in the mix.

I have only one response. "Why?"

"If you haven't noticed, I've got a bit of a drinking problem."

I eye him in warning. "Dad, you know that's not what I meant."

My father steps closer to me, winding his fingers around my upper arms. "Violet, that boy's in love with you."

My heart flutters in my chest. But then, just as quickly as it began, the weight of reality stops its excited movement and crushes it instead. "Sometimes that doesn't make a difference, Dad. You know that."

I see the pain flicker across his face. "Oh, you don't have to tell me that, sweetheart." He takes a deep breath. "Look, I don't know what he's done that's so unforgiveable. I probably don't even want to know. That's why I'm staying out of it."

"Going with him to AA meetings is hardly staying out of it, Dad."

"If you hadn't found out about it . . ."

"But I did. So tell me what's going on."

"He just wants to help you, Vi. Even if he can't tell you he's doing it, even if he can't be with you, he wants to make your life better. And he knows how much my . . . problem bothers you. How much it affects your life. How much it always has. And I do, too," he admits, casting his eyes down. "I never meant to hurt you, hon. I guess I just never thought of how my drinking impacted you. I only knew it gave me an escape when I needed one." He falls silent, a long pause stretching between us. Finally, he looks up at me, his expression serious. Pained almost. "But *he* did, Violet. He knew how much it hurt you, and that's why he wanted to help.

"He came to me while I was working at his father's place and asked me if I'd go with him. Said he had some problems and that he'd hurt you because of them. He said that we both had a chance to make your life easier, better. I never really thought of it that way, never really thought of *you* as a reason to get cleaned up. But he did. He only saw what was best for you. And I should've, too. So I went with him."

I pull free of my father's grip. I walk to the sofa, standing over it rather than sitting down. I think back to all the tiny and not-so-tiny things, all the seemingly coincidental and not-so-coincidental things that have happened in the past weeks, and I realize that not everything Jet did was to get my attention. Had Tia not cancelled on me, had I not needed to keep busy, had I not parked around back, I might never have known that Jet was taking my father to AA. He wasn't doing it to make a statement. Or to get credit. Or to win brownie points with me. He was doing it *just for me.* Seeking nothing more than my happiness, with or without him, he did it. Just for me.

My heart is crying out for me to act. It's on fire for me to take the risk, to say to hell with the smart thing, to just go with my gut and give Jet another chance. It's screaming at me, telling me that it's not only the right, the forgiving and the mature thing to do, but it's what I *want* to do. Desperately. Deep in my heart.

So I do.

Whirling around, I run for the door. I don't know where Jet went or how I'll find him, or really what I expect to find when I open the door; I just know that I have to move. To do. I have to go after him.

I hear my father's voice as I jerk open the door.

"Where are you going?"

I don't answer him; I just take off running down the walk to the street. It's when I get there that I realize I have no shoes, no keys, no purse and my car is parked around back.

Breathing hard, I turn a helpless circle, wishing I'd come to this conclusion just a little bit sooner. When Jet was still here.

It's before I turn and start to head back inside that I hear the slam of a car door. I jerk my head left, following the noise down the street. That's when I see Jet standing in the dark, bathed in the glow of moonlight reflected off the shiny black hood of his car.

I stop and stare, my heart swelling at the sight of him.

He steps onto the sidewalk and moves closer to me, walking slowly, cautiously, until only a few inches separate us. "Please tell me you were coming for me," he breathes quietly.

I'm shocked. And thrilled. And excited. I'm caught in the surreal moment like light caught in the facets of a diamond—trapped in the brilliance, in the beauty. I do the only thing I can and nod, turning to face him more fully.

"Tell me," he whispers. "I need to hear you say it."

My heart is pounding so loudly, I wonder that he can't hear it, too. "Yes, I was coming for you."

As though that's all he was waiting on, Jet raises his hands to cup my face, his touch desperate. "I'm sorry I hid it from you, Violet. I only did it because I love you. And I wanted to help you. But I knew you wouldn't want anything from me. Please, please, please forgive me," he says softly, closing his eyes and leaning his forehead against mine.

"There's nothing to forgive, Jet. I know why you did it."

He pulls his head back to look down at me, his eyes boring holes into mine. "I'm so miserable without you, it's the only way I can sleep at night. Knowing that I'm doing *something* to make you smile, *something* to make you happy. It's the only thing that has kept me going."

"But you don't have to do things like that."

"I know. But I wanted to. It was tearing me up inside to think that you believed I only wanted you in order to win a bet. Violet, you are the only thing in my life that makes it worth living. I knew that if I couldn't be with you, I'd still have to be involved in your life, in your happiness *somehow*, even if you didn't know it."

I smile. "Well, some of it I've figured out."

"You did?"

I nod. "Suspected, I guess. But still. There are only so many things I can write off as coincidence."

"Please don't be mad. I just wanted you to be happy. I just wanted to help you like you always help other people. Like you always helped me."

"You did. And I appreciate it."

"Will you ever be able to forgive me for what I did?"

"I already have. Why do you think I came out here?"

"When I saw the door open and you came running out, I prayed that you were coming for me. I promised God that if He would just make you run to me, that I'd never disappoint you again." Jet sprinkles kisses over my nose and my cheeks. "I'll never lie to you. Never hurt you. Never make you sad or give you reason to doubt me. I just want to make you happy, baby."

When he pauses, our noses touching and his lips hovering over mine, I feel the moist warmth of the sweetest words I've ever heard, settling over my skin and my heart like a soft promise. "I love you, Violet. I've loved you even before I met you. I had no idea what I needed in life until I found you. I didn't know that there was a person who could make me whole. I didn't know that there was a woman who could rock my world like no guitar ever could. I didn't know that all the music in my life was missing something until I found you. *You* are the beautiful notes in every song I sing. *You* are the beautiful face behind every lyric I write. *You* are my reason, my muse. You're the love I was waiting for, the one thing I can't live without. Please tell me that you love me, too."

"I love you, Jet," I whisper. "I loved you when I didn't want to because I couldn't stop. I won't ever be able to stop. You changed something inside me, something that can never go back to the way it was. Without you, I'm empty and miserable. And more alone than I've ever felt before."

Gently, Jet strokes the side of my face, brushing his lips over mine. "You'll never be alone again. You'll always have me. Always. Forever."

When Jet finally presses his lips to mine, I feel a sigh that permeates my entire being, body and soul. I melt into him like he's the missing piece of my puzzle. And he fits me perfectly. Because, even though neither of us knew we were missing our other half, we were. But now we're whole. Together, we'll always be whole.

FORTY-SIX: *Jet*

Violet's lush little body is plastered against mine. The taste on her silky tongue is awakening more than just my heart. I lean away from her so that I don't do something stupid like drag her into the woods across the street and pin her up against a tree.

"I can't remember the last time I actually looked forward to *life*. In one way or another, I've tried to drown out huge parts of it for so long, I feel like I've only been half alive."

I see Violet's lips curve into a suggestive smile as she swivels her hips against mine. "Let me guess which part is coming back to life first."

I growl, leaning forward to nip her full lower lip with my teeth. "It's a good thing I can't see you very well right now."

"And why is that?" she whispers, flicking out her tongue to taste me, her voice as sexy as ever.

"Because if I saw that damn little blush of yours, I'd probably do something stupid."

"Like what?"

"Like carry you into those woods right there," I confess, crushing her lower body against mine and then wishing I hadn't. "Dammit, why do we have to be right in front of your dad's house?"

"I can fix that, you know."

"Is that right?" I reach between us to pull her loose-necked shirt down enough that I can press my lips to the top curve of her breast. "Because as much as I love the taste of your mouth, there are other things I'm dying to dip my tongue into."

Violet arches her back, pushing against me, needing the contact as much as I do.

"Like what?" she asks again, her voice noticeably breathy.

"One thing in particular," I reply, moving my hand to her ribs, down her side and into the elastic band of her pants. I reach around to cup her ass first, grinding her into me, loving the way she gasps. "It's the sweetest thing I've ever tasted. I'd easily walk a hundred miles to have it. Just once." I move my hand to her hip, slipping my fingers under the thin edge of her panties and running them around to her stomach. "But once would never be enough," I groan into her ear. "I'm addicted. I'll never be able to get enough of you." I move one finger into her crease, rubbing the hard knot of her clit. "You're all I can think about. The way you laugh, the way you smell. And, oh God, the way you taste." I push my finger into her, my dick throbbing when her muscles clench around it, wet and hot.

"How would you feel about spending the night with me tonight?" she pants, her hips moving against my hand.

I thrust my finger in once more, going in deep and pulling out slow. "I think that sounds like heaven."

Violet exhales a shaky breath as she leans her forehead against my chin. I feel the tremble of her fingers when they sink into my biceps. "I can't go back in there like this," she admits.

"Then let me take you home. You can call him and tell him I'll bring you back tomorrow to get your car."

She looks up at me and smiles. "That sounds wonderful."

"Thank God it's not far to your house."

She laughs as I give her a smacking kiss on the lips and take her by the hand to lead her to my car. "Who says we can't make the ride interesting?" she asks.

The interior light hits her face when I open the car door, illuminating the blush that's coloring her cheeks. "Damn, I love you."

She grins and stretches up to kiss me. "I love you, too. Now get in," she says as she plops down in the passenger side.

I have to give her credit. For a shy girl who's *not* a sex addict, she really knows how to make a short car ride something spectacular.

EPILOGUE: *Violet*

Eight months later

"What are we doing here?" I ask when Jet pulls into the driveway of the gorgeous, single-story Spanish colonial house, complete with mission-style shingles and an arched front door.

"I just need to run in here real quick," he replies, cutting the engine.

"Is that Fiona's car?" I ask, nodding to the silver Cadillac parked in one side of the open garage bay. It looks like the one my dad's girlfriend drives.

"Yep," he answers, sliding out from behind the wheel to round to my side.

"What's she doing here?"

"You'll see," he says with a grin.

I note the mischievous twinkle in Jet's eyes. Whether it was because I was distracted and didn't see it before, or because it simply wasn't there, I don't know, but it's there now.

"What are you up to?"

"Why do I have to be up to something?"

"I know that look."

"What look?"

"*That* look," I say, pointing to him when his grin widens.

He just shrugs and winks at me, which makes me *even more* suspicious.

I let Jet lead me up the front steps to a tall, heavy wooden door with a wrought iron grill over it. He opens it and steps back, sweeping his hand out in front of him. "After you."

The foyer is beautiful with its vaulted ceiling and Spanish tile floor that flows seamlessly into a huge, empty living room.

Jet leads me between the dining room and living room to an amazing kitchen, and beyond it to a hall lined with doors. "Does no one live here?" I ask, surveying the blank walls and unfurnished bedrooms as we pass.

"Not yet."

I tug his hand to a stop and I gasp with the realization, "Ohmigod, are Dad and Fiona moving in together?"

"They just met a couple of months ago," Jet reasons.

"Yeah, but they get along so well and they have so much in common." Dad and Fiona met at an AA meeting. Jet knows her better than I do, since he still takes Dad each Thursday. But I like her. And, more importantly, so does Dad.

Thursdays must be popular nights for addicts, I think randomly, remembering that it was on a Thursday that I met Jet all those months ago.

"Yes, they do, but they're taking it slow. Which is smart. You know that."

"Yeah, I know that."

"But I wouldn't be surprised if they end up together like that."

"Neither would I. And they have you to thank for it."

"Why is that?"

"If you hadn't started taking Dad to those meetings, or if you'd stopped after we got back together . . ."

Jet shrugs again. "It's best for *you* if he still goes, which means I'll take him as long as he needs it. Or as long as he wants me to."

"I think he enjoys you going with him."

"Nobody should have to go through that alone."

"Now he has you *and* Fiona."

"One big happy family."

My heart swells at the way he says that. "Yes, one big happy family."

"What do you think of this room?" Jet asks as he drags me to the end of the hall into an enormous master suite.

"It's gorgeous!" I say, walking by the bank of windows to the right. I circle around to the bathroom and adjoining dual walk-in closets that are bigger than my current bedroom.

"Could you live here?"

"Of course! Who wouldn't love to live here?"

Jet takes my hand and pulls me back toward the windows overlooking a lush green backyard, replete with a brick patio and an outdoor fireplace. "Could you live here *with me*?" he asks, turning me to face him.

My heart speeds up and my mouth goes dry. "Why do you ask?"

"Fiona knows the contractor who built this house. It's only been finished for about two weeks. She talked him into letting us look at it before he puts it on the market. It's ours if we want it. If *you* want it."

I'm shaking as Jet turns me toward the windows again, coming around behind me to cross his arms over my waist. "Please say yes. I want to wake up beside you every day in this bedroom. I want to have breakfast with you every morning in that kitchen. I want to pick out paint and turn one of the spare rooms into a nursery. And, one day, I want to marry you right there," he says, pointing past me to the beautiful backyard, where I can now see my father and Fiona waving up at us. "Say yes, Violet. Say you'll live here. With me."

I feel Jet's lips brush the curve of my neck, his arms tightening around me. I turn in them, clasping my hands together at his nape. "I can't think of a more perfect life than the one you just described."

His smile is brilliant, and his eyes shine with a happiness that is mirrored in my heart. "Is that a yes?"

I return his smile, my soul bursting with a joy I never even dreamed of, much less sought. "That's a *big* yes!"

"Then let's go down there and welcome your Dad to our new house and get them the hell out of here so we can sneak back in and properly christen this room."

He ducks his head and his lips meet mine in a kiss that would steam up the windows if it were colder outside. I'm breathless and achy by the time he finishes exploring my mouth.

"Does that mean you're not tired of me yet?"

"I could never get tired of you. I'm addicted. Hopelessly, shamelessly, undeniably addicted."

"Then I'm happy to be your enabler."

"Forever?"

"Forever."

Addiction has never looked so promising.

ABOUT THE AUTHOR

New York Times and *USA Today* bestselling author **M. Leighton** is a native of Ohio. She relocated to the warmer climates of the South, where she can be near the water all summer and miss the snow all winter. Possessed of an overactive imagination from early in her childhood, Michelle finally found an acceptable outlet for her fantastical visions: literary fiction. Having written more than a dozen novels, Michelle enjoys letting her mind wander to more romantic settings with sexy Southern guys, much like the one she married and the ones you'll find in her latest books. When her thoughts aren't roaming in that direction, she'll be riding wild horses, skiing the slopes of Aspen, or scuba diving with a hot rock star, all without leaving the cozy comfort of her office. Visit her on Facebook, Twitter, and Goodreads and at mleightonbooks.blogspot.com.